JUN

W9-BTS-914

DAWN OF THE CLANS

WARRIORS

THUNDER RISING

WARRIORS

THE NEW PROPHECY

POWER OF THREE

MANGA

The Lost Warrior

Warrior's Refuge

Warrior's Return

The Rise of Scourge

Tigerstar and Sasha #1: Into the Woods

Tigerstar and Sasha #2: Escape from the Forest

Tigerstar and Sasha #3: Return to the Clans

Ravenpaw's Path #1: Shattered Peace

Ravenpaw's Path #2: A Clan in Need

Ravenpaw's Path #3: The Heart of a Warrior

SkyClan and the Stranger #1: The Rescue

SkyClan and the Stranger #2: Beyond the Code

SkyClan and the Stranger #3: After the Flood

NOVELLAS

Hollyleaf's Story

Mistystar's Omen

Cloudstar's Journey

DAWN OF THE CLANS

WARRIORS

THUNDER RISING

ERIN
HUNTER

HARPER

An Imprint of HarperCollinsPublishers

ISBN 978-0-06-206350-2 (trade bdg.)
ISBN 978-0-06-206351-9 (lib. bdg.)

Typography by Hilary Zarycky
14 15 16 17   CG/RRDH   10 9 8 7 6 5 4 3
❖
First Edition

Special thanks to Cherith Baldry

ALLEGIANCES

CLEAR SKY'S CAMP

LEADER

CLEAR SKY—light gray tom with blue eyes

FALLING FEATHER—young white she-cat

MOON SHADOW—black tom

LEAF—gray-and-white tom

PETAL—small yellow tabby she-cat with green eyes

QUICK WATER—gray-and-white she-cat

FROST—pure white tom with blue eyes

FIRCONE—tortoiseshell tom

NETTLE—gray tom

TALL SHADOW'S CAMP

LEADER

TALL SHADOW—black, thick-furred she-cat with green eyes

GRAY WING—sleek, dark gray tom with golden eyes

JAGGED PEAK—small gray tabby tom with blue eyes

DAPPLED PELT—delicate tortoiseshell she-cat with golden eyes

RAINSWEPT FLOWER—brown tabby she-cat with blue eyes

SHATTERED ICE—gray-and-white tom with green eyes

CLOUD SPOTS—long-furred black tom with white ears, white chest, and two white paws

JACKDAW'S CRY—young black tom with blue eyes

HAWK SWOOP—orange tabby she-cat

KITS

LIGHTNING TAIL—black tom

ACORN FUR—chestnut brown she-cat

THUNDER—orange tom with amber eyes and big white paws

ROGUE CATS

WIND—wiry brown she-cat with yellow eyes

GORSE—thin, gray tabby tom

THORN—she-cat with a short, thick gray coat and bright blue eyes

DEW—mangy tom with splotchy fur

RIVER RIPPLE—silver, long-furred tom

MISTY—gray-and-white she-cat

KITTYPETS

BUMBLE—plump tortoiseshell she-cat with yellow eyes

TURTLE TAIL—tortoiseshell she-cat with green eyes

THUNDERPATH

CLEAR SKY'S
CAMP

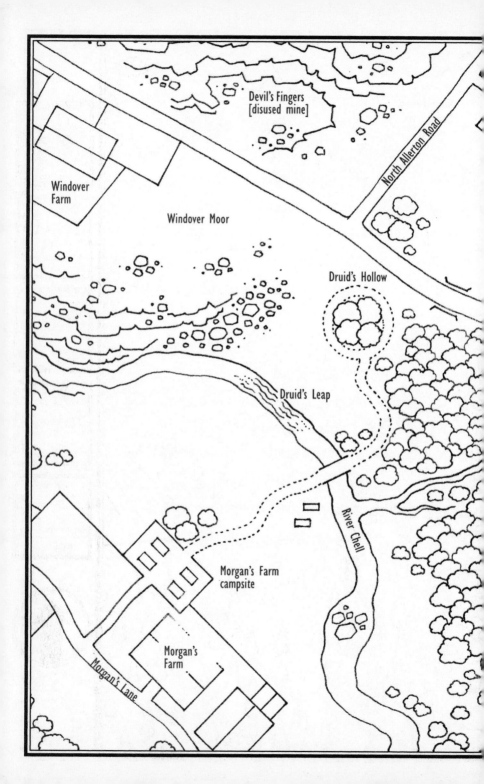

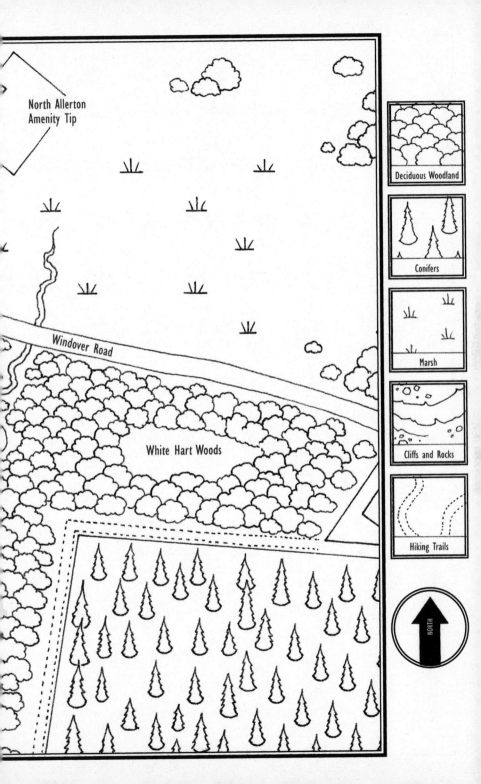

North Allerton
Amenity Tip

Windover Road

White Hart Woods

Deciduous Woodland

Conifers

Marsh

Cliffs and Rocks

Hiking Trails

NORTH

PROLOGUE

❧

All was dark over the moor, except for the glitter of far-off stars and the pale light of the moon. Thunder shifted on his haunches and closed his eyes to narrow slits as he gazed up at the silver circle where it hung close to the horizon. The night breeze rippling through his fur was cool and refreshing. The young cat began a luxurious stretch, then froze as another sensation joined the gentle ruffling. Something warm was rasping repetitively across his head.

Thunder turned his head and saw his mother, Storm, licking his ears as she used to do when he was a tiny kit. Back then she would soothe him to sleep against her soft belly fur. Thunder drew in his breath in wonder. *My mother!* It had been so long since he'd last felt the touch of her fur.

Storm paused. Thunder's gaze met hers and he felt like he was sinking into the green depths of her eyes. Reaching out with one paw, his mother drew him closer to her, and he felt the comforting beat of her heart.

Thunder's mind whirled with the strangeness of this meeting, yet at the same time he realized how familiar it felt. In the waking world he had never been able to remember his mother,

1

but now he recognized every marking on her fur. Even the faint scent of her breath was known to him, reviving memories of the dark, echoing Twoleg den where he had been born.

Seeing Storm again reminded Thunder of the she-cat who had taken care of him when Gray Wing brought him to the moor. *Hawk Swoop is kind to me.* Her tenderness had never failed. Yet the feeling of love and comfort was much more powerful coming from his own mother.

A purr rose in his throat. "Tell me the story again," he begged, even though he wasn't sure which story he meant, or where the urge to hear it was coming from.

Storm settled herself more comfortably around him, one paw protectively over his shoulders. Briefly she hesitated, gazing past Thunder as if she could see into some immeasurable distance.

"I first met your father in the forest," she murmured, the words awakening a familiar echo in Thunder's mind. "In the sheltered hollow where he lived. He was stretched out in front of a clump of brambles. Our eyes met, and then we . . . we just knew. I could sense the love in him."

Thunder's pelt prickled with confusion as if ants were crawling through it. "Why are things so different now?" he asked. "Clear Sky turned me out—my own father! Where did all that love go?"

He felt Storm shift uneasily. "It's still there," she replied. "It's just . . . Clear Sky doesn't know what to do with it. You'll help him find a way." She bent her head and drew her tongue along the side of his body with strong, comforting licks. "I know you will."

Thunder relaxed, but before he could close his eyes, he spotted a sudden movement in the distance. The dark shape of a cat, his head and tail raised, paced across the shining circle of the moon. Though he was far away, Thunder instinctively knew that the cat was his father.

Storm must have seen him too, for Thunder felt her heartbeat quicken. His own heart ached to realize that his mother still loved Clear Sky.

He half rose, intending to go after his father, but the paw that Storm had laid across his shoulders tightened, drawing him closer to her side. "Leave him be," she mewed softly.

"But you said—" Thunder protested.

"The time isn't right," his mother told him. "You will know when it is."

She began to lick his ears again, and gradually Thunder settled down. "But he's my father . . ." he murmured sadly.

"I know," Storm reassured him. Briefly playful, she patted him on the nose, her claws sheathed. "You have so much of him in you," she purred.

The ache in Thunder's heart grew more painful still, as if sharp claws were gripping it. "Then why won't Clear Sky acknowledge me?" he demanded. "Why can't I go to him?" His voice rose to a wail. "Everything feels so wrong!"

Storm's eyes were full of sorrow as she fixed her gaze on the full moon. The night breeze grew stronger, ruffling her fur, and she curled her body more tightly around Thunder, protecting him from the chill.

Thunder couldn't see her face anymore. He could only hear her as she began to speak again. "You will make things right," she murmured, her voice trickling through him like warm honey in his veins. "When the time comes, I know you will. . . ."

CHAPTER 1

❧

The new growth of moorland grass rippled under a warm breeze
that ruffled Gray Wing's fur, telling him that the cold season was coming to an end. Green shoots were springing from
the ground in all directions, and bright yellow flowers had
appeared on the gorse bushes that dotted the landscape. The
distant sound of birdsong promised abundant prey in the
moons to come.

A few tail-lengths away, Thunder was letting out excited
squeals as he wrestled happily with Hawk Swoop's kits, Lightning Tail and Acorn Fur. Gray Wing blinked affectionately
as he watched them rolling around on the soft grass, batting
at each other with flailing paws, their claws sheathed. He had
asked Hawk Swoop for permission to take them out for a
hunting lesson.

"Okay," the tabby she-cat had agreed. "But mind you don't
let them go too far from the camp." Now Gray Wing was
content to let the kits play for a few moments, enjoying their
carefree antics.

Farther across the moor, he could see Cloud Spots and Dappled Pelt returning from the direction of the river, bunches of

fresh herbs clamped in their jaws. Rainswept Flower emerged from a clump of gorse carrying the limp body of a rabbit. She dragged the prey into the hollow where Jackdaw's Cry and Shattered Ice were digging out more earth to open up a new sleeping tunnel. Hawk Swoop and Tall Shadow sat close together, grooming themselves while they talked.

This feels like home now, Gray Wing thought, remembering their long journey from the mountains and their struggles to establish themselves on the moor. It had been hard to accept Stoneteller's vision of a better home to be found if they followed the sun trail. The journey had been full of danger, and yet they had made it through. *Life's good here.*

"Lightning Tail, you be a hare." Thunder's voice brought Gray Wing's attention back to the kits. "I'll show you how to catch one."

"Okay." Lightning Tail began hopping from side to side, imitating the irregular movement of a hare.

Thunder glanced at Acorn Fur and meowed, "Watch this!" Flattening himself to the ground he crept toward Lightning Tail, who kept glancing over his shoulder to see whether the older kit was catching up to him.

Thunder waggled his haunches and shot forward in an enormous leap. When he landed on top of Lightning Tail the black kit let out a squeal and rolled over on his back, wrapping his paws around Thunder's neck, so that the two toms collapsed to the ground in a bundle of wriggling fur.

Clear Sky and I were just like that once, Gray Wing thought with a prickle of sadness. *How did we ever come to quarrel so badly?*

"You're dead!" Thunder yowled. "I killed you!"

"I want to do it for real!" Acorn Fur announced, bouncing up to them. "I'm going to be the best hunter ever."

"That's good," Gray Wing mewed, padding up to the kits. "But you've got a lot to learn before then."

"I can creep like Thunder." Lightning Tail pressed himself down and squirmed along with his paws scrabbling in the grass. "See?"

"Great," Gray Wing responded, ignoring the kitten's tail, which was waving around in the air. "But there's more to that than catching prey. Out here on the moor, prey can see you from a long way off, so what do you have to do?"

"Leap on them . . . like this!" Acorn Fur screeched, jumping on top of her brother and knocking him off his paws.

Thunder dived in to join them. They would never catch anything if they couldn't pay attention, but Gray Wing held back from reprimanding them. It felt good to watch the happy, healthy kits.

They're so big and strong . . . twice the size of poor Fluttering Bird.

A twinge of grief passed through him as he remembered his sister, who had died in the mountains because there hadn't been enough food for her during the cold season. He felt a rush of protective love for Thunder and the others; he was determined that they would grow into strong, healthy cats.

The cold season wasn't so hard. There was always enough prey. Gray Wing still found it difficult to accept that the snow here wasn't as thick as the snowfall in the mountains, and it didn't stay around for so long. The frosts burned off much earlier in the mornings. There had been few days when they couldn't hunt or find water to drink, especially in the forest, where the trees provided shelter from the worst of the cold weather. He suppressed a sigh. There were still times when he missed his home and his mother, Quiet Rain, but the easier life on the moor meant the kits had survived, and would soon see the warm season return.

Thunder and Lightning Tail kept wrestling, yowling loud enough to scare off all the prey on the moor. Acorn Fur broke away from them with a sudden shriek. "Watch me!"

She raced into the hollow and vanished down the tunnel opening where Gray Wing had seen Jackdaw's Cry and Shattered Ice working earlier. He headed after her, his heart beginning to pound. There was a whole network of tunnels underneath the moor, mostly burrows dug by rabbits. The cats had begun to enlarge them to make dens, but some places weren't yet safe. And being in the burrows never felt natural to Gray Wing. It was so dark and confining, he found it hard to breathe. *Besides, if she goes too deep into the tunnels we might not be able to get her out.*

To Gray Wing's relief, Acorn Fur reappeared almost at once, thrust into the open again by another cat close behind her. As the cat emerged, Gray Wing saw it was her father, Jackdaw's Cry. Shattered Ice stuck his head out behind the other two, an annoyed look on his face.

"Stay away from here," Jackdaw's Cry scolded Acorn Fur. "This tunnel isn't safe yet. Shattered Ice and I are still digging it out." He gave his daughter a sharp tap on the nose, his claws sheathed. "Aren't you supposed to be having a hunting lesson with Gray Wing?"

"She is," Gray Wing called down to him. "Thanks, Jackdaw's Cry."

The black tom gave Gray Wing a nod of acknowledgment before vanishing into the tunnel again with Shattered Ice.

Acorn Fur turned away, her tail drooping, and trudged back up the slope to the top of the hollow.

"Wow!" Lightning Tail exclaimed as she joined the others. "That was awesome! Now we know how to get our noses whacked."

Acorn Fur glared at him, but didn't reply.

"I think you should show us again," her brother teased her. "I'm not sure I could get it right."

"Really? Then *this* is how you get your nose whacked, fleabrain!" Acorn Fur hissed, swiping her paw across her brother's nose.

Lightning Tail leaped back. "Hey, that hurt!"

"That's enough," Gray Wing meowed, getting between the littermates before a fight could develop. "We're supposed to be hunting, remember?"

To his relief the kits began to settle down, scuffling about until they found comfortable spots to sit. They looked up at him with wide eyes.

Gray Wing glanced around for something to help the young kits learn. He noticed movement underneath a gorse bush; a rabbit moved a little way into the open, nibbling at the grass.

"Look over there," he told the kits, pointing with his tail, "but *don't* move. See the rabbit? I'm going to catch it."

The kits nodded, with sparkling eyes and impatiently twitching tail-tips.

"First," Gray Wing went on, "I'm going to let it come away from the bush a bit. It's likely that the entrance to its burrow is hidden there somewhere. And when I'm chasing it, I'm going to keep a careful eye on it so I can guess which way it's going to run."

While he had been speaking, the rabbit had moved even farther into the open. Gray Wing watched carefully, waiting for just the right moment. Then, in a spurt of energy, he took off after it, reveling in the sensation of his muscles stretching and the breeze streaming through his pelt.

He was within a few tail-lengths of it before the rabbit realized he was there. It fled with a squeal of alarm, its white tail bobbing up and down. Gray Wing kept his gaze fixed on it, racing across to intercept the creature as it tried to double back toward the safety of the bush.

The rabbit's paws skidded as it veered away again. But within a few strides Gray Wing had caught it, slamming his paws on its shoulders to thrust it to the ground, where he killed it with a bite to the throat. Satisfaction flooded through him.

Picking up the still warm body of his prey, Gray Wing trotted back to the kits, who were watching admiringly.

"Great catch, Gray Wing!" Thunder exclaimed.

"I want to do that," Acorn Fur meowed.

"You will, soon," Gray Wing promised, pushing the rabbit underneath the branches of a nearby gorse bush. *I'll come back to retrieve it when we've finished.* "In fact, you may have a try now. Who can find some prey?"

The kits sprang to their paws, gazing around and sniffing vigorously at the air. "All I can smell is that rabbit," Lightning Tail complained.

"Then let's move," Gray Wing meowed, leading them a few tail-lengths away from the hollow. "Thunder, can you see anything?"

Gray Wing had already spotted a mouse nibbling on some seeds in a clump of longer grass. As it slipped between the grass stems, the tops began to wave about, and Thunder spotted the movement.

"There!" he whispered, angling his ears toward the mouse.

"Okay, go for it," Gray Wing told him.

Immediately Thunder pressed himself to the ground and began to creep forward.

Gray Wing shook his head, still keeping his voice low so as not to alarm the mouse. "No. I already told you, that way of hunting might work in the forest, where there are plenty of places to hide, and sounds in the trees that would cover your approach. But it's no good out here, because your prey can see you from a distance. You've got to rely on speed."

"Oh . . . okay." Thunder rose to his paws again, the tip of his tail twitching in frustration, then hurled himself across the moor toward the grassy tussock where the mouse was hiding.

"Faster!" Acorn Fur shrieked.

"Stupid furball!" Lightning Tail slapped his tail across his sister's mouth. "Now look what you've done!"

The mouse froze, as if it had heard Acorn Fur and realized there was danger near. Then it shot out of the long grass, scurrying toward an outcrop of rock a few tail-lengths away. Thunder tried to put on an extra burst of speed, but somehow he managed to get tangled up in his own paws and lost his balance, landing on the ground with a thump. The mouse dived into a gap between two rocks and vanished.

Thunder scrambled upright, gave his pelt a shake, and plodded back to the others with his head down. "Sorry," he mumbled.

"It's okay," Gray Wing responded, resting the tip of his tail on Thunder's shoulder. "You'll do better next time."

Glancing at Thunder's huge white paws, he could understand why the kit was so clumsy. He was obviously going to grow into a big, powerful cat, but he was at the gangly awkward stage now, not in full control of his movements. *His time will come,* Gray Wing thought. *He just needs to be patient.*

"I want to try now," Acorn Fur meowed. "If you haven't scared all the prey away."

"What?" Thunder's eyes widened indignantly. "If you hadn't—"

Gray Wing raised a paw to stop the bickering. "We'll look for more prey," he began. "There's bound to be something."

"There!" Lightning Tail pointed with his tail.

Gray Wing turned to see a small flock of birds pecking at the grass near the rocky outcrop where the mouse had vanished. He nodded. "Go for it."

Lightning Tail at once dropped into a crouch like Thunder,

as if Gray Wing's instructions had passed right over his head.

"Run, flea-brain!" Acorn Fur squealed at her brother. She took off, racing across the grass with her tail streaming out behind her.

Watching, Gray Wing admired her speed, but she was letting out excited little squeaks as she ran. A few birds had already flown off at the sound of her first squeal, and the rest of the flock rose into the air long before she got anywhere near them.

Lightning Tail, who had followed her as soon as he realized his mistake in trying to stalk, halted and turned back with a disgusted expression. "Now who's a flea-brain?" he asked.

Gray Wing shook his head, trying to hide his amusement. "You all still have a lot to learn," he murmured.

He was waiting for the two kits to come back when he was distracted by Thunder thrusting himself into a tremendous leap. Gray Wing saw that one of the birds had alighted a short distance away. Thunder's front paws reached out and batted the bird to the ground as it fluttered up in a vain attempt to escape.

The young cat straightened up with the limp body of the bird in his jaws. His eyes were shining. "I got one!" he announced, his voice muffled by his mouthful of feathers.

For a moment Gray Wing couldn't give him the praise he deserved. That massive leap had reminded him too much of Clear Sky, Thunder's father. *Like when he killed that hawk, not long before we left the mountains.*

The pain of remembering the days when he and his brother

were so close washed over Gray Wing again. He hadn't ventured into the forest or tried to see his brother since Clear Sky had refused to acknowledge Thunder as his son, and that had been before the cold season started. At their last meeting, Gray Wing had even declared that Clear Sky was no longer his brother. The loss of his closest family member felt like a thorn in Gray Wing's heart, but he couldn't forgive him for the harsh rejection of Thunder.

Gray Wing sighed. *I've been trying to raise Thunder to show kindness and compassion—but is Clear Sky's character going to come out in him, no matter what I do?*

A soft *mrrow* of greeting sounded behind Gray Wing, distracting him from his dark thoughts. He turned to see a tortoiseshell she-cat bounding toward him. His eyes widened and delight flashed through him like a ray of sunshine at the sight of her. Turtle Tail! She'd come with them down from the mountains and been a faithful friend, until . . . *But no. I won't dwell on that now.*

"Turtle Tail!" he exclaimed. "How did you find us?" She'd left the mountain cats before they'd moved into their new camp.

"I went to the hollow where we used to live," Turtle Tail explained, "and it was empty . . . just a trace of stale cat scent." She shivered. "I thought at first foxes must have killed all of you. But I couldn't let myself believe that, so I went on looking until I picked up a trail, and here I am!"

"It's so good to see you!" Gray Wing told her.

Turtle Tail padded up to Gray Wing and touched noses with him. "It's good to see you, too," she purred. "It's been a long time." Glancing around at the kits, she added, "It looks as if you've got your paws full!"

Gray Wing nodded. He hadn't seen Turtle Tail since she helped him to rescue Thunder from the collapsing Twoleg den. Since then, she had spent all the cold season cozily in the Twolegplace, living the life of a kittypet. *I still can't believe she'd choose to do that*, Gray Wing thought, shifting his glance so that she couldn't see his expression. To choose a life where you didn't have to hunt prey and you wouldn't feel a dawn breeze ruffle your fur . . . it made no sense to Gray Wing. When she'd left, Gray Wing hadn't been able to hide his sense of betrayal, and Turtle Tail had become cold and aloof.

But it was clear that Turtle Tail's new life suited her; she was plump and healthy-looking, with a glossy pelt and bright eyes that glowed as she gazed at Gray Wing.

"And this huge cat is Thunder?" she asked, turning to the kit, who stood close by with his prey in his jaws, looking bewildered and a bit hurt. Gray Wing realized with a twinge of guilt that he still hadn't praised him for his catch. "He's grown! I remember how tiny he was when we brought him into the forest and named him."

When Thunder's mother, Storm, had died in the debris of the Twoleg den, Gray Wing and Turtle Tail had been able to save Thunder, but his littermates and mother had been lost forever. *Her fur was so soft, her eyes so beautiful* . . . Gray Wing's tail drooped and pain stabbed through his heart. *I'll never see her again.*

"Look, Thunder has caught a bird! He's going to be a great hunter." Turtle Tail's voice jolted him from his thoughts. When Gray Wing glanced at her, he saw instantly that she was being deliberately cheerful. *It's almost as though she could see what I was thinking. I suppose Turtle Tail knows me so well she even knows how to distract me if I'm sad.*

"So he is," Gray Wing agreed, shaking himself.

Thunder brightened at the praise, and the other two kits came crowding up. "We're going to be brilliant hunters too," Acorn Fur announced.

"I'm sure you are," Turtle Tail responded. Blinking, she turned to Gray Wing. "These must be Hawk Swoop's kits. They're big and strong, too. Look at them!"

"Maybe you've been away longer than you realized," Gray Wing meowed. But the hurt in Turtle Tail's eyes made him immediately regret his words. "I mean, long enough for . . . well . . . ," he stammered. "I missed you, Turtle Tail."

The she-cat's eyes shone. "I missed you, too, Gray Wing."

He turned to the kits, suddenly aware that they were watching the two adult cats and drinking in every detail of the conversation. "This is Lightning Tail, and this is Acorn Fur."

"Good names," Turtle Tail mewed, happiness returning to her face. "I'm Turtle Tail."

"Lightning Tail got his name because he's always hanging

around with Thunder," Gray Wing explained. "They're our own little storm in the making!"

Turtle Tail's eyes gleamed with amusement and she touched noses with each of the kits.

"Go and play," Gray Wing gently told them. He wanted to talk to Turtle Tail without the three of them listening in on every word.

They didn't need to be told twice. With yowls of pleasure the kits went racing off, chasing one another around the gorse bush.

"How are you getting on in the Twolegplace?" Gray Wing asked, feeling suddenly awkward. He didn't want Turtle Tail to think he was criticizing her again. "Did you make it through the cold season okay?"

"Yes, it was nice," Turtle Tail replied lightly. "Very cozy and comfortable. Bumble and I had extra company, too—not long after I went to live there, another cat came to join us."

"A rogue?" Gray Wing asked, finding that hard to believe.

"Oh, no," Turtle Tail replied. "The Twolegs went away, and when they came back, they were carrying a cat—a big tom. He told us he had lived with another Twoleg, but one day his Twoleg suddenly stopped coming to feed him."

You can't trust Twolegs, Gray Wing thought, but he had the sense not to say it out loud.

"So then the tom went to live in a place with a bunch of other cats. They were all really unhappy and whiny there, and he said that they could hear dogs barking close by. They were all cooped up together. Then the cat—they called him Tom, by the way—"

"Tom?" Gray Wing interrupted. "They called a tom, Tom? I'll never understand twolegs."

Turtle Tail shrugged. "Anyway, he was taken away from there by our Twolegs, and came to live with me and Bumble."

"Did you like him?" Gray Wing asked. "Was he friendly?"

Turtle Tail hesitated, looking down at her paws. "Oh, yes, he was friendly," she replied at last. "We got on fine." Then she gave her pelt a shake. "It was time to leave, though. I missed my friends on the moors."

Turtle Tail is returning to us! Pleasure raced through Gray Wing's body, but before he had a chance to say anything, the three kits came charging back, chasing one another in circles, and skidded in a patch of loose soil, unable to stop in time. Lightning Tail barreled into Turtle Tail, who lost her balance and fell onto her back, her legs and tail waving as she let out a yowl of pain and discomfort.

Gray Wing's eyes widened with shock as he looked at her, seeing her swollen belly for the first time. *She's expecting kits!*

"Are you hurt?" he asked anxiously as he went to help her up.

Turtle Tail leaned on his shoulder, panting as she regained her paws. For a moment she was silent. Finally she let out a short puff of breath. "I'm fine . . . I think."

Gray Wing's gaze swiveled back to the three kits. Lightning Tail was cowering behind Thunder, his expression horrified. Gray Wing beckoned him forward with a flick of his tail.

"Come and apologize to Turtle Tail," he ordered sternly.

Lightning Tail cringed as he approached, his head down and his tail trailing behind him. "I'm really sorry," he mewed.

"It's okay." Turtle Tail gave his ears a swift lick.

"Just remember not to go dashing around without looking where you're going," Gray Wing told him. He paused briefly, then added, "Now I thought I told you to go play."

He waited until all three kits had bundled off, squeaking excitedly. *Turtle Tail is having kits . . . who would have expected that?*

"So," he meowed to her, angling his ears at her swollen belly. "How did that happen?"

"How do you think it happened?" Turtle Tail hissed. Then her eyes softened. "I made a mistake," she went on. "I missed you all so much. Tom seemed strong and friendly, I thought I could move on and make a new life with him. But when I realized I was expecting kits, he . . . he changed."

Gray Wing felt a growl rising up in his throat. "If he hurt you . . ."

"Oh, no!" Turtle Tail assured him. "Tom was still friendly, but he didn't want to make any plans for the kits with me. And Bumble seemed uncomfortable any time I mentioned them." Turtle Tail flicked her tail-tip. "But neither of them would admit that anything was wrong."

"So what did you do?" Gray Wing asked.

"I begged Bumble to be honest with me. She didn't want to, but at last she told me that the Twolegs would take my kits away and give them to other Twolegs." Her voice shook a little. "I would never see them again once they didn't need milk from me anymore."

"That's dreadful!" Gray Wing exclaimed, pressing his nose into Turtle Tail's shoulder. How could a family be torn apart like that? In the mountains and now here on the moors, the cats pulled together. Everyone helped look after the kittens—it was unthinkable that any cat would give up on their young. *Well, until Clear Sky rejected Thunder*, Gray Wing reminded himself.

"Bumble said Tom had asked her not to tell me the truth. And now . . . well, I'll never trust kittypets or Twolegs again. I've learned who my real friends are, and all I want is to come back to you all." She fixed her gaze on Gray Wing, her eyes wide. "Do you think the rest of them will have me?"

He felt his heart melt under her earnest gaze. "How could they not?" he mewed, glancing again at Turtle Tail's rounded belly. For some reason, thinking of Turtle Tail carrying another cat's kits made him feel uncomfortable. "This is where you belong."

Gesturing with his tail, Gray Wing led Turtle Tail to the top of the hollow.

"Wow!" she exclaimed, her eyes stretching wide with admiration as she looked over their home. "What an awesome place! Much better than the old camp."

Gray Wing nodded. "We're safer and more sheltered here," he said, indicating the gorse bushes with his tail.

As they headed down the slope, Shattered Ice popped out

of the tunnel he was digging with Jackdaw's Cry, earth scattered over his white pelt. When he spotted Turtle Tail he halted, his eyes narrowing.

"What are you doing here?" he asked.

"Hi, Shattered Ice!" Turtle Tail greeted him. "It's good to see you again."

At first Shattered Ice didn't respond. Instead he glanced at Turtle Tail coldly, then meowed, "You turned your back on us when the weather got cold. What makes a *kittypet* like you think that you'll be welcome here now?"

Turtle Tail fluffed out her fur indignantly, almost hiding her pregnant belly. "You don't have the right to tell any cat they can't come onto the moor," she retorted. "Who do you think you are, Clear Sky?"

"Look . . . ," Gray Wing began, wincing at the mention of his brother.

Both cats ignored his attempt to intervene.

"Clear Sky has some good ideas," Shattered Ice muttered. "I'm taking you straight down to Tall Shadow," he went on. "She'll decide what to do with you."

"Turtle Tail doesn't have to—" Gray Wing began again.

"Don't bother trying to defend me," Turtle Tail interrupted, her ears flattening angrily. "I'd love to see Tall Shadow again. I've missed her, and I don't think she'll need any help putting Shattered Ice in his place."

Shattered Ice and Turtle Tail set off, joined by Jackdaw's Cry, who had emerged from the tunnel with a startled look at

Turtle Tail. Gray Wing turned to find the kits, and spotted them scrambling up onto a lichen-covered boulder, then hurling themselves off it with squeaks of excitement.

"Come on!" he called. "It's time to go home."

CHAPTER 2
❧

When Gray Wing and Turtle Tail reached the bottom of the hollow, they found Hawk Swoop, Dappled Pelt, Cloud Spots, and Rainswept Flower all standing in front of Tall Shadow.

"You need to get more power into your back legs," the black she-cat instructed them. "That way you can deal with any cat who creeps up behind you. Rainswept Flower, try it again."

Gray Wing saw that Tall Shadow had propped a big piece of bark against one of the rocks. Rainswept Flower got into position, then kicked out strongly at the bark, dislodging it and sending scraps flying into the air.

"Much better," Tall Shadow mewed. "Cloud Spots, you're next."

Gray Wing noticed that Jagged Peak was crouching a few tail-lengths away, looking on unhappily. A shiver of compassion ran through him. Life had been a struggle for Jagged Peak ever since he had fallen out of a tree and broken his leg. Clear Sky had driven him from the forest, saying he was unable to support a cat who couldn't hunt. The moorland cats had taken him in, but Gray Wing knew how guilty his young brother felt that he couldn't contribute much.

His ear twitched as Turtle Tail leaned over to whisper to him, distracting him from Jagged Peak's troubles.

"I'm surprised to see Tall Shadow training the cats in fighting techniques," she murmured. "Things must have changed around here."

Gray Wing opened his mouth to respond, but before he could speak, Shattered Ice dashed across to Tall Shadow. "We discovered a cat in our territory!" he yowled, pointing his tail in Turtle Tail's direction.

"Turtle Tail!" Rainswept Flower exclaimed, dashing over to touch her nose to Turtle Tail's ear. "Shattered Ice, she's not just *a cat*," she added, annoyance in her voice as she gazed at the white tom. "She's our *friend*."

Hawk Swoop followed her denmate, and brushed her pelt against Turtle Tail's. "It's good to see you," she meowed warmly.

The other cats held back, exchanging an uncertain glance, while hostility still radiated from Shattered Ice.

Suppressing a sigh of annoyance, Gray Wing waited anxiously for Tall Shadow's response. He knew very well how cautious the black she-cat was around strangers. *Of course, Turtle Tail isn't a stranger. But it's still not the best way to announce that she's back.*

"Since when do we talk about territories?" Turtle Tail muttered into his ear again. "Things have *really* changed."

Reluctantly Gray Wing admitted to himself that she was right. He and his denmates had become like Clear Sky and his group—much more defensive of their hunting area—since

Turtle Tail was last on the moor.

When the group had first split up, and Clear Sky had taken his cats to live in the forest, every cat had thought that they would come and go freely, visiting one another as often as they wanted. But it hadn't turned out like that, and the division between the two groups had become as hard to cross as a mountain chasm.

Tall Shadow padded over to Turtle Tail, her tail held high, while the rest of the cats gathered around curiously. Gray Wing was impressed by how noble and dignified she looked, confident in herself as their leader. *Surely she couldn't possibly be unwelcoming toward Turtle Tail?* All the same, he braced himself for an awkward conversation.

Tall Shadow dipped her head politely. "Greetings, Turtle Tail," she mewed. Flicking her tail toward the tortoiseshell's swollen belly, she added, "And congratulations. Who is the father?"

Turtle Tail scuffled her paws uneasily. "There's no father," she replied, "or none that I want involved in the kits' lives."

Tall Shadow exchanged a glance with Gray Wing, who could hear murmurs arising from the other cats. He could see that the black she-cat understood. *Turtle Tail went to live with Twolegs, and now she has kits fathered by a kittypet. The less said about that the better.*

Taking a deep breath, Tall Shadow turned to the other cats. "Good news! Turtle Tail has returned to the place where she belongs, and soon she'll give birth to kits. More cats to strengthen our group!"

"Or more mouths to feed," Shattered Ice protested. "I can't believe you're letting her walk back in here after the way she betrayed us!"

Tall Shadow whipped around, her neck fur bristling. "If you're so worried about food," she rasped, "you can go hunting."

Shattered Ice opened his jaws to protest, then caught Tall Shadow's warning glance. Muttering something inaudible, he turned and padded away, up the slope and out of the hollow.

Gray Wing watched him go. He could tell that Shattered Ice hated being humiliated in public like that. He had been one of the key cats who had led them down from the mountains. *But Tall Shadow has been leading us since Shaded Moss left her in charge, and she gets the final word here.*

Turning back to the others, Gray Wing saw that Thunder was intently watching Shattered Ice as he left the camp.

"I want to hunt too," the kit mewed.

"Not right now," Gray Wing told him. "Better leave Shattered Ice alone until he gets over his bad mood." *He always was a bit touchy. And it must be difficult for him; he's worked so hard on this new camp, and now Turtle Tail, who was gone all through the cold season, returns to enjoy it.*

"Come over here." Tall Shadow beckoned Turtle Tail toward a patch of moss. Gray Wing joined her, and the three cats sat together, watching Acorn Fur and Lightning Tail chasing butterflies. Jagged Peak limped up and settled down a couple of tail-lengths away, his eyes uncertain, as if he wasn't sure of his welcome.

"Jagged Peak, what happened to you?" Turtle Tail exclaimed, her eyes widening with shock as she saw the young cat's injury. "I thought you were living in the forest with Clear Sky."

"I was," Jagged Peak replied, scuffling his paws unhappily. "But I fell out of a tree and hurt my leg, and Clear Sky . . ." His voice trailed off.

"Clear Sky decided he only wants healthy cats," Tall Shadow finished for him. "So Jagged Peak came back to us. It might take a while, but he'll get better."

She looked kindly at Jagged Peak, who nodded, but Gray Wing knew very well that his brother wasn't at all certain that the injured leg would mend.

"I'm so sorry," Turtle Tail meowed, her green eyes full of sympathy.

"So," Tall Shadow continued. "What do you think of our new home, Turtle Tail?" Her eyes shone with interest. "Have we changed much? It's good to see you back. I'd love to hear more about what made you decide to return."

Turtle Tail was looking around the hollow, taking every-. thing in with an intense green gaze. Gray Wing tried to see the cats through her eyes: plump and happy, their pelts shining with health. She was impressed by the camp, he knew: the cover of gorse and rocks that stuck up out of the earth, and the wide tunnel dens.

"Aren't you glad we left the mountains?" Turtle Tail asked eventually, avoiding Tall Shadow's questions. "Do you remember how Stoneteller sent us on our way? What was it she said? 'There is another place for some of us, full of sunlight and warmth and prey for all seasons.' It seems so long ago now."

Gray Wing nodded in agreement. He thought of Turtle Tail's bounce and energy back then, the hope and spirit that had been so important when their journey got rough. She seemed different now; he could sense that she had gained wisdom and experience. *We've all changed, I guess,* he thought.

As Gray Wing watched his friend, he saw the happiness fade from her face. He opened his jaws to question her, but Tall Shadow got there before him.

"What is it?" she asked. "What's wrong, Turtle Tail?"

Turtle Tail dug her claws into the soft moss. "I'm not sure I can bring my strengths to help you anymore," she confessed. "Stoneteller used to praise me for my speed and sharp eyes, and look at me now." She gestured toward her heavy belly with one paw.

"You still have your sharp eyes," Tall Shadow mewed. "Your skills are needed here more than ever." She hesitated for a moment, then glanced thoughtfully around her. "I need some cat to be the eyes and ears of the hollow," she continued. "To watch the horizon and report back. Will you?"

Turtle Tail looked confused. "Why do you need a cat to keep such careful watch?"

"Things aren't quite as happy as they appear," Tall Shadow explained. "True, the cats are well fed and cared for, but things have changed. It's many moons since we laid eyes on Clear Sky, but when we've met his cats, they've made it quite clear that the forest is theirs now. They talk about cats trespassing, and if any of us sets paw under the trees, they chase us off."

Gray Wing nodded; regret pierced him like a thorn as he realized afresh how distant they had become from Clear Sky and his cats. As kits, he and Clear Sky had spent every waking moment together. *I never would have guessed we'd end up like this.*

"It feels as if they're hostile," he mewed.

"Have you seen any of them near the Twolegplace?" Tall Shadow asked Turtle Tail. "We need to know everything we can about them. Any detail, however slight, could be useful."

Turtle Tail shook her head, while Gray Wing felt his fur prickle. *Are we spying on Clear Sky now?*

But as Tall Shadow went on, Gray Wing realized that wasn't the most important thing on her mind. "If Clear Sky's cats don't want to share hunting rights in the forest, it's up to me to protect our hunting rights out here. As it is, we always seem to be arguing with rogue cats over prey."

"That was a problem before," Turtle Tail commented with a glance at Gray Wing.

"True," Tall Shadow meowed. "But it's definitely gotten worse. We'd achieved some kind of understanding with the rogue cats. We left them alone, and they did the same. Now . . . it's difficult to put into words, but there are tensions that we didn't have before. That's why we need your help. Can you let me know when strange faces appear or hunt near our home?"

"I'll do whatever I can," Turtle Tail promised. Gray Wing could see that her eyes were full of bitterness. "I should never have left," she admitted. "If I'd been here, I could have done more to help. And I can't believe that Clear Sky is behaving like that!"

Gray Wing felt that he had to defend his brother. "He's just doing what he thinks is best."

Turtle Tail flicked her tail, showing clearly that she wasn't convinced. "Since when does he have to be so protective about hunting rights?" she asked. "There's enough prey here for every cat."

A rustling sounded behind Gray Wing. He glanced over his shoulder to see that Jagged Peak had crept closer to listen to their conversation. He might have been permanently injured, but clearly the young cat had cunning enough to move silently. His eyes were gleaming with excitement.

"I can help, too!" he announced. "I can keep watch with Turtle Tail. I might not be able to run or scramble into trees, but I can guard the hollow." Glancing at Turtle Tail's swollen belly, he added, "Turtle Tail won't be as capable as she normally is, and I can't run like I used to, but between the two of us . . ."

Tall Shadow hesitated, her eyes compassionate as she surveyed the injured cat. "Thank you, Jagged Peak," she responded. "But all I want now is to see you rest and get well."

Gray Wing's muscles tensed as he saw the look of hurt and rejection on Jagged Peak's face. He knew Tall Shadow meant to be kind, but he also knew how desperately Jagged Peak needed to prove to himself that he could still be useful.

"Go on with the exercises Cloud Spots gave you," he mewed sympathetically to his brother. "You'll soon be out hunting again."

Jagged Peak turned away without replying, his head

drooping. Gray Wing knew that his brother didn't believe his encouraging words. Turtle Tail rested her tail on Jagged Peak's shoulder, but he shrugged her off.

Watching him slink away, hobbling on his damaged leg, Gray Wing asked himself whether Tall Shadow had made the right decision.

"Maybe you should have let him help," he murmured.

"It would make him feel better," Turtle Tail agreed. "And another pair of eyes can't be bad, surely?"

Tall Shadow's sharp gaze flicked from one to the other. "I'm supposed to be in charge," she mewed abruptly. "It's not easy." She sniffed and stalked off toward her den.

Gray Wing exchanged a glance with Turtle Tail, whose mouth hung open in shock. *Who put ants in her fur?* Gray Wing wondered.

CHAPTER 3
🍀

"*How about I give you a* tour of the hollow and the moors?" Gray Wing suggested to Turtle Tail. He wanted to dispel the tension left by Tall Shadow's departure. "You should get to know them again. Besides," he added, teasingly, "you might have gotten soft after living with Twolegs."

"Rude furball!" Turtle Tail exclaimed, batting at him with one paw, though there was a glimmer of affection in her eyes.

"Okay, not soft," Gray Wing agreed. "But come on, let me show you around anyway." The idea of being alone with Turtle Tail was comforting. *I missed her so much*, he realized. Now that she had returned, he could see the enormous hole she had left in his life when she went away.

But as they headed up the slope out of the hollow, Rainswept Flower called over to them. "Can I come too? I'd love the chance to catch up with Turtle Tail."

"Of course," Gray Wing replied, though not without a pang of regret. *I wanted Turtle Tail all to myself!* But then he cast a sidelong glance at her and felt a thrill pass over him. It didn't matter—she wasn't going anywhere. There would be plenty of time to talk. *And Rainswept Flower is such a great cat;*

we're lucky to have her in the hollow.

As Rainswept Flower raced to join them, Gray Wing spotted a flicker of movement and saw Jagged Peak emerging from his nest. "Can I come too?" the young cat asked.

Gray Wing shook his head. "No," he responded gently. "Stay in the hollow and build up your strength."

Jagged Peak looked stricken at his refusal, his tail trailing on the ground as he turned away.

"Jagged Peak, wait!" Rainswept Flower turned back and went to touch noses with the little gray tom. "When we come back, I promise I'll help you with your exercises."

"I'm sick of exercising," Jagged Peak meowed, his voice shaking. "It's so boring!"

Rainswept Flower glanced at Gray Wing, who was waiting with Turtle Tail near the top of the hollow. "I'll be back soon," she assured Jagged Peak. "We all will. Really, you're not missing out on anything special." Touching the young cat's nose again, she headed back toward Gray Wing.

As they turned to leave, Gray Wing could feel Jagged Peak's gaze boring into his back. "That was kind," he commented to Rainswept Flower.

Rainswept Flower blinked at him. "I think we all should do more to help Jagged Peak," she suggested. "It's no good constantly telling him that he *can't* do things."

"You may be right," Gray Wing admitted, with a twinge of guilt. "Thanks for being so sensitive."

The tabby she-cat twitched her whiskers. "It was nothing."

The three cats left the hollow side by side, and headed

across the moor in the direction of the river. Gray Wing reveled in the warm breeze that ruffled his fur, and the scent of fresh growing things that wafted along with it. They passed a moorland pool where reeds waved gently and sunlight glittered on the surface of the water.

As they were picking their way up a slope covered with gorse bushes, a rabbit suddenly darted across their path, its eyes wide with terror, then vanished into the gorse before any cat could try to intercept it.

"Hmm . . . ," Gray Wing commented. "Where there's a fleeing rabbit, there's bound to be—there she is!"

As he spoke, the rogue she-cat Wind emerged from one of the bushes, her brown pelt untidy and a disgusted expression on her face. "Stupid creature!" she spat. "I nearly had it!"

Gray Wing let out a *mrrow* of laughter. "You must be getting slow in your old age!"

Wind slid her claws out threateningly, which amused Gray Wing even more. He knew very well that Wind wouldn't attack him; they had come a long way since their first hostile meeting when Gray Wing had killed the rabbit Wind and her friend Gorse were chasing.

As if Gray Wing's thought had called him up, Gorse appeared now, a skinny tabby shape slipping out from the shelter of the bushes. Turtle Tail glanced at Gray Wing, looking cautious and worried, as the cat stepped forward. *Of course! She never knew the two rogues well when she lived on the moor.*

"It's okay," Rainswept Flower reassured her, brushing

Turtle Tail's shoulder with her tail-tip. "Gorse and Wind are our friends."

Gray Wing remembered talking to Tall Shadow a few moons ago, discussing whether it would be a good idea to invite the rogues to join them in the hollow. In the end, Tall Shadow had decided against admitting them. *But who knows what the future holds?* Gray Wing asked himself. *I won't say anything to Gorse and Wind now, but maybe in a while . . .*

"How has the hunting been?" Gray Wing asked Wind. He admired the way she would dive down into the tunnels to hunt the rabbits in their own burrows. She knew the whole network of tunnels that lay beneath the moor.

And that might be useful one day.

Wind gave a snort of disgust. "There's plenty of prey," she replied, "but hunting is becoming . . . complicated."

"Why don't you say it straight out?" Gorse demanded, with the beginnings of a snarl. "Clear Sky is refusing to let us hunt in the forest. Can you believe it? How dare Clear Sky tell us where we can and can't hunt?"

Wind nodded in agreement. "The problem is, all the hunting around here is awkward now. One argument after another." Flicking her tail angrily, she added, "The other day I met a couple of other rogues—Thorn and Dew—at the edge of the moor. They'd never been exactly friendly, but we mostly left each other alone, and we were happy with that. But that day we ended up chasing the same hare. It was big enough to feed all of us, and there was a time we would have shared it."

"That's right," Gorse put in. "But this time Thorn and Dew dragged the prey away. They threatened to claw our pelts off if we came anywhere near it." He shook his head in confusion. "It never used to be like this. Not until . . ." He glanced at them.

Gray Wing saw Rainswept Flower's tail begin to twitch, and she took a pace forward. "Are you blaming the mountain cats?" she demanded.

Turtle Tail gave Gray Wing an anxious look, as if she expected a fight to break out. Gray Wing rested his tail-tip on her shoulder. "It'll be fine," he murmured, hoping he was right, and realizing that he would have to report this to Tall Shadow.

Gorse's neck fur began to bristle, but Wind shouldered him away and faced Rainswept Flower. "We're not blaming you," she meowed. "At least, not all of you." Letting out a sigh, she turned to Turtle Tail. "I know you, don't I?" she meowed.

"Yes, this is Turtle Tail," Gray Wing responded. "She left the moor for a bit"—*no need to tell them she lived as a kittypet*—"but she's back now."

Wind narrowed her eyes and gave Turtle Tail an assessing look. "I think she's okay," she mewed to Gorse. "Should I show you some of the best hunting areas around here?" she added to Turtle Tail. "You need to know, if times are going to get more difficult."

"Yes . . . yes, thanks," Turtle Tail stammered, looking taken aback. *It must be hard for her, realizing that life out here isn't as perfect as she'd imagined.*

But once again Gray Wing was impressed by how kind and friendly Wind could be, even in the midst of her own troubles.

Rainswept Flower obviously realized it, too. "I shouldn't have taken offense," she mewed, blinking apologetically. "It's just that . . . well, you're right that times are more challenging now."

Wind twitched her whiskers. "It's okay."

Gorse and Wind led the way toward the river, following a tiny stream that trickled along a deep cleft in the moorland, a place where the mountain cats had never hunted before. The stream was edged with long grass and ferns that overhung the water.

"This place is no good for rabbits," Wind explained as Gray Wing gazed around in amazement. "But you can generally find a mouse or two, or a vole, where the plants grow thickest."

"Thanks for showing us," Gray Wing responded, enjoying the dazzle of sunlight on the ripples and the gentle gurgling sound the water made. "Why haven't we searched for prey here?"

Wind stifled a snort of laughter. "You just have to know where to look!"

"And now this way." Gorse leaped across the stream and scrambled up the side of the cleft onto the open moor again. "There are always a few rabbits around here," he panted as he waited for the others to join him. "You can see some of their holes over there," he added, pointing with his tail toward a steep rocky bank with a few scrawny bushes clinging to the thin soil between the stones.

Gray Wing tasted the air. Gorse was right; there was a strong smell of rabbit, and he spotted several piles of their droppings among the grass.

"You're carrying some extra weight," Wind mewed to Turtle Tail as they set off again.

Turtle Tail gave her shoulder a couple of embarrassed licks. "My kits should be here soon," she murmured.

"Then you need some easy hunting," Gorse told her. "Maybe a nice, fat pigeon that can't get too far. Let's head for the river."

The rest of the cats followed Gorse. Gray Wing pricked his ears, listening for the weird clacking call that would tell him there were pigeons around.

"Over there." Rainswept Flower angled her ears forward and Gray Wing picked up the sounds of several pigeons, though he couldn't see anything.

"Stupid birds," Gorse muttered. "They don't know when to stay quiet."

The cats prowled ahead more slowly. The moorland had given way to sandy soil and rocky outcrops with tussocks of wiry grass and bushes here and there. Gray Wing still couldn't spot any prey until Turtle Tail halted and raised her tail.

"Under that bush," she whispered.

Gray Wing peered hard and finally made out the pinkish breast of a pigeon that was pecking at something on the ground between two boulders close to the edge of the river.

"Your eyes *are* sharp," he breathed. *This is so great—hunting in a new place, and with Turtle Tail.*

"Yes!" Gorse flashed past him, clearly unable to resist making the catch.

The pigeon took flight with sharp flicks of its wings, but Gorse hurled himself at it and gripped its tail with his claws. Two or three more birds broke out of the bushes as he sprang, and soared upward, well out of danger. Gorse's pigeon struggled frantically; one of its wing tips caught Gorse in the face and he tumbled backward, losing his grip on its tail feathers.

Wind sighed. "I suppose I'd better finish the job."

As she spoke she raced forward and made a ferocious leap as the pigeon took off. Sinking her claws into its breast, she wrestled it to the ground again and held it until it stopped struggling.

Turtle Tail's eyes were glimmering with amusement. "Do you think we should show them how to catch birds?" she whispered to Gray Wing.

Gray Wing gave his head a tiny shake. "We might offend them." *But we made cleaner kills than that in the mountains.*

Wind looked up from her prey with a feather stuck between her teeth. "Come and share," she invited.

Gray Wing, Turtle Tail, and Rainswept Flower headed toward her, all three trying to hide amusement.

"I thought we were supposed to be showing Turtle Tail how to catch fat, lazy pigeons," Rainswept Flower mewed innocently.

"Well, I've certainly learned something," Turtle Tail responded.

When they were all crouched around the pigeon, taking bites of the warm flesh, she continued, "I'm glad I came back. Hunting has never looked like such fun!"

"Remember that there are tensions now," Gray Wing warned her, swallowing a mouthful.

"What tensions?" a new voice chimed in.

Gray Wing stiffened. Looking around, he spotted a silver-furred cat sitting on a rock in the middle of the river. Water swirled a mouse-length beneath his paws and his elegantly curled tail.

"Who's that?" Rainswept Flower exclaimed, shocked. "What cat likes sitting near water?"

The silver cat leaped neatly across a line of stones and climbed the bank until he stood beside them. He looked friendly and completely at ease. "Hi," he meowed. "My name's River Ripple."

Wind and Gorse exchanged a glance; clearly the newcomer was a stranger to them, too.

"Are you a rogue?" Gray Wing asked.

River Ripple shrugged. "I don't like giving myself labels. I live by the river"—he flicked his tail toward the opposite bank—"and that's all any cat needs to know."

"I'm Gray Wing, and this is Turtle Tail and Rainswept Flower," Gray Wing began with a polite dip of his head. "And these two are Gorse and Wind."

As he spoke, he noticed that River Ripple was only half listening; he was eyeing the remains of the pigeon. "That looks tasty," he remarked, swiping his tongue around his whiskers.

Gray Wing snorted with amusement, and pushed the rest of the prey over to the silver tom. *That was a pretty heavy hint!*

"Thanks." River Ripple bent his head and demolished the pigeon in a series of neat, rapid bites.

"I've never seen a cat eat so delicately," Turtle Tail commented.

Neither have I, Gray Wing thought. *So elegant, even when he's hungry!*

River Ripple met Turtle Tail's gaze, then shrugged. "I'm a cat full of surprises," he meowed. He dipped his head to the others, then, with a flash of his tail, raced back across the stones and plunged into the undergrowth on the opposite bank of the river.

Gray Wing and his friends looked at one another. "I think that was his way of saying good-bye," Gray Wing meowed. *I've never met such a strange cat!*

"Weird . . . ," Wind murmured.

Before any of the others could speak, a series of guttural, angry noises sounded above the rushing of the river. Gray Wing felt a prickle of uneasiness, and exchanged an alarmed glance with Turtle Tail. "What's that?" he asked.

The noises came again, louder and closer this time.

"Dogs!" Wind exclaimed.

A rush of panic invaded Gray Wing, and he fought to stay calm. "We have to find shelter!" he exclaimed. Even as he spoke, he realized that he had no idea where to go. *We don't know this place!*

Wind nodded. "You're right. Come on, Gorse. Let's go to

our nest—quickly." As she and the tabby tom slunk off down a gully, she glanced over her shoulder. "You'd better get back to the hollow as fast as you can," she told the mountain cats. With a flourish of her tail, she added, "It's that way."

Gray Wing and the others had already risen to their paws. Leaving the last scraps of the pigeon, they raced across the moor. Gray Wing would have liked to move even faster, but he had to match his pace to Turtle Tail's; with her extra weight, she was struggling to keep up. The barking continued behind them; Gray Wing couldn't tell if they were outpacing the dogs.

"Are you okay?" he asked Turtle Tail. He could hear her panting.

"Yes, I'm fine," Turtle Tail gasped. "Pull ahead if you need to."

"Never!" Gray Wing retorted. "I'm not leaving you."

Eventually the camp came into view. With Rainswept Flower in the lead they skidded down the slope.

"Dogs!" Gray Wing yowled.

More barking exploded into the air just behind them. How had the dogs been able to find their way here? Cold horror froze Gray Wing from ears to tail-tip. *We've led the dogs straight to the camp. Our fresh scent has given us away!*

Tall Shadow, who was sitting on the tall rock at the far end of the hollow, leaped to her paws. "Scatter!" she yowled. "Take cover!"

Hawk Swoop and Jackdaw's Cry dived down the nearest tunnel, pushing Acorn Fur and Lightning Tail in front of them. Dappled Pelt and Cloud Spots raced up the opposite slope and vanished onto the moor. Rainswept Flower thrust herself into a gap between two boulders.

Gray Wing guided Turtle Tail toward his own sleeping tunnel and followed her inside, turning so that he could look out into the camp. Turtle Tail cowered beside him, their flanks pressed together.

The barking grew louder still. Gray Wing's eyes stretched wide with fear and shock as two dogs shot over the lip of the hollow and down toward their friends. One of them was a rangy creature with a brindled pelt, the other was small and white. Their paws churned up moss as they bounded to and fro, sniffing at the mouths of the tunnels.

Tall Shadow still stood on top of her rock, her back arched and her fur fluffed out so that she looked twice her size. She was snarling and she had raised one paw, her claws out ready to strike if one of the dogs came within range. The small white dog pawed at the bottom of the rock for a few heartbeats, yipping in a frenzy, but he couldn't reach the black she-cat.

Meanwhile the bigger dog had found some discarded rabbit bones and was chewing them up; Gray Wing winced as he heard the bones cracking. The dog spat them out a moment later and began sniffing at the tunnel where Jackdaw's Cry and Hawk Swoop were trying to protect Lightning Tail and Acorn Fur.

"Oh, no!" Turtle Tail whispered. "Those poor kits!"

Gray Wing could hardly breathe with the tension, but he

gathered himself to leap out and attack from behind if the dog looked likely to force his way in.

The dog had begun to scrape at the loose earth around the tunnel mouth when another sound rose above the dogs' barking: the roar of a monster on the distant Thunderpath. The dogs paused, their heads on one side, listening. Then they headed back up the slope, chasing each other as they retreated the way they had come. Their yelping died away, but it was still many heartbeats before Gray Wing dared to emerge, with Turtle Tail nervously following him.

Tall Shadow leaped down from her rock and Rainswept Flower emerged from between the stones where she had been hiding. Jackdaw's Cry poked his head out of the tunnel. "Are they gone?" he asked.

It was Dappled Pelt who replied, reappearing at the top of the hollow with Cloud Spots. "Yes, they're running toward the river," she reported, padding down to join the others. "We're safe now."

Letting out a breath of relief, Gray Wing glanced around the camp. Then his muscles tensed again as he realized that one cat was missing. "Thunder!" he exclaimed. "Where's Thunder?" He raised his voice to a yowl. "Thunder!"

His cry echoed around the camp, but no cat replied.

"Who saw him last?" Tall Shadow demanded.

"He was here earlier, when Turtle Tail arrived," Rainswept Flower replied.

"Has anyone seen him since then?" Tall Shadow's gaze swept around the cats, who were huddled together, scared and shaken. "No? Okay, let's search the camp. Check all the tunnels."

The cats scattered, vanishing into the dens and beneath the lowest boughs of the gorse bushes, only to return a few moments later. There was no sign of Thunder.

Dread enveloped Gray Wing like cold, clinging fog. "Thunder must have followed Shattered Ice when he went out to hunt," he meowed, realizing that the two of them were on the moor, and vulnerable if the dogs spotted them.

Turtle Tail nudged him. "It's worse than that," she told him, her sharp eyes ranging across the hollow. "Jagged Peak has gone too."

CHAPTER 4

❧

Thunder took in a huge breath and let it out in a sigh of utter satisfaction. He couldn't imagine anywhere he would rather be than here in the forest. He loved the sheltering branches of the trees overhead, the rustling of prey in the undergrowth, and the exciting scents coming at him from all directions. He couldn't decide which of them he wanted to investigate first.

Bouncing gently on his paws, he exclaimed, "This is *brilliant!* So much better than trying to chase rabbits on the moor."

Shattered Ice, standing a couple of tail-lengths farther into the forest, gave him a suspicious look from narrowed eyes. "You got permission to come with me?" he asked.

Thunder felt his mouth turn dry. "Oh, yes . . . yes, I did."

Shattered Ice still looked suspicious; Thunder couldn't tell whether he believed him. *Please don't send me back to camp.*

The gray-and-white tom twitched his tail impatiently. "Okay then. Are you going to stand there all day?" he asked.

"No, I'm going to hunt!" Spotting a tiny movement in the shelter of a clump of ferns, Thunder crouched down. "Watch me!"

It felt so natural to be creeping forward like this, using the undergrowth for cover and making sure he didn't put his paws on a dead leaf or a twig that might alert his prey. His body was relaxed and his limbs moved fluidly; it was as if he knew instinctively what he had to do. *Gray Wing wouldn't expect me to run here*, he thought.

The grasses parted and a tiny dark-pelted creature scuttled out from under the ferns. Pushing off with powerful hind legs, Thunder pounced. His paws slammed down on the soft body and he sank his claws into it.

"Got it!" he exclaimed. "I've caught a—what is it, Shattered Ice?"

His denmate came to sniff at the small body with the unusually long snout. "It's a shrew," he told Thunder, and added disparagingly, "A scrawny thing like that isn't going to keep all of us fed. Come on, there'll be bigger prey farther into the forest."

Stung, Thunder considered carrying his prey back to the camp. But being in the forest was too exciting. He shoved the body of the shrew under the nearest bush, ready to collect when he came back, and pattered after Shattered Ice. *I'll show him!* he thought. *I'll show all the cats. I can hunt and provide for us all.*

He had never felt so free, able to follow his instincts without Gray Wing telling him he was doing it wrong. He would always be grateful to Gray Wing for saving his life. But now, he was ready to be his own cat.

Halting, he clawed at the ground in his frustration.

Shattered Ice stopped too, glancing over his shoulder. "What's the matter with you?" he asked.

Thunder hesitated. *I can't tell him what I was thinking,* he realized. *I'd feel like a traitor.* But Shattered Ice was still waiting for an answer.

Thunder glanced around, looking for a distraction. He remembered the stories he'd heard about Clear Sky's cats guarding the forest and driving off any intruders. A shiver of apprehension prickled his pads. "We shouldn't be here," he mewed, suddenly wondering whether any of his father's cats had spotted them. *It was foolish of me to think we were alone here.*

But Shattered Ice only let out a snort of amusement. "No, we shouldn't," he agreed. "Why do you think I came here in the first place? I won't be told what to do—not by Tall Shadow and not by Clear Sky's mange-ridden followers. I'll only listen to cats I respect, and I go where I like."

He looked disdainfully over his shoulder at Thunder, who was panting to keep up with Shattered Ice's long strides. "Why don't you go back to your kin, youngster? This place isn't for kits. I should never have let you come."

Thunder felt his neck fur bristling up. *I'm not just a kit. And I'm not going back to my kin!*

He stalked after Shattered Ice, ears pricked and jaws parted for the first sign of prey, so that he could prove himself. For a heartbeat his ears flicked toward the moor and he cast a swift glance to where he could still make out the rolling sweep of open country through the outlying trees. He could imagine what Gray Wing would have to say when he found out what he'd done.

Then he shrugged. *I'm not going back!* he resolved, determined to ignore his creeping sense of guilt. *Wait till they see what I can do.*

"I'll show you how I can hunt," he told Shattered Ice.

The trees were thinning out; there was a clearing just ahead, and in the middle of it was . . . a rabbit! The creature was nibbling on some grass, clearly oblivious to the presence of cats. *Stupid puffball*, Thunder thought. *Now's my chance!* He took off toward it, but forgot all about his earlier caution, barreling through the undergrowth. Dry, crisp leaves on the forest floor crackled under his paws.

The rabbit sat up, startled, then raced for the edge of the clearing and vanished into a hole among the roots of an oak tree. Thunder halted, frustrated. Shame throbbed through his whole body as he heard a *mrrow* of laughter from Shattered Ice.

Shattered Ice padded over, looking down at him, the laughter gone from his expression. "All right, all right," he sighed. "Don't look so upset. It's not the end of the world. I'll help you learn, okay?"

Thunder brightened up immediately. "Sure!"

"Start by getting low and listening for little animals in the bushes," Shattered Ice instructed him.

Obediently Thunder crouched. "Like this?"

Shattered Ice moved slowly around him, examining his position with a critical eye. "Not bad," he commented. "Move your forepaws back a bit, and keep your tail out of the way."

Thunder felt his denmate pushing his haunches down with one paw. The pose felt awkward for a moment, until he began to get used to it.

"That's the right position," Shattered Ice meowed. "Stay

like that for a moment so you remember—"

"Teaching your friend how to steal prey?" asked a sudden voice.

Thunder whirled around. Two strange cats had appeared at the edge of the clearing: a black-and-white tom and a smaller yellow she-cat. Thunder realized they must have approached them from upwind while Shattered Ice was showing him how to crouch. They were staring at Thunder and Shattered Ice with hostile eyes. *I was right*, Thunder thought. *We weren't alone.*

Shattered Ice had whipped around too, and was returning the strange cats' glares. "Leaf. Petal," he mewed, moving protectively in front of Thunder. "How *nice* to see you."

The newcomers padded forward and stalked around Thunder and Shattered Ice, their shoulder fur bristling and their tails lashing.

"You're trespassing," Petal snarled. "What should we do with them, Leaf?"

"Slash their noses to start with," Leaf growled. "And then rip their pelts off."

Shattered Ice slid his claws out defiantly. "I'd like to see you try!" Hissing, he added, "We're not thieves or trespassers. We're just cats like you, trying to survive."

Petal's eyes narrowed and she shoved her face up close to Shattered Ice. Thunder's belly clenched and he winced as he wondered how his denmate would react.

To Thunder's surprise, the gray-and-white tom didn't attack, which made Thunder realize that this encounter was even more serious than he'd thought. *Shattered Ice would never allow himself to be pushed around. Not unless he had no choice . . .*

"You and your friend here can go back where you came from," Petal hissed. "Pass on the message that you're not welcome in the forest anymore. If you dare to hunt here, there *will* be consequences."

The expression on Shattered Ice's face hardened. "What sort of consequences, dungface?" he demanded.

There! Shattered Ice had finally reacted, throwing one of the worst insults Thunder knew.

Petal's fur bristled and she drew back a paw to slash her claws across Shattered Ice's muzzle.

"No!" Thunder yowled before he could stop himself.

But suddenly there was a movement at one side of the clearing. A clump of ferns parted and two other cats strode into the open.

Relief flooded through Thunder as he recognized them: Falling Feather and Moon Shadow. Both of them had made the journey from the mountains; Thunder had met them when they had come to visit the camp on the moor.

"Petal, what are you doing?" Falling Feather asked, bounding forward. "Shattered Ice saved my life!"

"What?" Petal drew back grudgingly. "When?"

"When we were traveling from the mountains," Falling Feather replied. "He saved me from a bright red monster."

"Is that true?" Leaf asked.

Shattered Ice gave a curt nod. "Yes."

Leaf took a pace back, looking uncomfortable. "You know we're not supposed to let cats trespass on our territory," he protested to Falling Feather. "These cats were trying to hunt."

"We were only defending ourselves," Petal added.

"Don't worry." Moon Shadow puffed out his chest importantly. "I can escort these cats away."

Shattered Ice rolled his eyes. "You haven't changed then, Moon Shadow," he mewed. "Still showing off. We don't need escorting, thank you very much."

Thunder cringed as Moon Shadow flexed his claws and drew his lips back in a snarl. He hoped that Shattered Ice hadn't gone too far. "Would you prefer a fight, flea-pelt?"

Falling Feather pushed her way between the two toms before either of them could strike a blow. "Stop this!" she ordered. "I'll never turn my back on a cat who once saved my life. Still," she added, turning to Shattered Ice, "you have to understand that things have changed now. It's best that you don't come here to hunt. Clear Sky wouldn't be happy."

A pang struck Thunder like claws around his heart at the mention of his father. "Would Clear Sky really be so angry?" he asked. "He wouldn't deny his own son, would he?"

The other cats all looked at one another uneasily, and a nasty silence dragged out until Thunder wanted to yowl to break it. His heart sank as low as his paws.

At last Falling Feather turned to him. "Clear Sky is only concerned about helping every cat survive," she explained gently. "He can't have favorites. And so that all cats know where they can hunt, he's making sure that the boundaries are respected. That's all we're asking for—a little respect."

Thunder's pelt felt hot with shame as he listened to

Falling Feather. *Shattered Ice and I shouldn't have entered the forest, but they didn't need to be so hostile. We haven't done anything wrong!* He exchanged an uncomfortable glance with Shattered Ice. "What should we do?" he asked.

Before Shattered Ice could reply, a loud barking split the quiet air, coming from the direction of their camp. Thunder's heart began to pound. "Dogs!" he exclaimed.

"We have to go to the others!" Shattered Ice meowed.

Without another word he and Shattered Ice broke away from the forest cats, who were already disappearing farther into the forest. They pelted through the trees, heading for the moor. Thunder could only hope they wouldn't be too late.

CHAPTER 5

Thunder exploded from the trees, hard on Shattered Ice's paws, and raced up the slope, his paws pounding over the wiry moorland grass. He could still hear the dogs barking, but he couldn't see anything until he reached the ridge.

Pausing to catch his breath, Thunder looked down the hill. Now he could see the dogs in the distance, and hear their yelping and growling more clearly. Beyond them he spotted the small figure of a cat, hobbling and totally exposed as he tried to reach the camp. He kept glancing back over his shoulder as the dogs' powerful legs ate up the distance between them.

"That's Jagged Peak!" Thunder exclaimed, pointing with his tail. "What's he doing out here?"

"Never mind that. Come on!" Shattered Ice mewed. "We have to head off the dogs before they catch him."

Together the two cats rushed into the valley. But before they reached the dogs another cat appeared from the direction of the hollow. He was much closer to Jagged Peak, racing toward him with his belly fur brushing the grass and his tail streaming out behind him.

"Gray Wing!" Thunder gasped. "Oh, no! What's he doing?"

Gray Wing dashed straight past Jagged Peak, who halted to stare at him. Gray Wing yowled something at him and hurled himself at the nearest dog, a leggy brindled animal with a lolling tongue. Reaching out a paw, Gray Wing swiped his claws across the dog's nose, then instantly doubled back and darted away. Faintly Thunder heard him snarl, "Take that, flea-pelt!"

The brindled dog let out a howl of pain and fury and began to chase Gray Wing; the second dog—a small white creature—gave chase too, leaving Jagged Peak free to struggle on unharmed.

Shattered Ice reached the valley bottom and veered to one side to come up beside Gray Wing, but Gray Wing waved him off with a lash of his tail. "Help Jagged Peak!" he yowled, and pelted on with the dogs panting close behind him.

The air reeked of dog-scent. Thunder was close enough to see their gleaming eyes and the spittle flying from their open jaws. He shuddered at the thought of those murderous fangs sinking into Gray Wing.

Hurtling along behind Shattered Ice, Thunder saw Gray Wing heading for a copse of windblown trees on the ridge. The dogs were snapping at his paws as he reached it and scrambled up the nearest tree.

Crouching on a low-lying branch, Gray Wing looked down at the dogs, who were yelping and throwing themselves at the tree trunk.

"Flea-pelts!" he spat. "Useless mange-faces! Go away and leave us alone."

Thunder and Shattered Ice caught up with Jagged Peak,

flanking him on either side; Shattered Ice let the injured cat lean on his shoulder. "What are you doing out here, you stupid furball?" he asked.

"I can go where I like!" Jagged Peak gasped.

Shattered Ice just snorted in reply. Jagged Peak's neck fur was bristling, but Thunder could see that he was too exhausted to argue anymore.

"Not far now," Thunder meowed encouragingly. "When we get to camp we can hide in the dens."

But to his horror Thunder heard the yelping and whining of the dogs turn to full-throated barking. Glancing back, he saw that they had abandoned Gray Wing in his tree, and were heading back in their direction. "They're coming!" he gasped.

Jagged Peak bared his teeth. "Get out of here!" he snarled. "I can take care of this."

Thunder couldn't believe what he was saying. "We wouldn't ever leave . . . ," he began to meow.

Before he had even finished speaking, Shattered Ice put on a burst of speed, abandoning his place beside Jagged Peak. In moments he'd vanished over the next hill. Thunder stared after him disbelievingly. *I never thought Shattered Ice was a coward!*

"I'm not going," he growled at Jagged Peak. "We'll do this together, so get over it."

The dogs were drawing closer, eating up the distance with enormous bounds. Thunder realized that he wouldn't be able to get Jagged Peak back to the camp before the dogs caught up with them. Glancing desperately around, he spotted a narrow hole between two rocks that jutted out of the moorland soil.

Thunder threw all his weight against Jagged Peak, thrusting him across the grass and down the hole, then turned around and crammed himself in tail first. He had managed to push the two of them a tail-length from the opening when the dogs loped up, whining in excitement.

Most of the light from the hole was cut off as the big brindled dog shoved its snout inside. Thunder met its maniacal gaze. He could hear its excited panting and feel its hot, sour breath washing over him. It stuck a paw inside the hole; Thunder shrank back, barely able to stay out of reach of the thrusting claws. *If it gets in here, we're done*, he thought.

Behind him he could hear a continual muttering from Jagged Peak. "What do you think I am, a rabbit? Stupid, mange-ridden dogs . . . we should have stayed to fight. I could rip the throat out of one of them, no trouble. . . ."

Thunder flicked his ears. Despite Jagged Peak's words, he was happy to be safe in the tunnel.

Thunder had never been down one of the rabbit burrows before. Even discounting his fear of the dogs, he didn't like it at all. It was so different from the wide, comfortable tunnel mouth where he slept with Hawk Swoop and her kits. His fur itched with the dirt, and the damp walls seemed to press in on him from all directions. The dog's panting echoed loudly and he could hear it start to scrape at the earth around the hole.

"Please get me out of this," he muttered, then wondered who he was talking to. *I'm so scared I've got bees in my brain!*

Sliding out his claws, Thunder braced himself to attack the dog if he had to. More muffled sounds penetrated from outside, and he recognized the voices of Twolegs. The ground quivered with the stomping of their huge paws. There were angry noises, then Thunder glimpsed a Twoleg reach out and drag the dog away. The creature gave a howl of protest, but a heartbeat later light flooded into the burrow again as the dog's nose was withdrawn.

Thunder heard more Twoleg voices and another flurry of barking. They seemed to be growing more distant; the ground stopped shaking. *Are they really leaving?* He couldn't see any dogs or Twolegs through the narrow mouth of the tunnel. But he wondered whether they might be crouching outside, waiting for the cats to emerge.

"What's going on?" Jagged Peak asked.

"I'm not sure." Thunder felt too scared to poke his head out of the hole. His heartbeat was so fast and strong, it felt as if his chest was going to burst open. *Clear Sky said I was too young to look after myself. Maybe I am.* Then a spark of confidence began to flicker inside him. *But I saved Jagged Peak, didn't I?*

"Do you think the dogs are definitely gone?" he asked the injured cat.

Jagged Peak let out an exasperated sound. Thunder looked around to see his haunches pressed against the side of the tunnel, his pelt clogged with soil. "How would I know?" Jagged Peak asked in a muffled voice. "I'm facing down the tunnel, mouse-brain. I can't see a thing!" He paused and added, "We should probably wait a while, just in case."

The two cats crouched motionless in the burrow. Thunder strained his ears to make out what was happening outside.

"Thanks," Jagged Peak mewed at last. "For staying to help me."

Hot embarrassment flooded through Thunder from ears to tail-tip. It felt wrong that Jagged Peak had to thank him—he'd only done what he would have done for any cat. Except they both knew that most cats in their camp weren't permanently injured. Most cats would have been able to run away. "That's okay," he mumbled. "I'm sure Gray Wing would have led the dogs away again."

"I'm sure he would have tried," Jagged Peak meowed. A couple of heartbeats later he went on reluctantly, "One thing I've learned since I was a kit is that not even Gray Wing can fix everything."

Thunder squirmed uncomfortably.

As if Jagged Peak's words had summoned him, Gray Wing's head appeared at the mouth of the tunnel. He looked thoroughly shaken. "It's okay to come out," he meowed. "The dogs have gone. And what in the world were you thinking?" he added angrily to Thunder. "Going off like that without permission. I ought to claw your ears."

Thunder's belly clenched. "Sorry," he muttered as he scrambled out of the burrow at once, relieved to shake the dirt out of his pelt. Thin trickles of soil fell from the roof as he emerged.

"Where's Shattered Ice?" Gray Wing asked.

"He . . . he ran back to the camp," Thunder replied.

Gray Wing's eyes clouded. "Without you and Jagged Peak?" he asked incredulously.

"I told the others to go away and save their own lives,"

Jagged Peak called out angrily from his place in the tunnel.
"At least Shattered Ice *listened* to me."

Gray Wing let out a sigh. "I never thought he—"

A loud yowl interrupted him. Thunder looked up to see a
long line of cats appearing at the top of the hill and sweeping
down the slope toward them. Shattered Ice was in the lead;
Thunder recognized Dappled Pelt, Jackdaw's Cry, and Rainswept Flower. To his surprise, Wind and Gorse were with
them too.

"It's Shattered Ice!" he called to Jagged Peak in the tunnel.
"He's not a coward after all. He went for help."

"Jagged Peak, you can come out now," Gray Wing added.

Scuffling sounds came from the tunnel.

"It's not easy, trying to back out of one of these little rabbit
dens," Jagged Peak grumbled. "Especially with a bad leg. I—"
Coughing drowned out whatever he was trying to say.

"What's the matter?" Gray Wing asked.

"Nothing." Jagged Peak's voice sounded muffled. "I just
got a mouthful of dirt. It's getting sort of dusty in here," he
added nervously.

There were grunts and noises of discomfort as Jagged Peak
wriggled his way to the entrance. Thunder wondered whether
it might have been a bad idea to shove him in quite so roughly.
But what choice did I have?

There was a small yowl of displeasure, and then a noise
that made Thunder much more worried—a creaking, groan-
ing sound that came from the ground itself.

Gray Wing darted a glance to where Thunder had gone to

sit on the bank above the hole. "Get away from there—quick!" he ordered.

Thunder leaped off. He crouched to look into the hole. More earth was dribbling down from the roof of the tunnel. "Jagged Peak, hurry!" he mewed.

"Come on, come on," Gray Wing added, glancing anxiously at the bank. Thunder couldn't believe it: The packed earth was sinking into a hollow before their eyes. The tunnel was . . .

A soft thump sounded. A cloud of dust billowed out into the open as the mouth of the burrow suddenly collapsed.

Jagged Peak was buried alive.

CHAPTER 6

This can't be happening. Not to my brother . . . Gray Wing stared disbelievingly as the ground sank into a hollow and soil closed up the entrance to the tunnel. "Jagged Peak!" he yowled. His heart was pounding with fear as he flung himself at the mound of earth where the opening had been and began digging frantically.

Thunder was beside him, loose soil spraying everywhere as his paws scraped with all their strength.

But the earth was too soft. As quickly as they tried to dig out a hole, the loose dirt collapsed in on itself. His fear mounting, Gray Wing realized they were making very little headway.

How much more time do we have?

Gray Wing had only gone down a rabbit burrow once, when Wind was showing him how she hunted. He remembered how uncomfortable he had been, close to panic, and his heart broke for Jagged Peak, trapped beneath the weight of earth. He kept on clawing and digging, even while he was fighting despair.

"Jagged Peak, we're coming!" he yowled, hoping the young cat could hear him.

There was a scuffling sound behind him and then Shattered Ice and the other cats were crowding around, all trying to reach the collapsed burrow and dig.

"Let us help," Jackdaw's Cry gasped, shoving in front of Gray Wing.

Gray Wing found his way blocked, and when he tried to get closer to the tunnel he was almost knocked off his paws by Rainswept Flower. She was clawing frantically, her paws moving in a blur. Cats were screeching in panic, and even though he realized they were trying to help, Gray Wing knew they were only making this worse.

Time's running out, he thought, picturing Jagged Peak crushed down in the dark, his mouth choked with dirt.

Then a cat's voice—Wind's—rose up above all the others. "Get back, all of you! Let us deal with this!"

When the other cats paused, startled, Gorse and Wind sprang past them and began digging farther up the tunnel, above the place where Jagged Peak had been when it collapsed.

"We know these tunnels," Gorse explained rapidly as they dug. "We'll reach solid ground quicker this way."

"There's room for one more cat," Wind added. "Jackdaw's Cry, you'll do. The rest of you keep away."

Gray Wing worked his claws impatiently into the moorland grass. It seemed to take forever for the three cats to clear away the soil, but at last he glimpsed a patch of gray fur. "Jagged Peak!" he gasped, starting forward.

Wind raised her tail to halt him. She and Gorse leaned

over the hole they had dug and carefully lifted out the limp form of Jagged Peak. His head lolled and his fur was caked with dirt; Gray Wing couldn't see him breathing.

"He's dead!" he choked out. *I've already lost Clear Sky! I can't lose Jagged Peak, too.*

The mountain cats gathered around sorrowfully as Wind and Gorse laid Jagged Peak gently on the grass. He looked so small and thin, with his pelt plastered to his sides by soil. Gray Wing remembered how tiny Fluttering Bird had looked in death, and a pang of grief shook him from ears to tail-tip. *Why do things like this happen?* he asked himself.

"We all came safely through the cold season," Dappled Pelt murmured, her tail drooping. "And now Jagged Peak dies like this."

It's my fault, Gray Wing told himself. *I left the mountains to protect Jagged Peak. I've failed. . . .*

"We can't give up hope," Wind meowed, her tone brisk and bracing. "He may not be dead."

While she was speaking she slipped her paw into Jagged Peak's mouth and clawed out some of the dirt; she gave his nose a lick, clearing that too. Gray Wing waited tensely, then let out a gasp of relief as Jagged Peak started to cough, gagging on the soil, and vomited some of it up. A heartbeat later his eyes blinked open and he rubbed at them feebly.

"He's okay!" Rainswept Flower exclaimed. "Oh, Wind, thank you!"

Wind dipped her head. "You're welcome."

We owe these rogues so much, Gray Wing thought. *I'm going to talk to Tall Shadow about letting them join us. We'd be crazy not to welcome such generous cats.*

Wind and Gorse stepped back as the mountain cats gathered around Jagged Peak, using their paws and tongues to clean the earth off his pelt, and giving him comforting licks around his ears.

"No need to fuss," Jagged Peak grunted as his strength began to return. He tried to pull away from his denmates and sit up. "I'm not a kit. I can groom my own fur."

Gray Wing knew his young brother wasn't trying to be rude and ungrateful; he understood that Jagged Peak was quivering with embarrassment because he hated to seem weak.

"You shouldn't have been wandering around by yourself," Jackdaw's Cry meowed. "What if something happened and no cat was there to save you? You're lucky that Thunder and Gray Wing were nearby."

Jagged Peak flinched, and Gray Wing glared at Jackdaw's Cry. "Jagged Peak has a brain," he mewed. "He would have figured out a way to get away from those dogs if he had to."

Jackdaw's Cry opened his jaws to protest, then clearly thought better of it.

"It's time we went back to the hollow," Gray Wing meowed roughly.

Before any cat could move, Rainswept Flower turned to him, with a sidelong glance at Jagged Peak. She'd worked harder than any cat to free his brother from the collapsed tunnel.

"I think Jagged Peak should lead the way back, don't you?" she asked.

That's mouse-brained, Gray Wing thought, then a heartbeat later realized how clever Rainswept Flower was being. *Taking the lead will give Jagged Peak his dignity back.* "Good idea," he agreed. "Jagged Peak, we all dashed here so quickly, we're not sure of the best way back. Can you show us?"

Jagged Peak struggled to his paws and gave his pelt a shake. "I guess so," he muttered, as if he was reluctant, though Gray Wing could see his eyes brighten and his tail begin to rise with pride.

"Thanks, Rainswept Flower," Gray Wing murmured into her ear.

"It's the least I can do," she responded.

Jagged Peak began tottering toward the camp, with Rainswept Flower and Shattered Ice springing to support him on either side. As the other mountain cats followed, Gray Wing flicked his ears at Wind and Gorse, beckoning them over to him.

"I thought when the dogs arrived you went to hide in the undergrowth," he began. "How did you end up coming with the others to help save Jagged Peak?"

Wind and Gorse exchanged a glance.

"We decided we couldn't just abandon you," Gorse explained. "After all, we're good friends now."

Wind nodded. "So we went to the hollow to see how you were, and got there just as Shattered Ice turned up, out of breath and yowling about Jagged Peak stuck on the moor."

"Thank you," Gray Wing meowed from the bottom of his heart. His paws itched to invite the two rogues to join their group, but he knew that he would have to discuss it with Tall Shadow first. "Is there anything we can do to show you how grateful we are?"

"If it's possible, we'd like to join you," Wind responded, as if she had followed Gray Wing's thought. "We'd do all we can to hunt well and help out."

"That's right," Gorse assured Gray Wing. "Life has gotten much harder since the new cats came to live here, and we need allies."

"I'll see what I can do," Gray Wing promised.

Racing past the other cats, he headed for the camp, where he found Tall Shadow standing at the edge of the hollow. Her ears were pricked alertly and her gaze swept across the moor, constantly watchful.

When Tall Shadow spotted Gray Wing she took a few paces forward to meet him. "Are all the cats okay?" she asked, desperate anxiety in her voice. "Thunder and Jagged Peak— are they safe?"

"Yes." Gray Wing rested his tail on her shoulder. "They're both fine. And the dogs have gone."

Tall Shadow let out a long sigh of relief. For the first time Gray Wing could remember, she sank to the ground as if her legs weren't strong enough to hold her up any longer. "Thank goodness!" she breathed out. "I could never have forgiven myself if . . ." She couldn't go on.

"They're still alive," Gray Wing reassured her. "Thanks to Wind and Gorse."

He explained how Thunder and Jagged Peak had hidden in the burrow, and how the roof had caved in before Jagged Peak could get out.

"We were panicking, getting in each other's way," he meowed. "When we've all recovered, we might discuss making plans in case anything like that happens again."

Tall Shadow nodded. "Good idea. Especially now that we're living in these tunnel dens. But go on," she added. "How did you get Jagged Peak out?"

"We didn't," Gray Wing replied. "We owe that to Wind and Gorse."

He described to Tall Shadow how Wind had cleared the earth from Jagged Peak's mouth and nose after she and Gorse dug him out. "And remember that they came to the hollow to help. They could have just looked after their own pelts. We owe these cats," he finished quietly. "They want to come and live with us."

Tall Shadow looked up at him, her eyes thoughtful. "They can stay and share the evening with us," she mewed at last. "But then they must go. I need time to think," she added, as Gray Wing opened his jaws to protest.

Gray Wing realized that there was no point in arguing. He knew how cautious Tall Shadow was, and letting the rogues stay for just the evening was a huge concession for her.

But is she too cautious? he asked himself.

For the first time Gray Wing noticed that Turtle Tail had come up to him and was hovering nearby, waiting for him to finish his conversation.

"That sounds so frightening!" she exclaimed as he turned to her. "Are you sure you're okay?"

"Every cat is fine," Gray Wing assured her. "Look, they're coming back now."

The sun was going down, casting red light across the camp. Jackdaw's Cry was outlined against it as he appeared at the top of the hollow. He raced across to Hawk Swoop and their kits. As he began to tell his story, Acorn Fur and Lightning Tail listened with their jaws gaping in shock.

A moment later Jagged Peak padded into camp, helped by Dappled Pelt and Rainswept Flower. Shattered Ice followed, escorting Gorse and Wind, and led them down to the bottom of the hollow. Gray Wing padded up to Jagged Peak, with Turtle Tail close behind. "Come over here," he meowed. "You must be tired now. There's a soft patch of moss where you can rest."

Jagged Peak pulled away from him. "You don't have to look after me all the time," he muttered. "I can take care of myself."

Gray Wing twitched his whiskers. "Really? Did today prove that?"

Jagged Peak flinched. Without a word he staggered off and sat by himself on the moss, his back turned to Gray Wing, rejecting help even though his whole body was swaying with exhaustion. Gray Wing's heart twisted to see him so proud and so full of hurt. *Stupid!* he scolded himself. *Rainswept Flower made him feel better, and now you have to go and put your clumsy great paw in it.*

To his relief, Rainswept Flower followed Jagged Peak and sat down beside him. Gray Wing saw them talking quietly, their heads close together.

Gray Wing felt a comforting paw on his back. "He'll be all right," Turtle Tail said gently.

The rest of the cats had made their way to the bottom of the hollow.

Thunder excitedly told the story of how the dogs had chased Jagged Peak. "You should have seen Gray Wing!" he meowed. "He dashed right up to that big brute and clawed its nose! The dog looked so surprised. But Gray Wing only did it so the dogs would chase him and Jagged Peak could escape. He was really brave!"

Gray Wing wanted to hide behind a rock as he felt the gazes of all the other cats turned to him. Lightning Tail and Acorn Fur looked especially impressed, their eyes wide and shining.

"That was well done," Tall Shadow pronounced. "But don't forget what might have happened. We could have been grieving for dead denmates tonight."

Thunder's head drooped. "I know," he muttered, looking chastened.

Gray Wing knew that Tall Shadow was right, but he felt sorry for his young kin. "Why don't you tell them how brave *you* were?" he asked Thunder. "How you stayed with Jagged Peak and hid in the tunnel with him?"

"That was pretty scary," Thunder admitted, beginning to sound cheerful again. "Especially when the tunnel collapsed. But Wind was brilliant, knowing how to get Jagged Peak out like she did."

Dappled Pelt rose to her paws. "I'd better check on Jagged Peak," she mewed. "The last thing he needs is to get sick, on top of everything else." Weaving around her denmates, she approached Jagged Peak, who was crouched on the moss with his nose on his paws. "Come on, Jagged Peak," she ordered. "You have to let me clean up your scratches and scrapes before it gets too dark to see them."

For a heartbeat Gray Wing thought Jagged Peak would protest. Then he let out a long sigh. "Okay, do what you want," he muttered.

Gray Wing watched for a moment as Dappled Pelt deftly parted Jagged Peak's fur to examine his injuries. "I don't think there's anything serious," she mewed at last, settling down beside him and beginning to lick his scratches. "But you'll need to let me check again in the morning."

Satisfied that Jagged Peak wasn't badly hurt, Gray Wing signaled for Wind and Gorse to come close.

"I asked Tall Shadow if you can join us," he murmured. "She says you can stay for tonight; after that you need to leave. But she will think about it," he added as Gorse and Wind exchanged a disappointed glance. "She just needs time to come to the right decision and invite you to join us for good."

Wind nodded. "I can understand that."

"Yes," Gorse agreed. "It's a big step for her to take."

"Don't worry," Turtle Tail murmured, touching Wind's shoulder with her tail. "I wasn't sure if I would be invited back. But here I am."

Gray Wing glanced around to see Jackdaw's Cry still telling the story of Jagged Peak's rescue to his denmates. He beckoned them closer with a wave of his tail.

"You know Jackdaw's Cry, of course," he meowed to Wind and Gorse. "Have you met his mate, Hawk Swoop? And these are their kits, Acorn Fur and Lightning Tail."

"And I'm Shattered Ice," the white tom announced, bringing up the rear as the whole group padded up to greet the newcomers.

"Pleased to meet you," Wind responded, with a polite dip of her head, while Gorse murmured greetings.

The two kits crowded up, their eyes shining as they gazed at Wind and Gorse. "Do you really hunt rabbits down their burrows?" Acorn Fur asked. "Will you teach us how to do it?"

"All in good time," Gray Wing told her. He was glad to see how his denmates were welcoming the moorland cats, but he had to remind himself that they weren't part of the group yet. "Meanwhile, I'm sure Wind will tell you all about it. And maybe you'd like to share some prey?" he added to Wind and Gorse."

"We sure would!" Gorse replied, swiping his tongue around his jaws.

With the sun sinking below the horizon, the cats gathered together in the middle of the camp, grooming themselves or quietly talking to the newcomers. Gray Wing was pleased to see how well Gorse and Wind were fitting in, and hoped that Tall Shadow was taking notice. He was glad to see too that Turtle Tail had been accepted, and was crouching comfortably beside Rainswept Flower.

As Gray Wing watched, Rainswept Flower got up to bring out the rabbit she had caught earlier that day and Jackdaw's Cry contributed a couple of mice. Lightning Tail and Acorn Fur fetched Gray Wing's rabbit, which they had carried back to the camp.

"So what did you two catch today?" Cloud Spots asked Shattered Ice and Thunder. "You know, when you went off on your own."

Gray Wing saw the two cats exchange an embarrassed glance. "I caught a shrew," Thunder replied, "but I had to leave it behind when we heard the dogs."

Cloud Spots sniffed but didn't comment, only glancing around at the others as if he thought his point was made.

"And don't you dare do anything so stupid again." Tall Shadow gave Thunder a severe look. "No young cat should go out on the moor alone. You know how dangerous it is."

Thunder ducked his head. "Sorry," he meowed. "I'll be sensible in the future."

"And we need to talk about you leading the dogs right into our camp," Tall Shadow went on, flicking the same hard glance toward Gray Wing. "Didn't any of you *think?*"

"No, and I'm sorry," Gray Wing replied. "We panicked."

"And we haven't lived on the moor long enough yet to know where all the safe places are," Rainswept Flower pointed out defensively.

"That's a fair point," Dappled Pelt murmured. "Maybe we should do more exploring, and work out a few escape routes in case this kind of thing happens again."

"We'll help with that," Wind meowed eagerly.

Tall Shadow gave her a cool nod. "I'll think about it." Gray Wing guessed that she didn't want to encourage the rogue cats to get too involved with her group.

While the prey was being shared, Rainswept Flower tore off a portion of her rabbit and took it to Jagged Peak. "Won't you come and join us?" Gray Wing heard her ask.

Jagged Peak shook his head. He bent to sniff the rabbit, hesitated, then took a small bite. "Thanks," he muttered.

Rainswept Flower didn't try to persuade him anymore, just touched her nose to his ear before leaving him to it. Gray Wing was reassured that at least he was eating.

Gray Wing took some of the rabbit and went to sit beside Turtle Tail and Rainswept Flower. At once Rainswept Flower gave him an amused glance, rose to her paws and padded off to join Jagged Peak. Gray Wing blinked as he looked after her. *What's the matter with her?*

"I'm so glad you're all right," Turtle Tail purred as Gray Wing settled down beside her. "I wanted to come and help you, but Tall Shadow said I had to think of my kits."

"She was right," Gray Wing responded, pressing his nose into Turtle Tail's shoulder fur.

Twilight fell as the cats shared their stories of the day. Gray Wing told the others about the meeting with River Ripple beside the river; so much had happened since that it seemed like a long, long time ago The streaks of scarlet from the vanished sun died away, leaving an indigo sky where stars appeared one by one, glimmering peacefully above the camp.

It's so beautiful here, Gray Wing thought. *Who would ever imagine the danger we've been through?*

Gray Wing bent his head to eat his share of the rabbit. He realized that Turtle Tail was watching him with admiring eyes.

"It sounds as if you had quite an adventure," she mewed. "Jagged Peak would have died if you hadn't been so quick-thinking . . . and lucky."

Gray Wing sighed. "We were very lucky," he agreed. Hesitantly he went on, giving voice to a fear that he had kept secret for so long. "Maybe we were wrong to make our home here on these open moors. We're too exposed. There's nowhere to hide from dogs, or anything else that might threaten us. There were dangers in the mountains, but at least we had the shelter of the cave behind the waterfall. We were safe there."

Turtle Tail blinked, then flicked her ears in denial. "But where else could you have used your speed to distract the dogs and lead them away?" she asked. "Where else could Thunder and Jagged Peak have found such a good hiding place? Where else could the other cats have come to the rescue so quickly when the tunnel collapsed?"

Gray Wing began to nod slowly. What Turtle Tail was saying made a lot of sense.

"This is the perfect home for us," she went on, brushing her pelt against his. "Look at the kits," she added, flicking her tail-tip to point across the hollow to where Acorn Fur and Lightning Tail were stuffing themselves with prey. "They've survived, they're strong and healthy, and that proves this is a good place—as long as Clear Sky doesn't spoil it. I can't wait to see my own kits thriving here."

The question that had been burning inside Gray Wing for many moons rose up again. "If you're so sure we belong here, Turtle Tail, why did you leave us to live with Twolegs?"

Turtle Tail's ears flicked up and her eyes widened; clearly she was taken aback. "That had nothing to do with not being sure that the moor was the right place for us," she replied.

"Then why?" Gray Wing persisted.

Turtle Tail shook her head, still unwilling to talk about what had upset her. "This rabbit is delicious," she meowed a heartbeat later, pushing the last scraps over to him. "Much fatter prey than we caught in the mountains!"

"That's true," Gray Wing agreed, knowing he had to accept the change of subject. *But what is she keeping from me?* he asked himself, bewildered.

He looked up at the wide stretch of stars over the moor, brilliant in the clear sky. All around him he could hear the comfortable murmur of his denmates, full-fed and sleepy.

Turtle Tail is right, he thought. *This is home now.*

CHAPTER 7

The moon, almost full, was riding high, casting a silver light over the hollow. Gray Wing looked down affectionately at Thunder, who had settled at his side; the young cat's head was drooping drowsily, but he was struggling against sleep. Hawk Swoop had bundled Lightning Tail and Acorn Fur off to bed; Gray Wing guessed that Thunder didn't want to go with them, preferring to listen to the older cats talking instead.

Jagged Peak had crept closer, too, and lay stretched out, his eyes closed. Gray Wing was glad to see that his expression had cleared; he looked almost happy as he sank into sleep. Cloud Spots was giving himself a long stretch, while Dappled Pelt had curled up and was drowsing with her tail over her nose.

"I want to tell you more about the tunnels," Wind began. "They're full of rabbits, if you know where to look. There was one time, I followed a rabbit almost as far as the Twoleg-place—"

"That's enough." Tall Shadow rose to her paws, cutting off the brown she-cat. Gray Wing guessed that she didn't want Wind to encourage any of her cats to go near the Twoleg-place, or to risk themselves down unfamiliar tunnels. "Wind,

Gorse," she began, "we thank you for your help today. But now we must say good-bye. It's time for you to leave the hollow."

Shattered Ice and Jackdaw's Cry, who had been listening with intense interest, looked up indignantly.

"Surely Wind and Gorse aren't leaving?" Shattered Ice asked. "Everyone wants them to stay. Why don't they just spend the night here?"

The rogue cats' eyes widened hopefully, but Tall Shadow shook her head.

"No, they have to leave," she insisted politely. "This hollow is just for the cats from the mountains. We found it and we dug out the dens."

Wind and Gorse seemed disappointed, but they merely dipped their heads to Tall Shadow and glanced around at the others.

"Good-bye," Wind meowed. "Thanks for letting us stay, and for sharing your rabbit."

"Yeah, it was great," Gorse agreed. "We'll see you around."

Side by side, the two rogue cats bounded up the slope. The mountain cats watched in silence as they melted fluidly into the dark moorland. In a heartbeat they were gone.

"I don't see why they had to leave," Jackdaw's Cry grumbled after a while.

"Yes, they saved Jagged Peak," Hawk Swoop added as the cats returned to their nests. "They'd be really great cats to have with us."

Shattered Ice sprang to his paws and confronted Tall Shadow. "I think you should explain to us why they have to leave," he demanded, flicking his tail in the direction of the departed cats, "but Turtle Tail—who was a *kittypet*—gets to stay."

Turtle Tail let out a shocked gasp. Her neck fur fluffed out indignantly. "What do you mean by that?" she demanded.

"Loyalty is important," Shattered Ice replied coldly. "You shouldn't get to leave and then stroll back in again as if nothing happened."

"Fine!" Turtle Tail glared at the gray-and-white tom. "I'm not going to stay where I'm not welcome!" she hissed.

Appalled, Gray Wing rose to her side and curled his tail around her shoulders. "You can't go back to the Twolegplace now, not when that would mean losing your kits!" he protested. "And you can't survive on your own, not when they'll be born any day now."

He could tell from the look on Turtle Tail's face that she didn't really want to leave the hollow. "I don't care," she muttered. "I don't have to take that from any cat."

"Of course you care," Gray Wing told her, realizing how deeply upset she was by Shattered Ice's words. "You must stay," he went on gently. "Think of your kits."

Turtle Tail hesitated, then nodded, leaning in for a moment toward Gray Wing.

"Good," Tall Shadow meowed. "No cat here would turn you out at a time like this. Shattered Ice, apologize."

Shattered Ice glared at Tall Shadow, then turned to Turtle Tail. "Okay—sorry," he muttered grumpily.

Gray Wing drew a breath of relief, hoping that the near

quarrel was over, but Shattered Ice spun around again to face his leader.

"But you still haven't answered my question. Why did you make Wind and Gorse go?" he asked. "They saved Jagged Peak's life and probably others! You call yourself our leader, but you don't care what we think. What makes you so special?"

Tall Shadow stiffened at the white tom's accusing tone. "I—" she began, but Shattered Ice ignored her attempt to speak.

"All this time, while this was going on," he continued. "You were guarding the hollow! Some bravery! Some leadership! Gray Wing was out there, saving cats. You should follow his example. In fact, we all should. Gray Wing should be our leader!"

A babble of comment and protest rose up from the other cats at Shattered Ice's challenging words. The drowsy peace that had fallen over the camp was swept away.

"You can't change a leader just like that," Rainswept Flower protested. Tall Shadow looked on, her face blank with shock. *Don't rely on Rainswept Flower to stand up for you*, Gray Wing silently willed her. *Show your authority!*

"Yes!" Hawk Swoop yowled. "Gray Wing!"

"Now just a moment . . ." Cloud Spots shouldered his way forward, but anything else he might have said was lost in the rising clamor.

Tall Shadow drew herself to her full height. Her shoulder fur was bristling and her tail bushed out to twice its size. Fury snapped in her green eyes, but she still looked too stunned to say anything.

Shock pierced through Gray Wing like a bolt of lightning. The idea of taking over as leader made his fur rankle, particularly when that would mean displacing Tall Shadow. *Do they expect her to purr sweetly and start taking orders from me?*

Sudden words exploded out of Gray Wing. "Be quiet!" he ordered Shattered Ice. "Is this what we want—arguments among ourselves when there are serious dangers out there?"

"That's exactly what we want," Shattered Ice retorted. "Because there are dangers, we need a leader who's capable of dealing with them. Only today, Thunder and I were stopped by some of Clear Sky's cats in the forest. We could have ended up fighting if it wasn't for the dogs."

Gray Wing cast an angry glance at Thunder, who was struggling back to wakefulness as the argument erupted in the hollow. *You never told me about that!* But speaking to his young kin would have to wait. "Tall Shadow is the leader we need," he meowed sharply to Shattered Ice.

Shattered Ice lashed his tail. "I say she is *not!*"

Several gasps of astonishment followed, and Tall Shadow took a pace forward, a low growl coming from her throat. Gray Wing realized that she was within a heartbeat of attacking Shattered Ice.

Before Gray Wing could move or speak, Cloud Spots pushed his way between the two hostile cats. "Do you really want a leader who led *dogs* into our camp?" he asked Shattered Ice.

Fury pierced through Gray Wing. "What would you have done, flea-brain?" he demanded.

"Gray Wing was brave!" Thunder's voice was raised in protest. "He saved Jagged Peak."

Gray Wing realized that he should have kept his temper. Thunder was fully awake now, on his paws with his shoulder fur fluffed out as he glared at Cloud Spots. Guilt stabbed through Gray Wing and he tried to calm himself. *I shouldn't behave like this in front of younger cats.*

"I want a leader who'll *do* something," Shattered Ice retorted to Cloud Spots, ignoring Thunder's interruption. "Not sit around in the camp all day. And if you think any different, you're more flea-brained than I thought!"

"Who're you calling flea-brained?" Cloud Spots growled.

For answer, Shattered Ice leaped at him, his claws out, and caught him a blow over one ear. Cloud Spots reared up on his hind paws and hurled himself on top of Shattered Ice with a snarl.

Gasps of shock and loud protests arose from the other cats. For a heartbeat Gray Wing stood frozen, appalled at the sight of two of his denmates attacking each other.

"Stop!" he yowled.

He sprang forward, grabbed Cloud Spots by the scruff, and hauled him off Shattered Ice. Shoving Shattered Ice away, he stood panting between the two furious cats.

"That's enough," he meowed. "How can you raise your claws against each other, after all we've been through together? We must be united, or what hope do we have?"

Gradually both the toms grew calmer, their bristling fur beginning to lie flat on their shoulders. "Sorry," Cloud Spots muttered. Shattered Ice just glared, breathing hard.

Before Gray Wing could say any more, Tall Shadow bounded across the hollow and sprang up onto her rock. "Listen!" she yowled. "Shattered Ice," she continued when every cat was giving her their attention. "You have no right to talk to *any* cat as rudely as that, much less your leader. And then to attack one of your denmates! You—"

"But he has a point," Jackdaw's Cry interrupted. "Things have to change."

"Have to?" Tall Shadow gave him an icy glare. "We belong to each other and look out for each other, no matter what. That doesn't change." Her glance raked across the assembled cats. "I'm *sorry* if some of you felt offended because I was guarding the hollow. Next time I'll let the dogs sneak up on us without warning."

"That's a good excuse." Jagged Peak struggled to his paws. "It meant you didn't have to do anything when Thunder and I were in danger. You just left us to the dogs."

"Foolish creature!" Tall Shadow hissed at him. "You wouldn't have *been* in danger if you hadn't gone off without telling any cat."

With a last furious look flung at Shattered Ice, she leaped down from the rock and stalked off into the darkness. Before she disappeared, she glared over her shoulder at Gray Wing, the accusation in her eyes making him feel like a traitor.

But I didn't ask for this! he protested silently. *I didn't ask for any of it.*

The voices of his denmates rose again around Gray Wing, continuing the argument in hushed tones. Gray Wing hesitated, knowing that he had to intervene, but not certain what he should say.

"Jackdaw's Cry," he began at last, trying to keep his anger under control, "there was no need for you to take Shattered Ice's side."

"There was every need," Jackdaw's Cry responded swiftly. "Tall Shadow is making a mistake by forcing us to live like we did in the mountains. She's set in her ways. Now is the time for change—and that change is you! You should be our leader, Gray Wing. What do you say?"

Hawk Swoop nodded, moving closer to her mate. "Things are changing in spite of Tall Shadow," she agreed. "For one thing, there weren't other cats in the mountains! Now, we're scrambling for space to hunt, and dogs are attacking us."

"That's true," Dappled Pelt put in. "Prey was scarce up there, but at least it was all ours."

"There's plenty of prey for every cat here," Cloud Spots pointed out. "We don't need to be fighting over it. All these arguments about hunting rights are ridiculous. We should all be able to hunt where we want."

"Tell that to Clear Sky," Shattered Ice flashed back at him. "He's the one setting boundaries. At least he's making sure that all his cats are well fed."

"Do we really want a leader like him?" Rainswept Flower countered. "If you ask me, we're better off as we are." She flicked a glance at Gray Wing. "I'm sorry. That's just how I feel."

Gray Wing felt Turtle Tail press up against him. "How can they talk like this?" she whispered.

"I told you things weren't perfect here," Gray Wing responded in a murmur before striding into the center of the circle. "Don't apologize to me, Rainswept Flower," he meowed. "I didn't ask to be leader—that's the foolish idea of other cats." He waited for the yowls of protest to die down and didn't dare make eye contact with Shattered Ice. He knew he would pay later for such a statement, but for now . . . *I need these cats to know that I won't lead them, and I won't see Tall Shadow undermined.*

He padded around, gazing at the collected cats. "Is this what we all want?" he asked. "Arguing among ourselves over a visit from two rogue cats? We all ought to be glad to be alive tonight—instead we're turning on each other. I think we should retire to our nests and think hard about what's gone on this evening. Then, tomorrow morning, we can apologize to whichever cats we offended. But please don't ask me to lead you again. That's not the way things are meant to be. Tall Shadow led us here, and she'll carry on guiding us along the right path. You need to have faith."

Some of the cats began to pad away, back to their nests. Jackdaw's Cry, however, was staring hard at Gray Wing. "That's a nice suggestion, but I still think we need to do what Clear Sky is doing," he argued. "Organize our boundaries, defend our territory and our prey, bring cats who agree with us into our group, and keep the others out. It doesn't matter whether they started out with us in the mountains, or whether they're rogues." He lashed his tail. "You're right, Shattered Ice. We need a new leader. If it's not Gray Wing . . ."

Gray Wing couldn't believe the change that had come over his denmates. He glanced at Jagged Peak; his brother had hardly spoken, but was following the argument carefully, his gaze flicking from one cat to another. Thunder was watching carefully, too. Gray Wing had no idea what either of the young cats was thinking.

One thing was certain in Gray Wing's mind. *I don't want to be a leader like Clear Sky.* As soon as the words had formed themselves he felt full of guilt. *Clear Sky is my brother! I know he's only doing what he thinks is best.*

"Jagged Peak, what do you think?" Jackdaw's Cry asked. "You lived in Clear Sky's group for a while. What was it like?"

Jagged Peak twitched his whiskers, looking pleased that one of the older cats was asking his opinion. "I wasn't welcome there once I was injured," he responded drily. "If we're planning to organize ourselves like Clear Sky's group, will we be throwing out injured cats or motherless kits? How about cats who get old or sick?"

Jackdaw's Cry stared at Jagged Peak, clearly startled. "We're not planning anything like *that*," he replied in a shocked tone. "We just want to get more organized and have more cats join us so we can defend our territory."

Rainswept Flower nodded eagerly. "Please, Jagged Peak,

won't you show us something that can help? Something you learned from Clear Sky and his cats?"

Jagged Peak hesitated, as if he was about to refuse, then shrugged and dragged himself on top of a boulder. The rest of the cats gathered around him; even the ones who had been heading for their nests returned to listen.

Glancing around the crowd of his denmates, Jagged Peak let out a sigh of resignation. Even so, Gray Wing could tell by the gleam in his eyes that he was glad to have a chance to share what he knew.

"First, you've got to promise not to tell any cat I told you this," he began. "I don't want it getting back to Clear Sky that I gave away his secrets."

"We promise," Rainswept Flower mewed.

"Sure," Jackdaw's Cry added, and a murmur of agreement rose from the rest of the cats.

"Okay," Jagged Peak continued. "Now I want you to think like Clear Sky and his cats. What are your special skills? What do you do best? Hunt or chase? Can you climb trees or burrow through tunnels?"

"You're best at burrowing," Shattered Ice observed wryly.

A few snorts of amusement followed his words, though Gray Wing shivered at the memory of his brother buried in the tunnel.

Jagged Peak rolled his eyes. "Suppose we organized ourselves into groups," he went on. "Rainswept Flower and Jackdaw's Cry each have a good sense of smell and Turtle Tail has keen eyes.

They would be good at patrolling the hollow and the territory around it. Cloud Spots and Dappled Pelt are best with healing herbs, so that would be their job. Gray Wing, you're fast, so you would be a good hunter. This is how Clear Sky organizes things. Each cat has a special role." His gaze fell to the ground and his voice was quieter as he added, "Even I had a role, until . . ."

"Thank you, Jagged Peak," Shattered Ice meowed.

Gray Wing realized that Tall Shadow was still missing. *She should have heard what Jagged Peak suggested*, he thought. *It's her job to organize us.*

A loud voice broke in on his thoughts. "But I don't *want* to patrol!" Jackdaw's Cry insisted. "I'm better at hunting."

"No, you're not," Shattered Ice snapped back. "You missed that rabbit the other day—"

Within a couple of heartbeats it seemed to Gray Wing that every cat was arguing over who should hunt, who should go on patrol, and who should guard the camp.

"That's enough!" he yowled, raising his voice to make himself heard over the bickering. As the noise died down he shook his head sadly at Jagged Peak. "I'm sorry," he mewed. "They're not ready for this yet."

"It was only a suggestion." Jagged Peak climbed stiffly down from the boulder and headed into the darkness.

Rainswept Flower began to follow him, but Gray Wing raised his tail to stop her. "I know you want to help, but I think it's best to let him be for now," he advised. "He needs some time alone."

The tabby she-cat looked as if she would have liked to argue, but after a moment she dipped her head politely. "Whatever you say, Gray Wing."

Somehow, her deference disturbed Gray Wing. He turned away from her, only to realize that the other cats were crowding around him, talking excitedly among themselves.

"Remember how Gray Wing and Jagged Peak were clever enough to make it out of the mountains on their own?" Hawk Swoop meowed.

"That's right," Turtle Tail agreed, with an admiring look at Gray Wing. "I'm sure I couldn't have done it. And he saved Thunder when the Twoleg den collapsed, and Storm and the other kits were all killed. I've never been so scared in my life, but Gray Wing was really brave!"

"He helped to save Jagged Peak today," Rainswept Flower pointed out.

"He's one of the fastest hunters on the moors," Dappled Pelt added. "And he can get cats to work together. What more could we possibly want? He should be our new leader."

Gray Wing had heard enough. "Stop it, all of you," he protested. "Did you hear anything I said? I'm not a leader, and I don't want to be. I saw how Clear Sky changed when he started thinking about boundaries and territories instead of individual cats." He hesitated for a moment, the pain of estrangement from his brother sweeping over him like a cold wind. "Clear Sky is not the cat I used to know," he finished.

"Oh, you're just being modest," Cloud Spots meowed. "We know you wouldn't end up like Clear Sky."

A chorus of agreement followed this declaration. Gray Wing raised a paw for silence and waited until the voices died away.

"Okay, I'm brave, or I try to be," he began. "But I don't have the skill of planning or the special authority that a leader needs." He glanced around at the others, encouraged to see that they were at last listening to him. "Surely you remember Stoneteller?" he went on. "She wasn't just brave; she knew how to take care of each cat like they were her own kit. I don't have that in me."

"Yes, you do!" Thunder interrupted, glaring indignantly up at Gray Wing. "I know—because of how you've cared for me, and because of what all the other cats say about you."

"I don't," Gray Wing meowed abruptly. "None of us do. And I'd rather have Tall Shadow, who listens to every cat and tries to keep us together fairly, than Clear Sky, who thinks he can control who deserves to be in the forest."

"But that's what we've been telling you," Shattered Ice declared. "You don't *have* to be like Clear Sky. You would learn from his mistakes. You'd be a great leader."

"A leader? Me?" Gray Wing felt anger surging inside him again as he thought of the chasms that had opened up since they left the mountains with such high hopes. "I couldn't even keep my own family together! And look at you—all you've done today is bicker among yourselves. Now do as I asked, and go to sleep. It's been a long day."

To his relief, no cat seemed inclined to go on arguing. Gradually they began to drift away to the edge of the hollow or the tunnels to sleep. There was still no sign of Tall Shadow. *She should have been here*, Gray Wing thought. *She shouldn't have abandoned the argument so early.* Lots had been said—words Tall Shadow should have heard.

"Things need to change," Shattered Ice muttered as he headed for his nest, and Gray Wing heard some murmurs of agreement.

Thunder pressed up against Gray Wing, as if he was trying to offer comfort. "How could you have kept your family together?" he asked. "It's not your fault, the way Clear Sky is behaving."

Gray Wing sighed. "It feels like it."

Jagged Peak was watching them both silently, his eyes narrowed and the tip of his tail twitching. Something about the way the young cat was looking at Gray Wing made him uneasy.

"Thank you for trying to talk to the cats," Gray Wing meowed, padding over to him.

"That's just it, though," Jagged Peak responded. "I *tried*. I didn't succeed. They didn't really listen to what I was telling them."

Gray Wing suppressed a sigh. *When will Jagged Peak learn to like himself again?*

CHAPTER 8

The sun was going down, casting long shadows across the moor. Gray Wing and Thunder were on their way back to the hollow after a session of hunting practice; Gray Wing was carrying a rabbit. He felt tired but satisfied, enjoying the last of the sunlight and the cool breeze ruffling his fur.

To his relief, when the cats woke after the dispute on the previous night, they had all settled into their usual routines without mentioning a change of leader again. Tall Shadow had reappeared and was organizing the camp with her trademark efficiency. Gray Wing hoped that they had heard the last of the argument. *It was all so stupid. I don't even know why we were talking like that.*

He had intercepted Shattered Ice when the white tom was heading for the tunnel he was digging out with Jackdaw's Cry. "I . . . uh . . . I'm sorry about last night," Gray Wing meowed. "I didn't mean to call you stupid."

Shattered Ice had hesitated for a heartbeat, then dipped his head. "It's okay. Maybe we all said things we didn't mean."

"I tried really hard, and I didn't catch anything," Thunder mewed despondently, breaking into Gray Wing's thoughts.

He had to admit that Thunder was still having problems. All his instincts were to hide and stalk; he didn't seem to appreciate that out on the moor there was nowhere he could hide. *Not unless he can make himself invisible,* Gray Wing thought wryly.

Before they reached the camp, Gray Wing spotted a young bird hopping awkwardly across the grass, one wing trailing. He halted, dropped his prey, and touched Thunder on the shoulder with his tail-tip. "Look," he murmured. "It must have fallen out of its nest."

Thunder let out a sigh. "That's not really hunting, is it? A young, injured bird?"

Gray Wing suppressed a hiss of exasperation. "Prey is prey, and you need all the practice you can get."

Still looking reluctant, Thunder crouched down and began to creep up on the bird as it hopped toward a gorse thicket.

Just run after it! Gray Wing wanted to yowl the words aloud, but he knew that he had to let Thunder work it out for himself.

As he watched, Thunder set his paw down on a twig; it cracked under his weight with a sharp sound. The bird's head swiveled toward him and it let out a squawk of alarm as it dived into the center of the thicket. Thunder dashed after it, only to be brought up short by the barrier of thorns.

"Oh, Thunder, come on!" Gray Wing bounded over to his young kin, his tail lashing. "How many more times do I have to tell you? Out here, you don't stalk, you run."

Thunder swung around on him. "Stop criticizing me!" he spat.

Gray Wing couldn't believe he had heard that, or how hurt he felt at the young cat's words. "What have I done wrong? I'm trying to teach you what you need to learn."

Thunder shook his head in frustration. "Can't you see, Gray Wing? I'm tired. It's the end of the day, and I've had enough. You don't have to keep pushing me all the time."

"Pushing you?" Gray Wing echoed.

"Yes, pushing me! And watching over me all the time as if I was a kit. I'm *not* a kit anymore!"

Pain clawed at Gray Wing's heart as he saw the rebellious look in the young cat's eyes. "I only want what's best for you," he meowed.

Thunder muttered something under his breath.

"What was that?" Gray Wing snapped, anger rising inside him, blotting out the pain. "Speak up!"

Thunder stared at him, his eyes blazing with fury. "You don't always *know* what's best for me!"

Silence stretched out between them. Gray Wing had to clamp his jaws shut to stop more hurtful words from pouring out of him. Finally he swung around, collected his rabbit, and began to stride back toward the hollow.

"I'm sorry! I didn't mean it!" Thunder called after him.

Gray Wing didn't respond.

Thunder caught up to him at the edge of the hollow. "I'm sorry," he repeated.

Gray Wing set his prey down and nuzzled the young cat affectionately to show him that their quarrel was over. "It takes time to master your own techniques," he reassured

Thunder. "I know that. I should give you more room to grow. You'll get there, I'm sure of it."

Thunder lashed his tail in frustration. "I caught a shrew when I went into the forest with Shattered Ice," he complained. "I felt as if I knew what to do when I had all the cover in the undergrowth. But out here, I keep messing up. I feel like I'm letting you and all the other cats down. I want to be a cat you can depend on. Especially after everything that happened yesterday."

"You will be—" Gray Wing began.

He broke off as Thunder suddenly whipped around and raced toward a clump of gorse bushes. Gray Wing stared after him, startled, until he spotted a mouse crouched under one of the outlying branches. *Well spotted, Thunder!* he thought, feeling his fur prickle with pride in his kin. He could see the young cat's courage and strong sense of honor. *He'll grow into an outstanding cat. . . .*

Before he could see whether Thunder made his catch, a cry came from the hollow. "Come quick! Turtle Tail is having her kits!"

For a heartbeat Gray Wing froze. *So soon! She's lucky she came back to us when she did.* He pictured Turtle Tail giving birth alone in some exposed spot on the moor, and then trying to hunt for herself and care for her kits at the same time. He was glad that she was safe in the camp.

Abandoning the rabbit, Gray Wing burst into movement and hurtled down into the camp. Thunder raced along beside him, his hunt forgotten.

Rainswept Flower was standing in the entrance of Turtle Tail's tunnel with Jagged Peak beside her. "Keep back, all of you," she ordered.

Gazing past her, Gray Wing could see Turtle Tail lying stretched out on a bed of moss and dried ferns. Cloud Spots and Dappled Pelt were with her; Dappled Pelt was stroking her belly, while Cloud Spots bent his head over a tiny mound of wet fur. Gray Wing's relief intensified. *Dappled Pelt and Cloud Spots can help her through this. . . .*

He wriggled his way through the crowd until he stood in front of Jagged Peak and Rainswept Flower. "Let me through!" he demanded.

Jagged Peak limped forward to bar his way. "Not yet," he meowed. "Turtle Tail needs her space."

Gray Wing gave his brother a surprised glance. "You'd stop me?"

Jagged Peak dipped his head. "I'm only doing what's necessary."

"That's right," Rainswept Flower agreed. "You can go in and see her when she's ready."

I won't be kept away! Gray Wing barely understood the emotions that made him push past the two cats to enter the tunnel. He stumbled to a halt beside Turtle Tail. She was breathing in shallow rapid pants. The atmosphere was warm and stifled; there was a tang of blood in the air. As Gray Wing approached she raised her head a little and let out a feeble purr.

"I said you couldn't. . . ." Rainswept Flower had followed Gray Wing, outraged, but Cloud Spots raised a paw to silence her.

"It's okay now. Say hello to the new kits," Cloud Spots told Gray Wing, his voice shaky. Gray Wing was surprised. For all his experience with herbs, Cloud Spots looked slightly queasy at the sight of the three damp, blood-streaked bundles.

Gray Wing looked down, and was instantly fascinated by the tiny creatures as they squirmed in the bedding alongside their mother, their eyes still closed. He remembered seeing his brother and sister, Jagged Peak and Fluttering Bird, just after they were born, and he felt the same deep connection with these kits, amazed at how perfect they were.

"They're wonderful," he whispered. "Turtle Tail, the little tortoiseshell is just like you."

"Two toms and a she-cat," Dappled Pelt meowed. "You're all done, Turtle Tail. Three strong, healthy kits."

Two of the kits were already vigorously drinking Turtle Tail's milk. The third was scrabbling blindly among the moss, letting out pitiful squeaks as he sought his mother. Gray Wing reached out a paw and gently nudged him so that he could find Turtle Tail. The squeaking stopped as the kit began to suck next to his littermates.

"They're small," Gray Wing murmured, gazing into Turtle Tail's eyes, "but they're fighters. You'll make the best mother in the world."

For some reason, his praise made pain flood into Turtle Tail's face. She glanced down at her kits. "If only they had a father . . . ," she whispered.

When she turned to Gray Wing, he could read her questioning expression and the depth of love in her eyes. *Love for her kits, surely. She can't possibly mean* . . . Suddenly unsure of himself, Gray Wing took a hasty step back. "I'll leave you in peace," he mewed. "You need to sleep."

Rainswept Flower followed him out of the tunnel and raised her voice above the babble from the cats gathered around the entrance. "Turtle Tail has three healthy kits!" she announced.

Gray Wing heard the yowls of approval as he padded back to his own mossy nest. He tried not to think of the pain and love in Turtle Tail's eyes, or of what it meant. *I need time to think* . . . Not just about Turtle Tail, but about his own behavior. He'd insisted on forcing his way through to see her. Why? He wasn't the father; he had no right there. And yet, something had made him want to be one of the first cats to meet Turtle Tail's new kits.

Gray Wing woke to the sound of rushing water in his ears. He sneezed as a feather tickled his nose, and opened his eyes to find himself in the cave behind the waterfall.

What . . . ? How did I get back here?

He sprang to his paws, gazing around him wildly. Moonlight shone from behind the falling water, turning it into a screen of icy starlight.

In the frosty shimmer Gray Wing saw that the cats were all sleeping. He spotted his mother, Quiet Rain, alone in her nest, and Dewy Leaf curled around two healthy-looking kits. He couldn't see any of the cats who had made the journey with him from the mountains.

They all look well fed, Gray Wing thought as he padded from one sleeping hollow to the next. *It's as if we did the right thing to leave. I must be dreaming . . . but oh, I wish it were true!*

"Gray Wing!"

The clear meow came from the back of the cave. Gray Wing turned toward the sound and saw Stoneteller standing there, her white pelt turned to glowing silver in the light from the cave opening.

"Gray Wing, come with me," she invited, beckoning him with her tail.

Without waiting to see if he would follow, Stoneteller led the way down one of the tunnels that led out of the far end of the cavern. Apprehension prickled at Gray Wing's pads. He knew that the tunnel led to Stoneteller's den, the Cave of Pointed Stones.

He padded into the darkness, aware of damp rock beneath his paws, and Stoneteller's scent wafted back to him. Soon gray light filtered into the tunnel from somewhere up ahead, and he saw the outline of Stoneteller's head before she stepped aside and left the end of the tunnel clear.

Gray Wing emerged and halted, staring, awe trickling through him like icy water. The cave was much smaller than the main cavern where the Tribe lived, lit by moonlight that shone through a jagged crack high above his head. Pointed stones rose up from the floor and others hung down from the roof; some had joined together so that Gray Wing felt as if he was standing on the edge of a forest made of stone.

On the floor of the cave, puddles of water gleamed with reflected moonlight. Stoneteller stood beside one of them, still beckoning him closer with her tail.

"Welcome, Gray Wing," she mewed as he padded up to join her. "This is the Cave of Pointed Stones, where I read the signs our ancestors send us."

Gray Wing's mind spun with confusion. "How . . . how did I get here?" he stammered. "Did you bring me?"

Stoneteller shook her head. "We both walk in dreams, dear friend," she replied, her voice deep and soft in spite of her age and frailty. "And my heart tells me that I have a message for you."

Gray Wing's ears pricked alertly. "What is it?"

"A new life awaits you, Gray Wing," the white she-cat told him. "You must turn your paws onto a new path."

"I . . . I wondered about that, Stoneteller," Gray Wing meowed eagerly. "Turtle Tail's kits need a father. . . ."

Stoneteller dipped her head. "That may be so," she responded. "And yet I think there is another reason that your dream has led you here, into the place set apart for the leaders of our Tribe."

"But *I'm* not—" Gray Wing began to protest, then broke off, staring appalled at Stoneteller. "Tall Shadow is our leader," he went on after a moment's silence. "She should be here, not me."

Stoneteller blinked. "Who can tell what lies ahead in the

seasons to come?" she asked. "Be ready, Gray Wing. And may you walk your new path with courage. . . ."

As her voice died away the moonlight faded, leaving Gray Wing standing in darkness. Before he had time to feel afraid, he was waking in his own nest, with his denmates sleeping around him.

The next morning dawned dull and chilly, with a slap of rain in the wind. Gray Wing emerged from his nest, fluffing up his pelt against the damp cold. The camp was quiet; he guessed that most of the cats were still asleep, though Tall Shadow was already perched on her rock, keeping watch in spite of the weather.

Of course she's our leader, Gray Wing told himself, pushing the disturbing dream to the back of his mind.

As he gave himself a quick grooming, he spotted Thunder emerging from the tunnel he shared with Lightning Tail and Acorn Fur. As soon as he saw Gray Wing, the young cat bounded over to him.

"Can I see Turtle Tail's kits?" he asked eagerly.

"I'm not sure . . . ," Gray Wing began. "She needs peace and quiet, to sleep and get her strength back."

"Nonsense." Gray Wing turned to see Cloud Spots appearing from Turtle Tail's tunnel. "She'd love some visitors. Why don't you go hunting and bring a mouse for her? She'll be hungry."

"Okay, why not?" Gray Wing agreed.

He was afraid that with the sudden change in weather all

the prey would be snugly down their holes, but they hadn't gone far when Thunder spotted a mouse sheltering under a gorse bush.

With a glance at Gray Wing, who nodded encouragingly, he took off after it, leaping on the mouse with a triumphant yowl and padding back to Gray Wing with the limp body dangling from his jaws.

"Great catch," Gray Wing meowed, relieved that this time Thunder had caught the mouse without any trouble. "See, I said you would get there in the end."

Thunder's eyes were shining. "Can we go and see Turtle Tail now?"

"Let's see if we can find something else first," Gray Wing replied, wondering if he was deliberately delaying. "Turtle Tail must be starving, and one mouse isn't all that much."

Thunder left his mouse in a crack between two rocks, and the two cats headed away from the hollow, stalking quietly around a clump of gorse. This time Gray Wing was the first to spot prey: another mouse that scuttled away from him in a panic, straight into Thunder's paws. Thunder sank his claws into it and gave it a good shake.

"Two catches!" Gray Wing praised him. "You're a real hunter now."

"That one was really yours," Thunder mewed modestly. "I'd have had to be blind and deaf and clawless to miss it."

Returning to the rocks, Thunder collected the first mouse and carried both of them swinging from their tails as Gray Wing led the way back to the camp.

Turtle Tail was gazing down at her kits when they entered her den. All three were safe in the curve of her belly, squirming blindly on the moss and letting out tiny mews.

To Gray Wing's surprise, Jagged Peak was sitting beside Turtle Tail, watching the kits keenly and patting them back toward their mother if they strayed too far away. Rainswept Flower was there, too, tucking fresh bedding around Turtle Tail and her litter.

"What are you doing here?" Gray Wing asked his brother.

"He's being helpful," Rainswept Flower replied before Jagged Peak had a chance to speak. There was an edge to her tone. "Aren't you happy that the kits are being looked after and we're all pulling together?"

"Uh . . . sure," Gray Wing responded. "I didn't mean to criticize."

"That's okay." Jagged Peak sounded more content than he had since being cast out of Clear Sky's group.

Rainswept Flower gave a last pat to the fresh moss. "We could do with some more of that," she mewed, more like her cheerful self again. "Jagged Peak, come and help me collect it. We don't want to crowd Turtle Tail."

As she slipped out of the den, Jagged Peak rose to his paws and limped after her, giving Gray Wing and Thunder a nod as he passed.

"See you later, Jagged Peak," Turtle Tail called after him, and added to Gray Wing, "He seems to be feeling better. I'm so glad!"

"So am I," Gray Wing meowed. "Look, we brought you

some prey. Thunder caught them."

"Really? Good job, Thunder," Turtle Tail responded. "And thank you. My belly feels so empty!"

Thunder dropped the mice beside her and scuffled his forepaws in embarrassment. "I couldn't have done it without Gray Wing." He gazed down at the kits, his eyes wide with wonder. "They're so small and helpless," he murmured. His gaze gradually grew distant; Gray Wing guessed that he was remembering his mother, Storm, and his littermates, now gone forever.

Turtle Tail began eating one of the mice with rapid, famished bites. As she ate, Gray Wing watched the kittens, fascinated by their tiny, perfect bodies. Their fur was dry and fluffed out now; one of the toms had a dark gray pelt, while the other was a gray tabby with a splotch of white fur on his chest. The little tortoiseshell she-cat kept tumbling over onto her back, waving white paws in the air.

"Do you like them?" Turtle Tail mumbled around a mouthful of mouse.

"Like them?" Gray Wing could hardly find words to express what he was feeling, joy and pain at once. "They're . . . they're so trusting and innocent."

Turtle Tail let out a *mrrow* of laughter. "You won't think like that for much longer. Kits can be naughty, too!"

Gray Wing's pads prickled with embarrassment. *Of course I know that! What's the matter with me?*

"Have you given them names yet?" Thunder asked, stretching out one paw tentatively to stroke the tabby tom on his head.

"Not yet," Turtle Tail replied. "It's so difficult to decide. I think I'll wait at least until their eyes are open." She met Gray Wing's gaze, her expression soft, as if she realized she had hurt his feelings by laughing. "Come closer," she invited. "Maybe you could help the little she-cat—she's not very coordinated!"

Gray Wing took a step forward and righted the tiny tortoiseshell, who had tipped over again and was flailing her paws frantically as she let out a loud series of squeaks. Once upright, she stumbled forward and flopped down beside Turtle Tail; her wailing stopped abruptly as she started to suckle.

The two toms snuggled in beside her. Gray Wing watched as the three of them nursed, thinking back to how Turtle Tail had said that they needed a father.

After Storm died, I accepted that I'd never have kits of my own. But now . . . His heart fluttered excitedly at the thought of helping Turtle Tail to bring up her kits.

Turtle Tail's eyelids were drooping; she still looked exhausted, and she hadn't managed to finish the second mouse.

"We'll let you sleep," Gray Wing murmured, touching Thunder on the shoulder with his tail. As they headed out of the den, he added, "Come on, let's do some more hunting."

Excited squealing roused Gray Wing from sleep. Blinking drowsily, he emerged from his nest and arched his back in a good long stretch. The sun shone down on the camp; the sky was a clear blue, dotted with little puffs of white cloud. A warm breeze blew from the moor, bringing the scent of prey and fresh green growth.

Across the camp, Turtle Tail's kits had tumbled from their sleeping tunnel and were playing with Jagged Peak, who was gently pretending to fight with them and letting them climb on his back. A moon had passed since the kits were born, and all three of them were growing strong and active. Gray Wing felt warmth surge through him to see how close his brother was to the kits.

Turtle Tail sat at the entrance to the den, keeping an eye on them as she groomed her fur. Rainswept Flower and Hawk Swoop were observing them, too, from a little farther away. Hawk Swoop raised her tail to keep Lightning Tail and Acorn Fur back. "You can't play with them yet," she meowed. "They're too little."

On the other side of the camp Tall Shadow was grooming herself in her den, while Shattered Ice and Jackdaw's Cry were on the way out to hunt. Cloud Spots was sorting through a pile of herbs, tossing out the ones that were shriveled.

Optimism rose inside Gray Wing at the sight of daily life continuing peacefully in the camp. He bounded over to join Turtle Tail. "Hi," he meowed. "The kits are lively this morning."

Turtle Tail nodded, her eyes full of love as she gazed at her litter. "Jagged Peak is being such a help," she purred. "It's wonderful to have another cat to keep an eye on them when I'm tired and you're out hunting."

"Jagged Peak is happier, too," Gray Wing mewed.

As he spoke, the three kits came charging back to their mother. Jagged Peak waved his tail in farewell and settled down to give himself a thorough wash.

"I finally named them," Turtle Tail told Gray Wing as the kits scrambled around her. "The gray tom is called Owl Eyes."

As she spoke, the kit she named whipped around and stared at Gray Wing with wide, brilliant amber eyes.

"That's a really good name," Gray Wing commented.

"The tabby tom is Pebble Heart," Turtle Tail went on, "because of the white mark on his chest, and the tortoiseshell is Sparrow Fur."

"We like having names," Pebble Heart informed Gray Wing, giving an excited little bounce.

"And Mother says we can go out on the moor today," Sparrow Fur added. She butted her head against Turtle Tail's side. "Come on! You're groomed enough!"

Gray Wing felt amusement bubbling up inside him. Turtle Tail had her paws full with the kits, even though they were only one moon old.

"Are you sure it's safe to take them out?" he asked Turtle Tail.

"They have to leave the camp sometime," Turtle Tail replied. "And we're not going far: just to the top of the hollow."

"I'm going to catch a mouse!" Owl Eyes boasted.

"I'll come with you if you like," Gray Wing offered. "I think it might take two of us to keep them in order."

"I think you're right," Turtle Tail responded, a gleam of

pleasure in her eyes. "All right, kits, let's go."

The three kits charged off up the slope; Turtle Tail caught up with them and made them wait until Gray Wing had ventured onto the moor and checked that there was no sign of trouble.

The kits halted in amazement as they scrambled over the edge of the hollow and gazed around.

"It's huge!" Pebble Heart exclaimed. "I never knew the world was this big."

"It's much bigger than this," Turtle Tail meowed. "Remember the story I told you of how we traveled for days and days to get here from the mountains?"

"Can we go and see the mountains?" Sparrow Fur asked.

"Not today," Gray Wing replied. "Today we're just exploring around the camp."

He and Turtle Tail strolled side by side, always staying within tail-lengths of the hollow, while the kits ran excitedly here and there, chasing butterflies and batting at beetles in the grass. It was nice to see the world through the kits' eyes.

Owl Eyes leaped onto a caterpillar, squashing it flat. "I killed it!" he announced proudly. "I can hunt!"

"So you can," Turtle Tail purred, and added softly to Gray Wing, "That poor caterpillar never stood a chance!"

Enjoying the kits' antics, Gray Wing felt even happier that the recent tensions in the camp seemed to have died down. His denmates hadn't gone on insisting that he should take over as leader. That was a huge relief, even though Tall Shadow had been cool with him since the night of the argument.

She stalked off and never heard me refuse to be leader, he realized. *I hope she doesn't think I'm trying to undermine her.*

Gray Wing might have taken offense that his leader didn't trust him, but he was enjoying the kits too much to give Tall Shadow more thought. She was still keeping watch over the camp, almost constantly perched on her rock since Turtle Tail's time was taken up with her kits.

Wind and Gorse had visited the camp several times, and had shown the mountain cats more good places to hunt. Gray Wing hoped that Tall Shadow would soon see the sense in allowing them to stay permanently.

He relaxed, enjoying the unusually warm day as the sun soaked into his fur. He drank in Turtle Tail's scent, strong beside him in the sun's heat. Then Gray Wing stiffened. He had picked up the scent of another cat, which at first he couldn't identify; something about it reminded him of the Twolegplace. *Not one of my denmates; not Gorse or Wind . . .*

Then there was a flash of white paws, and a cat leaped clumsily out from a clump of gorse.

"Bumble!" Turtle Tail cried in astonishment.

Gray Wing stared at the plump tortoiseshell. This was the cat Turtle Tail had gone to live with in the Twolegplace. *What is she doing here?*

Bumble padded forward and dipped her head awkwardly to Turtle Tail, who didn't respond for a moment. Gray Wing remembered how confident Bumble had been when they first met her at the place with four oaks. She looked strained now, unsure of her welcome.

I remember Turtle Tail told me that Bumble kept the truth from her, that the Twolegs would take her kits away. Is that why she looks so unhappy now?

The kits were tumbling around Bumble's paws, but for once none of the adult cats were paying them much attention. Gray Wing picked up the smell of dried blood on Bumble's fur; looking closer, he could spot some scratches on her legs and flanks.

Turtle Tail had noticed them too. "Who did that to you?" she asked gently, flicking her tail toward the injuries.

The kittypet lowered her head; Gray Wing could sense the pain and misery she was feeling, but she said nothing.

Turtle Tail padded up to her and touched her nose to Bumble's ear. "Come on," she coaxed. "You can tell me."

"Yes," Gray Wing added. "There's no reason to be scared of us."

Bumble still hesitated for a moment, blinking unhappily. "It was Tom," she admitted at last, her voice shaking. "He turned against me once you left, because he blamed me for telling you the truth. He's been bullying me; he swipes and scratches at me, but he's clever enough to do it where the Twolegs won't notice unless they really look hard."

"I'm so sorry," Turtle Tail mewed, giving Bumble's ear a comforting lick.

Bumble looked up at her with desperate yellow eyes. "I don't want to live with the Twolegs," she declared. "Can I come and live with you? I know I treated you badly, but I can't live with Tom anymore."

Gray Wing glanced at Turtle Tail and moved instinctively closer to her, seeing his own alarm reflected in her eyes. *There's no way this could work!*

The kits, who had been listening to all this with wide eyes, began bouncing up and down with excitement.

"Come and live with us!" Pebble Heart squeaked excitedly.

"Yes, come and live with us!" Sparrow Fur repeated.

"Hush!" Turtle Tail told her kits sternly. "Bumble, I want to help you," she went on. "You were a good friend to me when I needed one. But you've been a kittypet all your life. There's no way you'd survive in the wild, hunting for your food."

Gray Wing knew his friend was right. Bumble was plump, with a glossy pelt and soft belly. She had a thin tendril around her neck, with a tiny glittering thing that made a tinkling sound as she moved. *That would frighten off all the prey!* And she had lost all her former confidence, hardly able to meet their eyes, her voice shaking as she spoke. *She'd be useless and terrified, living out here.*

"I could—" Bumble began.

"You spend most of your days sleeping!" Turtle Tail interrupted. "You'd be so vulnerable out here."

Bumble looked crushed by Turtle Tail's refusal, and for a heartbeat Gray Wing thought she was going to turn back to the Twolegplace. Then the kittypet seemed to brace herself. "Please, take me to see Tall Shadow," she begged. "Let me ask her. I can be very convincing!"

Yes, you convinced Turtle Tail to go and live with you. Gray Wing would have refused, but Turtle Tail gave a reluctant nod, and the kits were already racing excitedly back to the hollow. Bumble followed them, with Gray Wing and Turtle Tail a pace or two behind.

Gray Wing felt a pang of resentment against Bumble, for interrupting his time with Turtle Tail and the kits. He tried not to let that influence him, but he knew that it would never work for Bumble to join them. "Tall Shadow won't agree," he murmured. "You know how cautious she is around other cats. She refused to take in Gorse and Wind, remember."

"That's why I want Bumble to ask her," Turtle Tail responded. "Tall Shadow is bound to refuse, and then maybe Bumble will understand that she can't live with us, and go back to the Twolegplace."

Gray Wing nodded in agreement, then put out a paw to halt Turtle Tail before they reached the top of the hollow. "You were so kind to her," he mewed.

Turtle Tail sighed. "I don't have it in me to hold a grudge," she replied. "You above all cats should know that."

Her answer puzzled Gray Wing. "What do you mean?" he asked.

Turtle Tail looked briefly confused, as if she'd said more than she intended. "Well," she stammered, "you know, you weren't exactly pleased with me when I made friends with Bumble."

Guilt clawed at Gray Wing. *I had no right to tell Turtle Tail what to do.* "I'm sorry," he meowed. "I shouldn't have been so quick to judge. Can I make it up to you now?"

"You already are," Turtle Tail purred, brushing her muzzle against his. "You make it up to me every day you spend with the kits."

Sudden happiness flooded through Gray Wing. "That's easy then," he responded. "Come on. Race you back to the hollow!"

CHAPTER 9

Gray Wing and Turtle Tail caught up with Bumble and the kits at the top of the hollow. Before they could head into the camp, Gray Wing heard a voice calling his name; Wind and Gorse appeared from behind an outcrop of rocks and bounded toward them.

"Hi," Wind meowed, with a curious glance at Bumble. "Who's this?"

Turtle Tail dipped her head in greeting to the two rogues. "This is a kittypet friend of mine," she explained. "Her name's Bumble."

"A *kittypet?*" Gorse spluttered, his eyes stretching wide with scorn he didn't bother to hide. "What are you doing, hanging out with a kittypet?"

Bumble raised her head defiantly and faced the two rogues. "I'm tired of being a kittypet," she asserted. "I want to lie in the sun all day and catch mice and climb trees. I'm going to ask if I can join Tall Shadow's group."

Wind twitched her whiskers. "Good luck with that," she muttered.

Gray Wing gave her and Gorse an uncomfortable glance.

They really want to join us, and Tall Shadow won't allow it, in spite of all they've done. And now this kittypet thinks she can just stroll in. . . .

He expected that Wind and Gorse would be furious, but all Gorse did was shrug. Wind mewed, "I'll come with you. This should be interesting."

Gray Wing wasn't sure that was a good idea, but there was no way of stopping Wind as she headed beside them down the slope into the camp.

Tall Shadow was sitting on her rock, keeping watch as usual. No cat had taken up Jagged Peak's suggestion of organizing groups with duties such as patrolling the edge of the hollow.

When Tall Shadow spotted Gray Wing and the others she leaped down and padded over to them. Other cats too were gathering around, casting curious glances at Bumble.

"Who's *that?*" Jagged Peak asked. "She doesn't look as if she's short of prey!"

Turtle Tail's kits ran ahead, bouncing excitedly up to Dappled Pelt and Cloud Spots. "Bumble is coming to live with us!" Owl Eyes announced.

Dappled Pelt and Cloud Spots looked startled, while Tall Shadow cast an accusing glance at Gray Wing. "What's gotten into you?" she muttered. "Why have you brought her here?"

Gray Wing gazed back at her. "She just showed up, wanting to join us. What could I do?"

"You could tell her what a mouse-brained idea it is," Tall Shadow replied, beckoning Gray Wing a pace or two away, so that they could talk without Bumble overhearing. "Send her back to her Twolegs."

"It's not my job to send her anywhere," Gray Wing responded, nettled at his leader's tone. "She can wander all over the moor for all I care."

Tall Shadow's tail-tip twitched. "Including into our camp?"

"If guests aren't welcome, it's the first I've heard of it," Gray Wing meowed. "I know as well as you do that she can't stay here. But doesn't she have the right to come and ask?"

Tall Shadow sniffed, then turned to Bumble, her eyes narrowed. "Why do you want to live with us?" she asked stiffly.

Bumble seemed unaware of the tensions among the cats. Gray Wing noticed that her confidence had returned, now that she had to argue her way into the camp. *A few moments ago, she couldn't even look Turtle Tail in the face!*

Bumble dipped her head politely to Tall Shadow. "There's another kittypet, Tom, who's come to live with my Twolegs, and he's been pushing me around," she explained. "Just look at the scratches he gave me!" she added, thrusting a leg forward. "Have you ever seen anything so awful?"

Oh, yes, Gray Wing thought. *We've seen much worse than that. And so will you, if you stay here.*

"But why would this other cat attack you like that?" Tall Shadow asked.

Bumble slid a glance toward Turtle Tail. "I think he's angry because she left."

Shocked, Gray Wing took in a sharp breath. *Is she suggesting that this is Turtle Tail's fault?*

Turtle Tail blinked at Bumble, obviously hurt. She was

opening her jaws to speak when Sparrow Fur butted her leg. "Who's Tom?" the kit asked.

The question distracted Turtle Tail from Bumble. "Never mind that," she told Sparrow Fur, sounding flustered. Sweeping her tail around to gather all the kits together, she added, "Come along, all of you. It's time for your nap."

In spite of the kits' shrill protests, Turtle Tail bundled them away across the camp to their den. Bumble blinked unhappily as she watched her friend leave.

Gray Wing stayed where he was. He wanted to see what was going to happen, and intervene if he had to.

Tall Shadow hesitated, seeming to struggle for the right thing to say. "Is there any way of making your peace with Tom?" she asked Bumble eventually. "Can't you find a way of living happily together?"

Bumble shook her head. "You should be saying that to Tom, not me," she declared. "I haven't done anything to him."

Tall Shadow seemed to be at a loss. "Well, then . . . why not make yourself extra nice to your Twolegs," she suggested. "Purr at them, or whatever kittypets do."

"Lick their fur," Lightning Tail suggested.

"Mouse-brain!" Acorn Fur gave her brother a shove. "Twolegs don't *have* fur!"

"There must be something you can do," Tall Shadow went on, with a severe glance at the kits. "Then maybe the Twolegs will give you extra treats that will make it worth staying."

Bumble let out a snort of scornful laughter. "You think *treats* are going to make my life okay? You've seen my scratches!"

Gray Wing could see that Tall Shadow was trying to break it gently to Bumble that she couldn't stay. *But "gently" isn't going to work. Bumble has to be told so she understands what a mouse-brained idea it is.*

Before Tall Shadow could speak again, Wind thrust herself between her and Bumble. "I'm sorry you've had such a bad time," she told the kittypet. "But there's absolutely no way you can come and live in the hollow with these cats. You're a *kittypet.* You don't know how to hunt, you're soft and lazy, and you're used to eating too much food."

Bumble flinched back at the harsh words, her eyes wide and hurt. Some cat in the group that surrounded them—Gray Wing wasn't sure who—made a small sound of protest, but Wind ignored it.

"You wouldn't be able to contribute to the group," she told Bumble sternly, "and not only that—your presence would put the lives of other cats in danger. There's simply no place for a weak cat in the wild." Wind looked over her shoulder. "Isn't that right, Tall Shadow?"

Gray Wing realized that the gaze of every cat in the hollow was trained on Tall Shadow. *If Tall Shadow agrees, it will look as if Wind is in charge. And if she doesn't agree, it might mean finding an excuse for Bumble to stay.*

Tall Shadow began to pad forward, trying to circle around Wind. "I'll escort you back to your Twolegplace," she told Bumble.

But before she could reach the kittypet, Wind called out to Gorse, who came racing down into the camp to stand beside her. Together they flanked Bumble. "We'll take care of this," Wind meowed.

Before any cat could argue, she and Gorse began to march Bumble away; Bumble looked too taken aback to resist. "You let me down!" she yowled back at Turtle Tail as she and her escorts disappeared over the top of the hollow. "After all I did for you! I'll never forgive you!"

Why is this Turtle Tail's fault? Gray Wing wondered. *I'll never understand kittypets. . . .*

Tall Shadow perched back on her rock, her face fixed on the horizon. Gray Wing guessed that she didn't want any cat to see her expression.

He leaped up beside his leader. It was a long moment before she acknowledged him. Then, still without looking at him, she meowed, "I'm sorry I've been distant with you, Gray Wing. I suppose it's hard for me, knowing that some cats would prefer you as leader."

Gray Wing dipped his head. "I understand. And I want you to know that I would never dream of challenging you. I don't want to lead."

Tall Shadow let out a little sigh. "Do you think I should let Gorse and Wind join our group?" she asked. Her voice was shaking. It sounded almost as if she couldn't trust herself to make the right decision anymore.

"Wind might have overstepped a bit just now," Gray Wing began carefully. "But I trust her and Gorse. They've helped us hunt, and they've saved lives."

Tall Shadow twitched her whiskers thoughtfully, but didn't respond.

"I know Wind probably wants Bumble out of the way so that there's room for her and Gorse in the camp," Gray Wing went on. "But Bumble would never really fit in here."

"Do you think I don't know that?" Tall Shadow snapped. "Isn't that what I was trying to tell Bumble myself?"

"Of course, of course." Gray Wing soothed his leader with his tail-tip resting on her shoulder. *Except you never actually said so. . . .*

Tall Shadow looked down at the other cats. Acorn Fur and Lightning Tail were tossing a ball of moss to each other, while Hawk Swoop and Turtle Tail looked on. Cloud Spots and Dappled Pelt were having an earnest consultation over a heap of herbs; Thunder was sharing some prey with Rainswept Flower. None of them seemed interested in Tall Shadow or Gray Wing, up on the rock.

"They asked you to be leader," Tall Shadow mewed after a moment. "And just now I let Wind take over. Maybe it is time to let some other cat take charge."

"Never!" Gray Wing protested.

Tall Shadow fixed her gaze on the horizon again. "Have you never, ever questioned the leadership here?" she asked. "Have you never thought about how things could be different? I wouldn't blame you."

Gray Wing remembered the dream when he had returned to the mountains and met with Stoneteller in the Cave of

Pointed Stones. *She implied I would become leader,* he thought, shame throbbing through him. *But I can't tell Tall Shadow that.* "Never," he protested weakly.

Tall Shadow turned to look at him, her gaze deep and searching. For a moment she said nothing, only sighed deeply, then turned away again to scan the rolling moorland. "Leave me to my thoughts—please," she murmured.

Gray Wing wanted to find words to reassure his leader, but he knew that nothing he could say would do any good. Reluctantly he jumped down from the rock. He felt that something had changed in the hollow. Something big. If only he could see into the future, to what would happen in a few moons.

And I've learned something new about Wind, he thought. *She took control so smoothly and bundled Bumble out of the hollow. She's clever. . . .*

CHAPTER 10

Gray Wing found himself in a vast open space with lush grass beneath his paws. A rabbit ran past him and instinctively he gave chase. It was odd, but however hard he pushed himself, he couldn't seem to go any faster. Then the rabbit vanished and the open space gave way to a wide forest ride, with trees arching overhead to form a green tunnel. Gray Wing knew that something hugely important was waiting for him at the end.

But wait! What's that scent? As he raced along, the scent of prey and growing plants was suddenly blotted out by the smell of smoke. He halted; his nose twitched and he rubbed it with one paw. There was movement to one side of his vision—a darting, flickering orange. The crackle of flames. *Fire!*

Startled, Gray Wing jerked awake. He found himself in his mossy nest under the gorse bush. *I was dreaming.* But in the next moment he realized that the smell of smoke and the orange glow in the sky were still terrifyingly real. He leaped to his paws.

"Fire!" he yowled. "Fire in the forest!"

Some of the cats were already awake and in a panic. Hawk

Swoop dashed past him, hard on the paws of Acorn Fur and Lightning Tail, then herded them back toward their den. Jackdaw's Cry bounded up to the top of the hollow, took one appalled look, then raced back down, his fur bristling and his tail bushed out. Rainswept Flower was crouching in her nest, her eyes wide and scared as she gazed up at the sky.

Struggling to control his own terror, Gray Wing stuck his head into Turtle Tail's sleeping tunnel. Her kits were still asleep in a furry heap beside their mother, but Turtle Tail was awake, her head raised as she gazed out fearfully.

"What's happening?" she asked.

"Fire in the forest," Gray Wing repeated. "Stay here with the kits. It won't get this far."

Relieved at the she-cat's nod of acknowledgement, Gray Wing raced to the top of the hollow and looked across the moor. Fire was sprouting from the edge of the forest. Even at that distance he could hear the crackling. The blaze stretched up like a flaming foreleg swiping at the trees.

Clear Sky! Gray Wing felt his heart begin to pound so hard he could hardly breathe. *He and his cats are in there somewhere. They might be trapped!*

"Come on!" he yowled. "We have to help."

As the cats began to emerge from their dens, Gray Wing spotted Jagged Peak hobbling toward him. "I know I can't come with you," the young cat meowed. "But is there anything I can do?"

Gray Wing turned back to meet his brother. "Yes—can you protect the kits in the hollow while we're away?"

Jagged Peak's eyes shone and he puffed his chest out importantly. "Of course I can!"

"Great!" Gray Wing rested his tail on his brother's shoulders for a heartbeat. *Jagged Peak is finding a new role for himself,* he
thought as he dashed back up the slope. *And just in time . . .*

Reaching the top again, Gray Wing clambered over
the edge of the hollow and hurtled across the moor. All his
instincts were shrieking at him to flee the other way, but he
forced his fear down and kept going.

Casting a rapid glance over his shoulder, he realized that
Thunder, Tall Shadow, Jackdaw's Cry, Rainswept Flower,
Cloud Spots, and Dappled Pelt were following him. Thunder was the most determined of them all, picking up the pace
until he was running along at Gray Wing's shoulder. "Do you
think any cats are hurt?" he panted.

Gray Wing didn't reply. *I don't even want to think about that.*

As they approached the forest Gray Wing and his compan-
ions slowed, moving more cautiously. The fire on the edge of
the forest was dying down, but farther into the trees it still
raged on, sending hot red sparks swirling into the sky.

"Now what do we do?" Rainswept Flower asked.

"We have to find Clear Sky," Gray Wing responded,
appalled at the sight of the blaze and finding it hard to get his
breath as the surge of hot air hit him in the throat.

"But we need to stay together," Tall Shadow meowed, raising her voice so that all the cats could hear her. "Follow me,
and keep your eyes and ears open."

Tall Shadow took the lead as the cats picked their way

cautiously among smoldering, glowing branches. "What's this?" she muttered.

Gray Wing padded through the swirling smoke and drifting, charred leaves to see a circle of stones in the middle of a black patch of earth, with a heap of ash and burnt branches inside it. There were huge dents in the earth around the circle of stones. "Some sort of Twoleg thing," he responded. "Look, you can see the marks of their paws. This could be where the fire started."

Tall Shadow sniffed at the dents. "I guess the Twolegs tried to stomp out the fire," she murmured.

Gray Wing nodded. "Maybe they didn't get it all," he suggested. "If there were embers, they could have set the bracken on fire and then the flames could have spread to the trees."

Jackdaw's Cry snorted. "Trust Twolegs to do something flea-brained. That's one thing we never had to deal with in the mountains."

The branches around them were glowing with bits of fire. The cats crouched down as one of them exploded in a shower of sparks and Rainswept Flower let out a sharp screech as a spark singed her fur.

Gray Wing stiffened as he looked up and saw that the sparks had rekindled several small fires. Fresh orange patches sprang up all around them, including one back the way they had come. Retreating was going to be hard.

But I'm not retreating yet. . . .

Bracing himself, Gray Wing turned toward the heart of the forest, where flames still roared greedily around the trees. *My brother is in there somewhere. . . . I'll do everything I can to find him.* Only then would he be ready to find a way out.

All the tensions there had been between Gray Wing and Clear Sky vanished in that moment. He remembered how they had played together as kits and how they had supported each other on their journey. *I didn't come with him out of the mountains to see him die in a forest fire!*

Gray Wing raced toward the flames that blocked the way into the deeper forest, running back and forth as he tried to find a way to pass the fiery barrier. But every time he spotted a gap in the flames that he might fit through, it closed up in front of him.

"Gray Wing!" Rainswept Flower called out. "You must get away!"

"You'll set your fur on fire!" Jackdaw's Cry added.

"Yes, come back." Tall Shadow spoke in a voice of authority.

"No!" Gray Wing meowed. "Clear Sky and his denmates are in there! We have to help get them out." He could picture his brother and the other cats, crouching, terrified, in the middle of the fire as the blaze drew closer.

But the other cats were drawing back, clearly terrified by the crackling flames. Only Thunder stayed near Gray Wing, uncomfortably close to the blaze.

"Get back!" Gray Wing snapped. "The heat is worse for you, being so small."

Thunder shook his head determinedly. "I'm staying with you."

Gray Wing had no time to argue further. *He's flea-brained, but so brave! Just like his father . . .*

Thunder remained beside Gray Wing as they darted toward a gap between the fire-damaged trees.

"Through there!" Gray Wing gasped, struggling to breathe in the smothering heat. "Clear Sky's camp is down this way. If we can reach it, we can lead them out." *If the fire doesn't spread farther,* he thought, then pushed the idea away.

Gray Wing believed they could make it through the blaze, but then one of the trees began to groan and tilt alarmingly, so that they had to scramble back before it collapsed.

"What can we do?" Thunder asked. "Do you think we could jump over the flames?"

Gray Wing looked up at the edge of the fiery wall, trying to work out if he could make it to the other side. A branch fell from the tilting tree, closing up the last of the gap, flames leaping many tail-lengths into the sky.

Then Gray Wing saw movement beyond the blaze; a heartbeat later a cat came hurtling across the barrier from the other side. He gasped with shock as he recognized Moon Shadow.

The black tom's paws didn't quite clear the flames. He let out a yowl of pain and instinctively tried to curl up in midair, abandoning his strong leaping posture. He landed with a hard thump on the ground, in a chaos of waving paws and tail. Fire crept through his pelt and along his tail.

"Help me!" he screeched.

Gray Wing, Thunder, and Tall Shadow raced toward him, battering at him with their paws to put out the flames. But panic held Moon Shadow in its grip. He rolled over, and tried to scramble up and flee before the flames were out.

Thunder leaped after him, throwing his whole weight across Moon Shadow's lower back. "Keep still!" he yowled.

Gray Wing and Tall Shadow went on crushing out the fire. Gray Wing hissed with the pain of his scorched paws, but he had to ignore it to help Moon Shadow, who was moaning in agony.

As the flames died, Gray Wing's nose twitched, picking up the smell of charred flesh. He spotted a patch on Moon Shadow's side where the fur had been burned away, revealing an area of angry red skin. Spots of dark blood welled up and spread, running into one another.

The cats stood around Moon Shadow, briefly frozen with fear as they watched his life leaking away. Then Cloud Spots gave his pelt a shake. "Come on, Dappled Pelt," he meowed. "We'll find some healing herbs." To Moon Shadow he added, "Don't worry. This doesn't have to end badly." Moon Shadow groaned and turned his head away.

Cloud Spots and Dappled Pelt vanished into the darkness, weaving their way between smoldering branches. The rest of the cats pulled the limp form of Moon Shadow away from the fire and the heat.

Gray Wing stared at him, thinking of Clear Sky. Was he lying somewhere, injured and helpless in the path of the devouring flames? He felt a tingle of determination run through his paws. *If my brother is behind that wall of fire, I will save him.*

Straightening up, he began to race toward the barrier of

flame. A chorus of desperate meows followed him.

"No, Gray Wing!"

"You mustn't!"

"Come back—you'll die!"

Gray Wing ignored the voices. He was readying himself to jump when a weight crashed into him from one side and he was bowled off his paws. He looked up to see Thunder, who was holding him down with both forepaws on his chest.

"Get off!" he gasped, trying to wrestle himself free.

Thunder didn't move. A moment later he was joined by Jackdaw's Cry. "There's nothing you can do," the black tom insisted.

Gray Wing stopped struggling, letting out a long sigh. *I know they're right . . . but oh, Clear Sky, where are you?* Thunder let him get up, and Gray Wing padded back through a fog of misery toward the other cats.

They had formed a protective guard around Moon Shadow, who was still moaning with pain. Tall Shadow stood beside her brother, her green eyes wide with fear and grief. Seeing her made Gray Wing's anxiety grow even sharper, and he crouched beside Moon Shadow.

"Was Clear Sky with you?" he asked urgently. "Do you know if he's safe?"

But Moon Shadow only stared at him with glazed eyes and let out another drawn-out groan. Gray Wing realized that he was too badly hurt even to understand the question.

Tall Shadow bent her head to nuzzle Moon Shadow's shoulder. "Don't worry," she mewed. "Cloud Spots will be back soon with something to make you better. Every cat knows he's the best at finding healing herbs." Her voice shook, as if she wasn't quite certain of what she was saying, but she steadied it again. "You know that, Moon Shadow. Everything will be all right."

Seasons seemed to pass in flickering scarlet and the crackling of flame before Cloud Spots and Dappled Pelt returned, darting between the patches of fire. Hope kindled in Gray Wing as he saw the bunches of leaves in their jaws, but sank again as they dropped their bundles beside Moon Shadow. These weren't healing herbs, just random collections of grass and weeds.

Cloud Spots bowed his head, looking helpless. "The fire has left so little," he mewed.

Making a huge effort to ward off despair, Gray Wing tried to encourage him. "Come on, let's chew up the grasses and dribble the juice on Moon Shadow's wound. It's bound to do *something*, if only to stop the bleeding."

"We can try," Cloud Spots responded, though he didn't sound hopeful.

The cats gathered around and began grinding the leaves and grasses with their teeth as best they could, placing the chewed-up lumps on Moon Shadow's burnt patch. But within moments the lumps turned an angry red as Moon Shadow's blood soaked into them.

"He's bleeding too much," Dappled Pelt muttered.

Suddenly, to Gray Wing's surprise, Moon Shadow lurched to his paws, swaying. For a moment he stood shakily. "I *will* walk," he hissed determinedly.

Gray Wing knew that the cats had no choice but to retreat with him. If they left Moon Shadow here alone he would certainly succumb to the flames and smoke.

A fresh wave of heat surged over Gray Wing's body, making him shrink back. Looking up, his eyes stinging from the smoke, his breathing rough and irregular, he saw that the fire was creeping closer. While they had tried to save Moon Shadow, they had taken their eyes off the angry flames. Now the blaze was slowly stalking them.

The cats' control was slipping away. Seeing the flames advance, they began retreating and scampering around in tight, chaotic circles as they tried to find a way of escape.

"We'll never get out!" Jackdaw's Cry wailed.

Gray Wing struggled with a mixture of fury and dread. *This is the worst disaster we've ever faced*, he thought as he scanned the fiery circle where they were trapped. *Somewhere in there Clear Sky could be dying—and there's nothing I can do about it.*

CHAPTER 11

❧

We have to do something!

Thunder saw that Gray Wing's head was drooping and his breathing was harsh, as if he had lost the will to fight. Desperately he looked around, to see that he and his denmates were trapped in a circle of fire. Flames had caught on the grass and were spreading fast.

"This way!" Thunder heard an unfamiliar voice coming from beyond the fiery barrier. He peered through the smoke, trying to work out who was calling to him, but he couldn't see any cat. "You have to jump the flames!"

Thunder didn't need telling twice. Not allowing himself to think, he broke into a run.

"Thunder! No!" Tall Shadow yowled after him.

Thunder ignored the command. *Some cat has to do this. It's our only chance!*

As he drew closer he could just make out, beyond the dancing flames, the glimmer of water.

A stream! Thunder thought, relief surging over him. "Come on," he called to the others. "There's water here!"

Making a tremendous effort, he launched himself high

into the air, feeling the heat on the tender skin of his belly as he soared over the flames. He landed in a soft roll on the other side and leaped to his paws.

A silvery, long-furred tom was looking down at him. Thunder had never seen this cat before in his life, but he couldn't stop to talk to him. He spun around and called once more to the others. "Jump! Come on. You can do it!"

His heart was beating fast and he felt a strange exhilaration come over him, like the first time he'd made a kill. The silver tom padded across and touched noses with him.

"Who are you?" Thunder asked.

"My name is River Ripple. You did well, young one."

Thunder could barely stay still long enough to enjoy the praise. He remembered Gray Wing telling him about meeting this cat beside the river, but until now he had forgotten. He padded up and down beside the flames, calling again to his denmates. "Tall Shadow! Gray Wing! Hurry! It's safe here!"

Jackdaw's Cry was the first to appear, clearing the flames in a strong leap and landing hard on the other side. "Made it!" he gasped.

Rainswept Flower followed, then Dappled Pelt and Cloud Spots. The black-and-white tom dabbed irritably at sparks on his long-furred body, and muttered, "Never again!"

Thunder realized that the fire was beginning to die down here, as the collapsed tree burned itself out.

Peering through the flames and smoke, Thunder spotted Gray Wing, Tall Shadow, and Moon Shadow hesitating on the other side. "Take a long run up," he called out, "and then leap into the air as if you were catching a bird."

"Moon Shadow can't make it," Tall Shadow snarled in reply.

Then what are they going to do? Thunder asked himself anxiously. *They're all trapped—they'll die if they can't get out.*

Jackdaw's Cry padded up beside Thunder. "Gray Wing, you jump," he meowed. "Then we'll work out how to help Moon Shadow."

The smoke from the forest was growing thicker and thicker, almost hiding the stranded cats. "Come on, Gray Wing!" Thunder yowled desperately. "You *have* to do it!" Even as he spoke he wondered whether Gray Wing could manage the leap. He seemed so shaken by the danger and Moon Shadow's injuries.

As a breeze fluttered the flames, Thunder saw Gray Wing and Tall Shadow exchange a quick word. Then Gray Wing backed up. He raced toward the fire, but as he leaped a cloud of smoke billowed into the air and he disappeared from view.

"Gray Wing, where are you?" Thunder yowled.

A rolling ball of fur landed heavily at one side. Thunder and his denmates darted across to find Gray Wing, his eyes streaming as he lay curled up in the dirt. He was coughing so hard that he could scarcely breathe.

Thunder could see that Gray Wing's hind paws were scorched, and the tip of his tail was on fire. Pouncing on the tail-tip as if he was catching a mouse, Thunder crushed out the flame, ignoring the pain in his paws. *All that matters is that Gray Wing is safe.*

"I'm fine," Gray Wing choked out through his hacking

coughs as the other cats closed around him. "We have to help Moon Shadow. He can't move fast enough to dodge the flames. Tall Shadow ordered me across, but she won't leave him." Coughing overtook him again and he sounded angry as he continued, "What are we going to do? We can't leave them there. They'll burn to death."

Thunder felt a cat prod him in the side, and turned to see Jackdaw's Cry. "I've got an idea," the black tom mewed. "But I need some help. Are you up for it?"

Thunder nodded tensely. "What do you want me to do?"

"Follow me." Jackdaw's Cry padded down to the stream and plunged in, crouching down to dunk all his body under the surface. He rose up again with water streaming off his pelt. His body looked skinny as the fur clung to his ribs. "Get yourself wet like this," he told Thunder. "Then we're going through the fire to fetch Moon Shadow."

Hope flared into life inside Thunder. *Of course! If we're completely wet, the flames won't harm us.*

He jumped into the stream beside Jackdaw's Cry, making sure his fur was thoroughly soaked. His whole body trembled from the cold shock, but he set his teeth, determined to do whatever he had to. Then he floundered out again and headed back to the line of fire.

Tall Shadow and Moon Shadow were still trapped on the other side. As Thunder had feared, the flames seemed to be closing in on them. He could hardly see the two cats anymore.

"Tall Shadow!" Jackdaw's Cry called out. "Get your tail over here! We're coming for Moon Shadow."

"I'm not leaving him," Tall Shadow snarled in reply.

"You have to!" Jackdaw's Cry responded. "Thunder and I are coming through, and there isn't room for four cats over there."

Silence for a moment, except for the roar and crackle of the flames, and the sound of Gray Wing coughing.

"Do you promise?" Tall Shadow demanded at last. "You won't let Moon Shadow die?"

"We promise!" Thunder called back. "We'll do everything we can."

There was another brief silence; then Thunder spotted a flash of movement beyond the blazing undergrowth. Tall Shadow appeared, skimming so closely over the top of the flames that Thunder caught his breath in horror, certain that her belly fur would catch fire. She landed hard and flopped onto one side, panting.

"Now get Moon Shadow out," she gasped.

Thunder gulped. *We have to get this right! If we fail, Tall Shadow will never forgive us.*

For a heartbeat he gazed at the flames, feeling instinctively that it was wrong to run straight into them. He wasn't sure that his paws would carry him forward. *Is this a crazy idea?* he wondered. *But there's no other choice.*

"Thunder, no!" Rainswept Flower exclaimed. "You're too young for this. I'll go."

"Come on!" Jackdaw's Cry exclaimed at the same moment.

There was no time to respond to Rainswept Flower's brave offer. Thunder stayed by Jackdaw's Cry's side as he pelted forward and plunged into the flames, squeezing his eyes tight shut. Heat flashed around him for a heartbeat; then he was through, almost stumbling over Moon Shadow, who was crouching on the last untouched piece of ground, whimpering as sparks showered down onto his fur.

Jackdaw's Cry gave him a nudge. "On your paws," he meowed. "You're going to walk through the fire. Thunder and I will stay on either side of you, so the flames can't get at you."

Moon Shadow looked up at him, his eyes glazed with terror, reflecting the red of the fire. Thunder wasn't sure if he understood what he had to do, but he struggled to his paws.

Together, with Moon Shadow between Jackdaw's Cry and Thunder, the three cats faced the flames again. "Now!" Jackdaw's Cry rasped.

He and Thunder sprang forward, half pushing, half carrying Moon Shadow. Thunder flinched as he felt the heat, but forced himself to keep moving. His pelt was drying now; he picked up the scent of scorched fur, and sharp pain shot through his pads.

Then, somehow, they were on the other side. Thunder and Jackdaw's Cry let Moon Shadow sink to the ground; Cloud Spots and Dappled Pelt hurried up to examine him.

"Quick!" River Ripple meowed to Jackdaw's Cry and Thunder. "Soak yourselves again—there are sparks in your fur!"

Jackdaw's Cry launched himself into the stream; there was a hiss, and steam rose from his pelt. Thunder saw flames licking at his own fur and bounded over to join him, thankful this time for the icy shock.

"We did it!" he exclaimed, up to his belly in water.

Jackdaw's Cry flicked his tail. "Are we amazing or what?" he asked.

Suddenly feeling exhausted, Thunder shivered as he crawled up the bank. His pelt was clinging to him, but he couldn't feel any more pain. He padded over to Gray Wing, who was still curled up and struggling to breathe.

"Are you okay?" he asked anxiously. "There's a burnt patch on your rear paw—"

"I'm fine," Gray Wing interrupted, his voice a rough whisper. "I'm not badly hurt, and my fur will soon grow back. You don't need to fuss."

Thunder flinched at Gray Wing's sharp tone. *Didn't he see how brave I was?* Looking around he saw that the patch of forest where they were gathered wasn't burning yet, but they needed to get farther away from the flames.

He realized that River Ripple was still watching, and turned to him. "Thank you for helping us," he meowed. "Now, how do we get out of here?"

CHAPTER 12

Gray Wing watched through a haze of pain as Thunder and River Ripple talked together. His hind paws hurt more than any injury he had ever felt, and it took all his courage not to let the other cats see his pain or the trouble he had breathing.

What hurt even more was that Thunder—barely more than a kit—had taken the lead to save his denmates. *These cats wanted me to be their leader—and I couldn't get them out of the fire. Instead I was the cat who led them into danger!* He knew too that if Thunder hadn't spurred him on, he would never have found the courage to jump. *Thunder saved my life.*

Gray Wing remembered how Thunder had rebelled and said that he didn't need Gray Wing to watch over him. *He's certainly getting his wish now.* . . .

At last Gray Wing could manage to breathe, though he still felt as if he had swallowed fire. He couldn't understand how he could be in so much pain on the inside, where the flames had never touched him. Struggling to his paws, he opened his jaws to speak to the other cats, when River Ripple forestalled him.

"Not every cat would find it in him to jump over fire," the

silver-furred tom meowed. "Most of them would panic until it was too late."

Gray Wing winced at River Ripple's words: they came a bit too close to home for his liking.

"It's good to see you again, Gray Wing," River Ripple continued, as calm as he had been the day they had met by the river.

"My name is Tall Shadow." The black she-cat shouldered her way to the front. "I'm the leader of these cats. Thank you for your help."

She was trying to sound in control, but her voice was shaking and Gray Wing could tell that she was almost overcome by emotion.

"Can you really get us out of here?" she asked River Ripple.

"Certainly," the silver tom assured her. "I can show you the way out of the fire and back to your hollow, but you have to trust me."

He turned away and padded to the bank of the stream.

Tall Shadow stared after him. "Are you birdbrained?" she asked. "We're not all going to be able to swim the stream. Cats don't like water. Jackdaw's Cry and Thunder only went in because they had no choice."

Gray Wing winced at her sharp tone, when River Ripple was only trying to help. But he recognized how stressed she was, and besides, he had to admit she was right. Just here the stream was wide, swirling into pools; he couldn't see how deep it was. He didn't feel like plunging into it, injured as he was, and Moon Shadow was certainly too weak to manage it.

River Ripple didn't respond to Tall Shadow. Instead he padded down the bank and out into the stream. The ripples swirled around him, barely covering his paws.

Gray Wing let out a gasp, and Thunder exclaimed, "You're walking on the water!"

River Ripple turned back; in the light of the flames Gray Wing could see a gleam of amusement in his eyes. "No, I'm not," he replied. "I'm walking on rocks and stones just below the surface. They'll hold any cat's weight."

Gray Wing tried to clear his throat. "I'm sorry," he croaked, "but I can't go yet. I'm sorry I led the rest of you into danger, but the whole reason I came here was to look for Clear Sky— he's my brother," he added to River Ripple.

The silver tom gave him a long, hard stare. "You think that Clear Sky can't look after himself and his cats?"

Gray Wing hesitated. "Well . . . he can," he admitted. "Clear Sky's excellent at surviving."

River Ripple's eyes narrowed. "Oh, yes, he's very good at that."

Suddenly the air was full of tension that had nothing to do with the encroaching fire. *Have I been really stupid?* Gray Wing asked himself. *Have I been utterly reckless, leading my denmates toward the fire in the first place? Have we risked our lives for nothing?*

River Ripple returned to the bank and padded up to Gray Wing. "Your leader is struggling," he murmured. "Your spirit is strong, and now you need to be strong for every cat." Glancing around, he added in a louder voice, "First we need to get you all to safety. Then we can think about helping Clear Sky and his group—if they need helping."

"Right," Gray Wing agreed. Relief and gratitude surged through him that River Ripple had presented him with a clear plan. "Let's do that."

As River Ripple led the way down the bank of the stream, Gray Wing tried to control a fresh bout of coughing that threatened to explode out of him. *We're still in danger. I don't have time to be ill.* Suddenly a terrible thought came over him: *What if the fire spreads to the moor?* His heart pounded at the thought of flames encroaching on their camp, the others yowling in fright. . . . He struggled to take a breath and calm himself. *Right now, we need to get out of danger. Then I'll have time to worry about what the fire might do next.*

Cautiously the cats formed a line, with River Ripple in the lead to show them where to put their paws. One by one they stepped onto the rocks in the river, picking their way along.

"Go on, Thunder," Gray Wing meowed when only they remained on the bank. "I'll bring up the rear."

"I should do that," Thunder protested. "Just in case there's trouble."

Gray Wing shook his head. *I don't want any cat to see that I'm limping.* "Just go," he ordered. *And when did Thunder start protecting me? When did he grow up?*

Thunder blinked at him, looking slightly disconcerted at Gray Wing's tone, then turned to follow the other cats. Gray Wing paused at the edge of the stream, bending his head to lap at the cool water—but not even that could douse the burning in his belly. He was in far more pain than he would ever admit, and the knowledge sent a dark pulse of fear racing through him.

As he hobbled from rock to rock, Gray Wing spotted plump and delicious-looking fish swimming in the stream. He couldn't stop his forepaw from lifting, but he resisted the urge to swipe at the prey. *I'd never keep my balance, not with these sore paws.* The last thing he wanted was to be rescued from water right after being rescued from fire. He let the enticing fish swim by and concentrated on keeping his balance as he walked from rock to rock.

Thanks to River Ripple, all the cats eventually reached the safety of the opposite bank, well away from the fire. Gray Wing realized that they had emerged from the forest not too far from the hollow, near the place where he had first met the silver tom.

Every cat crowded around River Ripple, gazing at him with awe.

"Thank you for saving our lives," Tall Shadow meowed, dipping her head with deep respect.

"Yes," Cloud Spots added. "Who knows how many of us the fire would have eaten before it was full?"

His words jolted Gray Wing. Clear Sky was still in the forest! Turning back to the stream, Gray Wing began yowling his brother's name, as loudly as he could from his damaged throat.

River Ripple came to sit beside him and joined in his calls, but the only response was the growing roar of the fire, the crackle of sparks and soft thumps as branches fell to the ground.

"Clear Sky! Clear Sky!" Gray Wing went on crying out his brother's name. Clear Sky might be dead—most likely was dead. *I can't have lost him!*

Thunder joined him too, his frantic look increasing Gray Wing's desperation.

"Clear Sky!" Thunder wailed. "Clear Sky, where are you?"

A sudden gust of wind made the crackle of the flames subside. Gray Wing's ears pricked and relief flooded over him as he heard an answering yowl.

"That's him!" he exclaimed. "He's alive!"

Clear Sky was close by, but he was still on the wrong side of the water, close to the devouring flames. *He needs my help.* Gray Wing wished he had never allowed River Ripple to persuade him to cross the stream.

Gray Wing hobbled back to the water's edge and peered across. Though he was safe from the flames, smoke and sparks still billowed over him, catching in his throat and making his eyes sting. He gazed through the fire and the trees, catching blurred glimpses of gray that he knew must be his brother's fur.

The fire was starting to die back, moving farther into the forest, but a barrier of burning undergrowth separated Clear Sky from the stones where Gray Wing and his denmates had crossed the stream. A rocky outcrop was holding back the flames from where Clear Sky stood.

"Clear Sky, can you hear me?" Gray Wing called out. "You'll have to swim! It's safe if you keep to the far side of that rock."

Clear Sky emerged into the open followed by a bedraggled line of forest cats. Relief surged through Gray Wing again as he recognized his old denmates Quick Water and Falling Feather. All the cats were on the verge of panic, glancing around fearfully as they headed for the stream, their fur bristling and their ears flattened.

"Watch out for that bush!" Gray Wing yowled, seeing a line of fire creeping through the grass.

Clear Sky veered away sharply as the bush burst into flames. He raced for the stream and plunged in, struggling desperately across. His cats launched themselves into the water behind him; Gray Wing raced along the bank to the point they were heading for, ready to haul them out. Thunder and River Ripple came to help, until Clear Sky and the rest were all safely on firm ground again.

"Thanks," Clear Sky gasped, glancing around to reassure himself that all his denmates had made it across.

Clear Sky's pelt was clinging to his ribs and his chest heaved with deep panting breaths. But gazing at his brother, Gray Wing felt a flicker of hope. *We're working with each other again. . . .*

Clear Sky and his denmates huddled close together. Water was streaming from their fur and they all looked exhausted.

Gray Wing stepped forward and dipped his head to his brother. "You're welcome to share the hollow with us," he mewed. "It'll be crowded, but you'll be safe there."

As soon as the words were out of his mouth, he darted a

glance at Tall Shadow. The offer should have come from their leader; he'd been too quick to speak. But what could he do— these cats needed a secure place to sleep.

Thankfully, Tall Shadow nodded. "You're all welcome," she told Clear Sky.

As his fear ebbed, Gray Wing felt glad to see his brother alive, even though he looked ready to collapse, with his fur sodden and plastered to his sides. He and Clear Sky stood looking into each other's eyes for a long time. Then Clear Sky dipped his head. "We owe you our lives," he murmured.

Gray Wing was about to respond, when he heard the sound of another cat approaching. Glancing around, he saw Thunder gazing up at his father with wide eyes. This was the first time Thunder had seen his father since Clear Sky rejected him as a tiny kit.

"Come closer," Gray Wing invited gently, angling his ears toward Clear Sky.

Thunder padded forward nervously. He still looked bedraggled from his dip in the river.

"This cat saved my life," Gray Wing told Clear Sky, pride in his eyes as he looked at Thunder. "If it wasn't for your son, neither of us would be alive now. Would you like to thank him?"

Gray Wing could see Thunder's chest rising and falling rapidly as he struggled to contain his emotions.

Clear Sky stared at his son for a long time. Then at last he dipped his head in acknowledgement. "You're a brave young cat," he meowed. "But try to keep away from fires in future!"

Gray Wing let out a snort of laughter in sheer relief; he could hear several of the others doing the same. Thunder was still gazing at Clear Sky; not a single mew had come out of his mouth.

"Don't you have anything to say to your father?" Gray Wing asked, giving him a gentle shove.

He sensed tension in the cats around him as they wondered what might come out of Thunder's mouth.

For a couple of heartbeats Thunder scrabbled at the ground with his forepaws. Then he raised his head and met Clear Sky's gaze once more. "Did you love my mother the first time you met her?" he asked.

Where did that question come from? At a time like this! Gray Wing felt prickles of apprehension all through his pelt. He knew that his brother didn't like any cat to mention Storm since she died.

"Of course," Clear Sky replied, with an uneasy glance at Gray Wing. "It was something neither Storm nor I could resist." Shaking his pelt, he added, "Come on. Are you going to take us to your hollow?"

"Yes," Tall Shadow replied, turning to River Ripple. "Would you like to come with us?" she invited.

River Ripple shook his head. "I'm a rogue," he told her. "I sleep with no other cats. But I wish you all the best." He turned and bounded off into the darkness.

"Thank you!" Gray Wing called after him. When he looked around, Thunder was still gazing up at his father, and Clear Sky was meeting his stare.

Tall Shadow gathered the cats together and led the way across the moors toward the hollow. Cloud Spots and Dappled Pelt flanked Moon Shadow, supporting him as he stumbled forward. Thunder padded along at Clear Sky's side.

The first pale streaks of dawn were creeping into the sky. When Gray Wing looked back he could still see a sullen glow over the forest, but out on the moor the cool, misty air was soothing on his burnt pelt and streaming eyes.

The nightmare is over, he thought with a sigh of relief. *We're safe now.*

CHAPTER 13

I've met my father again! As he padded across the moor, Thunder couldn't ignore the flutter of excitement in his chest. *He said I was brave.* Maybe Clear Sky would realize he'd made a mistake when he sent Thunder away. *He didn't know me then. But now he's seen what I can do. . . .*

He stayed close to Clear Sky as they headed toward the camp. His father kept glancing around, checking on his denmates, counting them to make sure no cat had been left behind. *He's such a good leader. I wonder what it's like to be part of his group. . . .*

Before they reached the camp there was a flash of movement in the darkness and a couple of rabbits dashed across their path. Their eyes were rolling in terror; Thunder realized the forest fire must have spooked them so that they hardly knew that they were fleeing through a group of cats.

Clear Sky halted, looking after the rabbits. "They'd fill our bellies, don't you think?" he mewed to Thunder.

Thunder didn't need any more encouraging. Forgetting his exhaustion, he took off after the rabbits, and Clear Sky raced along beside him, leaving the other cats behind. *They're safe now . . . and if we can get some prey, it'll really help them.*

"Do you like hunting on the moors?" Clear Sky asked him as they ran.

"Not really," Thunder admitted. "I get along better in the cover of undergrowth and trees." His paws tingled at his father's approving nod.

"As soon as I can, I'll be back in the cover of the forest," Clear Sky muttered. "But for now, let's get these rabbits!"

Thunder put on a sudden burst of speed and pulled ahead. He had lost sight of one rabbit; the second was just dodging around an outcrop of rocks. Thunder ran up to the top of the tallest boulder and saw the rabbit beneath. With a yowl of triumph he hurled himself down onto it.

Thunder and the rabbit rolled over and over on the short moorland grass, the rabbit's legs kicking out fiercely. He sank his jaws into its throat and felt hot blood stream out over his fur. Giving a final, vicious jerk of his head he heard a bone snap in the rabbit's spine. When he let go, the rabbit flopped to the ground, its eyes rolling back in its head. Thunder felt his stomach squirm with disgust, but he forced back the feeling, enjoying the success of his kill and the knowledge that his denmates would eat well.

Thunder turned to his father, expecting to hear his congratulations. But Clear Sky said nothing. He was looking out across Thunder's head, his gaze fixed on another spot on the moors.

Glancing around, Thunder spotted three rats racing toward him. His heart started to pound as he saw their whiskers quivering and their long, greasy tails whipping through the grass.

They want to steal my prey!

The rats were almost as big as him, and they attacked all together, their teeth bared and their claws swiping at him. Tiny malignant eyes gleamed in their narrow, wedge-shaped faces.

Desperately Thunder tried to remember the fighting techniques Gray Wing had shown him. He leaped on the leading rat before it could reach him, knocking it onto its back and slashing his claws over its belly.

One dealt with! Thunder thought, then let out a screech of pain as he felt teeth sinking into his tail. Whipping around again he shook off the rat and realized that Clear Sky was by his side. The remaining two rats drew back a pace, as if they didn't want to face two hostile cats.

"We'll fight as a team," Clear Sky meowed.

"But I don't know how!" Thunder protested.

Annoyance flashed through Clear Sky's eyes. "Attack one rat together," he explained rapidly. "You take this side, I'll take the other."

As soon as he had finished speaking, Clear Sky darted at the nearest rat, slashed his claws down its flank and leaped backward again. Getting the idea, Thunder did the same on the other side, throwing himself clear just in time to avoid the snapping teeth.

Meanwhile Clear Sky had whirled to attack the third rat, jumping onto its back and balancing there while he clawed at its eyes and mouth. The rat squealed with pain; Thunder raced forward and sank his claws into its haunches.

Clear Sky leaped free and crouched for another attack. But the foul creatures backed away from him, terror in their eyes, and fled into the gorse, abandoning the dead rabbit. The rat Thunder had wounded at first was dragging itself away, whimpering and bleeding.

Thunder's fur was dripping with blood: his own mixed with that of the rabbit and the rats. Clear Sky padded across and looked him up and down.

"Good job, young one," he meowed. "Did Gray Wing never teach you to fight like that?"

Thunder shook his head, immediately feeling guilty, as if he was betraying Gray Wing. "Not yet . . . ," he admitted.

Clear Sky's expression softened. "Then you learned something new today, didn't you, thanks to your father? But you'll need another dip in the stream." He glanced down at the rabbit. "Shall we take this back to the others?" he meowed.

He picked up the front legs while Thunder got a grip on the back legs in his jaws. They set off across the moor and soon settled into a regular pace, moving well together.

As Thunder followed his father in silence, he went over the events of the night in his mind. He had survived the fire, and more than that: He had helped Gray Wing and Moon Shadow. He had met his father, killed prey, and defended himself against the rat attack. *And I've lived to tell the tale.*

For the first time in his life, Thunder experienced the feeling of knowing he had done well. *Better than any cat could have asked for.* It was a good feeling, warm and exhilarating.

Before they reached the hollow, Clear Sky halted and set down the rabbit. "You're very quiet," he meowed to Thunder. "What are you thinking about?"

Thunder dropped his end of the prey. He hesitated for a moment, then decided just to tell the truth. "I'm proud of myself for surviving," he replied.

Clear Sky's eyes glowed with approval. "And so you should be. I know that feeling."

"When you journeyed from the mountains?" Thunder guessed, remembering the stories Gray Wing had told him.

His father nodded. "That was a hard time. I'll never forget when we were attacked by eagles. One of our cats . . ." His voice trailed off and his eyes clouded. "That was when I decided we couldn't allow ourselves to be victims."

"What happened?" Thunder asked. "What do you mean?"

Clear Sky gave his pelt a shake. "It's all over now, a distant memory." He looked at Thunder again, and Thunder thought that he could see affection in his eyes. "I made the journey to save my family," Clear Sky went on. "*All* of my family."

When they arrived back at the camp, the sky was pale with dawn and a golden flush on the horizon showed where the sun would rise. Thunder saw Gray Wing standing at the top of the hollow, waiting for them; his anxiety was evident in his working paws and twitching tail. Thunder was faintly surprised. Usually Tall Shadow was the one to watch over the cats, but now it was Gray Wing.

Gray Wing's gaze flicked over the prey and rested on

Thunder, examining him closely. "What have you been up to?" he demanded. "No rabbit bleeds that much."

"Wouldn't you like to congratulate Thunder on hunting down food for us all?" Clear Sky interrupted sharply. "He's done well—can't you acknowledge that?"

"Of course Thunder has done well," Gray Wing responded. "I'm just concerned about him, that's all. You took off without giving us any warning."

"Oh, sorry," Clear Sky meowed. "I didn't realize a father had to ask permission to hunt with his son. Come on, Thunder. Let's take the rabbit over to the others."

Clear Sky strode off with the rabbit, and Thunder followed him, not daring to look at Gray Wing's face. His buoyant mood had vanished completely.

I've done nothing wrong. So why do I feel like I've betrayed Gray Wing?

CHAPTER 14
&

Gray Wing watched Thunder and Clear Sky pad down into the hollow. His relief that they had returned safely was mingled with pain at Clear Sky's renewed hostility, and even greater uneasiness at the bond that seemed to have sprung up so easily between his brother and Thunder.

Yes, he's your son. But he meant nothing to you until now!

Another worry was tugging at Gray Wing's heart, and he guided his paws toward Turtle Tail's den. He had told her not to follow the other cats into the blazing forest, and he hoped she had been sensible enough to stay in the safety of the camp with her kits.

His anxiety vanished like dew in sunlight as he reached the den and poked his head inside. Turtle Tail was curled up in her nest, her belly curved around her kits, who were asleep in a tangled heap of fur.

Turtle Tail looked up, her eyes glowing in the dawn light, and raised her tail-tip for silence, angling her ears toward the sleeping kits. Gray Wing's throat was tight with emotion; he would have liked to stay with her, but instead he nodded and turned away.

Glancing around the hollow, Gray Wing saw that Jagged Peak was welcoming the forest cats, pointing out places where they could make nests, and doling out bracken and moss for bedding.

Gray Wing padded over to him. "How was everything, while we were away?"

"Fine," Jagged Peak replied. He was looking much more like himself, and Gray Wing realized what a good idea it had been to give him some responsibility. "Everything was quiet." He glanced around at the other cats. "It looks as if you had it tough over there."

Gray Wing nodded. "You could say that. But at least no cat died."

By this time all the cats had settled down and were sharing prey: the rabbit that Thunder had killed, and a hare that Hawk Swoop had caught on the previous day. Gray Wing noticed with a jolt of tension that the two groups of cats were sitting separately; even Falling Feather and Quick Water, who had come from the mountains with the others, had chosen to stay with the forest cats. The only exception was Moon Shadow, who was crouching beside Tall Shadow, twitching with pain and feebly licking at his injuries.

There was a sense of coldness, too, between the two groups; Gray Wing caught a furious glare from Petal, and guessed that she was still angry with him for killing her brother Fox. When Hawk Swoop padded across with a portion of the hare and offered it to Frost, the big white tom nodded stiffly, seeming grateful but unwilling to be friendly.

This is all wrong, Gray Wing thought. *The fire should have brought us together, but it seems as if nothing has changed. We risked our lives to help them, and this is how they repay us.*

He headed toward Clear Sky, in the faint hope that he might be able to do something to dispel the hostility. But he spotted Tall Shadow signaling to him with her tail.

Gray Wing padded up to his leader, who sat beside her injured brother. Seeing Moon Shadow more closely, he became painfully aware of the black tom's suffering. His eyes were glazed, and his breath came in shallow pants; Gray Wing wasn't sure that he realized where he was.

"Sit down, Gray Wing," Tall Shadow mewed. "There's something I have to say to you." Her gaze was fixed on her brother as Gray Wing settled down beside her. "I have to concentrate on Moon Shadow now," she continued. "He needs me to care for him." Turning her head, she looked Gray Wing in the eyes, and apprehension tingled in his paws. "Gray Wing," she asked, "can you take over as leader?"

Shock crackled through Gray Wing, as fierce as the spreading fire.

"Are you sure?" he asked.

His leader's eyes were full of pain and regret. "Can't you see why I have to do this?" she asked. "The other cats don't want me as leader any longer. Even Wind thought it was okay to take over when Bumble wanted to join us." She let out a deep sigh. "Where was I when it came to true leadership during the fire?" she continued. "Cowering behind the flames. If it wasn't for Thunder and Jackdaw's Cry, I would be dead."

"That was because you wouldn't leave Moon Shadow," Gray Wing protested. "How would you feel now, if you'd left him to burn?"

Tall Shadow only flicked her tail in a gesture of denial; Gray Wing could see that guilt was almost overwhelming her.

"You've been a good leader," he argued. "You've always been brilliant at strategy, and you helped lead us down from the mountains. You were the obvious choice to take over when Shaded Moss was killed."

"That was then." Tall Shadow's shoulders sagged. "Can't you see how tired I am? The only thing I've had strength for is watching over the camp." She shook her head helplessly. "No, this is the right time. Gray Wing, you should take over." With a wry twist of her mouth she added, "Just don't rub my nose in it, okay?"

"You should know me better than that," Gray Wing responded gently. "I would never dream of hurting you." He wanted to tell her that he had been injured in the fire too; his paws still hurt and his breathing didn't feel right.

But Tall Shadow had already turned back to her brother, licking his ears in an attempt to comfort him. *How can I refuse?* Gray Wing thought sadly as he moved away, leaving the brother and sister to care for each other. *Is this what Stoneteller was trying to say in my dream? That I should take the leadership despite my doubts?*

Cloud Spots and Dappled Pelt were moving among the other cats, checking for injuries. Gray Wing noticed that Frost had a bad burn on one leg. A sense of responsibility crashed over him, but he realized there was nothing he could do that Dappled Pelt and Cloud Spots weren't doing already.

I need to get some sleep. Even though the sun was high and bright, Gray Wing staggered toward his nest. He was almost thankful for the exhaustion pulling at his body; it dampened the pain in his paws. *Maybe things will look better after a rest, and I'll feel more like taking over the leadership from Tall Shadow.*

But before Gray Wing reached his nest, he noticed that Clear Sky was standing at the top of the hollow, gazing out across the moor. Jagged Peak was hovering nearby, clearly trying to pluck up courage to talk to him, but he might as well have been on the other side of the moor for all the attention Clear Sky was paying him.

Gray Wing couldn't see Clear Sky's expression because his brother was facing away from him. *But I know he must be unhappy to be forced from his home in the forest. I should go and talk to him. . . .*

His paws felt heavier than rocks as he dragged himself up the slope, but when he reached the lip of the hollow he spotted Thunder padding up to Clear Sky. Gray Wing lowered himself to the ground and watched.

Thunder sat down beside Clear Sky with a respectful dip of his head.

Clear Sky turned to look down at him. "I heard about how you took the lead in the forest fire," he meowed. "The way you showed the other cats how to leap over the flames. You should be proud."

Thunder's eyes glowed as he gazed up at his father. "Any cat would have done the same," he responded.

"No. *You* were the cat who did it. And you hunted well, too—I enjoyed being with you."

Gray Wing noticed that Jagged Peak was trying to join the other two cats, creeping up slowly and keeping low to the ground.

Clear Sky spotted his younger brother, too, and whipped around to face him. Jagged Peak jumped, startled.

"And you? What have you done to prove yourself?" Clear Sky demanded, scorn in his voice and eyes. "Well," he added sneeringly, "you survived. That's as much as you can do, now."

Jagged Peak's shoulder fur bristled. "Actually," he began, "I was responsible for looking after the camp and the cats who—"

"So you stayed behind, where it was safe," Clear Sky interrupted.

Gray Wing couldn't ignore that. He sprang to his paws and padded up to the group. "Jagged Peak is being really useful," he mewed sharply. "Injured leg or no injured leg. He protected the cats who stayed in the hollow, and in case you didn't notice, he did an excellent job of welcoming your cats into our camp. We need him, Clear Sky."

Turning toward Jagged Peak, Clear Sky gave him a long look from intense blue eyes. "I'm sorry," he told the young cat. "I take back what I said."

But Jagged Peak's gaze was still full of pain and anger. "It's too late!" he spat. "You clearly think I'm a waste of space. Why else would you have thrown me out of the forest? And now that I'm beginning to prove myself, you need Gray Wing to *tell* you what I've done." He shook his head. "Will I ever be good enough?"

"I told you I'm sorry . . . ," Clear Sky began.

But Jagged Peak wasn't listening. Turning his back on Clear Sky, he limped away to join Rainswept Flower.

Clear Sky let out a sigh as he watched him, then turned to meet Gray Wing's gaze. "I didn't mean . . ." His voice trailed off.

Gray Wing twitched his whiskers in exasperation. "You never do mean anything, do you, Clear Sky?"

"I'm just trying to do my best for every cat!" Clear Sky protested, instantly defensive.

"By humiliating your brother?"

Thunder was watching the two of them, drinking in every word. Gray Wing couldn't help feeling glad that the young cat was seeing firsthand that Clear Sky wasn't perfect. But even thinking that made Gray Wing squirm with discomfort. *Why do I care so much? Why shouldn't Thunder be happily reunited with his father?*

"Well, I can't help it!" Clear Sky snapped, his neck fur beginning to rise. "It's not my fault Jagged Peak fell out of that tree. Every cat has to contribute, and weak cats just don't count." He gave a single lash of his tail. "It's about survival!"

Gray Wing dug his claws into the ground. "We're all doing a pretty good job of surviving," he pointed out, forcing himself to sound calm. "There's enough prey here for every cat.

Stoneteller was right to tell us to leave the mountains; I can see that now. You need to let yourself relax a little bit. We've done what we set out to do. This is the time to enjoy it."

"Okay, we've survived for now," Clear Sky meowed. "But who knows what tomorrow brings? We have to be prepared— always."

As he finished speaking, Clear Sky turned his attention to Thunder. His eyes were full of approval. Gray Wing tried desperately not to feel his heart sink as he saw how close the two cats were becoming. *I allowed them to discover each other. I even encouraged it.*

"You're growing up into a brave and tactical fighter," Clear Sky meowed approvingly, touching Thunder's shoulder with the tip of his tail. "I like that in a cat. Storm was brave, too. It's good to see that quality in her son."

Thunder's eyes sparkled, all his attention on Clear Sky. "Tell me more about my mother," he begged.

"All in good time," Clear Sky responded. He seemed to hesitate, before asking: "How would you feel about coming to live in the forest with me?"

"No!" Gray Wing protested, but neither cat was listening to him.

Thunder gazed wide-eyed at his father. "Do you mean it?"

"Of course," Clear Sky told him. "Who wouldn't want a fearless young cat in their group? You'll be an asset."

"Thunder," Gray Wing began hesitantly, "you still have a lot of growing up to do. Maybe you can make this decision when you're a bit older." He couldn't help the anger that was churning inside him. Thunder would have died on the moor as a kit, if it hadn't been for him!

Thunder turned to look at him. "I'm not a kit anymore," he mewed.

"Well, Thunder?" Clear Sky asked, before Gray Wing could speak. "Are you coming into the forest with me, or staying here in the hollow with the other kits?"

Gray Wing's pelt prickled all over as he waited for Thunder's reply.

The young cat hesitated for a moment, his eyes troubled. "Is that true, what you said?" he asked Clear Sky eventually. "That we don't know what tomorrow brings?"

Clear Sky glanced across at Gray Wing, almost as if he was asking permission, but Gray Wing didn't respond, not even to twitch a whisker.

"Yes, I truly meant that," Clear Sky eventually replied. "There's food and comfort now, but no cat knows how things might change. What about your skirmish with the dogs?"

Thunder gaped in astonishment. "How do you know about that?"

"I have friends all over the place," Clear Sky meowed. "Rumors have a way of reaching me. You *did* have trouble with some dogs, didn't you?"

Thunder nodded. "It was scary," he admitted with a shiver. "But I survived! We all did."

"Yes, you're clearly a survivor." Clear Sky's voice was filled with approval. "And you need to help other cats to be the same. Thunder, I would like you to join my group. Troubled times lie ahead of us, and the more strong cats I have by my side, the safer we'll all be."

Gray Wing had to clamp his jaws shut to stop himself from interfering. *Why is Clear Sky playing these games with Thunder, talking about survival and making him think back to the dog attack? Any cat would think we were still up in the mountains, starving to death, terrified for our lives. Clear Sky can say what he likes, but we are safe and well fed here, most of the time.*

Though his tail lashed angrily, Gray Wing managed to keep silent. *This has to be Thunder's choice. He accused me of not knowing what's best for him. Well, not this time.*

He was relieved to see that Thunder still looked anxious as he peered up at Clear Sky. "There's just one thing . . . ," he mewed uncertainly. "When I was a kit, you didn't want me. You sent me away. If it wasn't for Gray Wing, I might not be alive now."

At first Gray Wing thought his brother wouldn't have an answer for that, but Clear Sky seemed unworried. "Congratulations on passing the test," he purred.

Thunder looked bewildered. "What test?"

No, Gray Wing thought, as understanding dawned. *Clear Sky has to be kidding.* Was he really going to try and pretend that this had all been part of a bigger plan?

"You can't . . . ," he started to interrupt, but his brother quickly spoke over him.

"Don't you see, young one?" Clear Sky's voice was smooth,

persuasive. "I wanted to see if you could survive without me. You did. So now is the time for us to grow together. I did all of that for *you*."

I've heard some twisted arguments in my time . . . , Gray Wing thought. The father who rejected Thunder was convincing the young cat that he had been spurned out of love.

Thunder stretched out his neck as if to give Clear Sky an affectionate nuzzle, then stopped short, clearly uncertain whether Clear Sky would appreciate the gesture. Gray Wing himself wasn't sure. But Thunder's agreement was obvious. Gray Wing had no chance of standing between the young cat and his father. The decision had been made. Clear Sky looked over at Gray Wing, and he could see the challenge in his brother's eyes—it was a challenge he wasn't ready to meet.

Thunder will be leaving soon. All I can do is prepare him.

CHAPTER 15

"Let all cats gather around to listen!" Tall Shadow yowled.

She stood on her rock, outlined against a scarlet sky as the sun went down over the moor. The day after the fire was drawing to an end.

Following his confrontation with Thunder and Clear Sky, exhaustion had overwhelmed Gray Wing; he had stumbled into his nest and slept for most of the day.

When he awoke he discovered that Rainswept Flower and Shattered Ice had made an expedition with Petal and Quick Water to find out the full extent of the damage in the forest. They reported back that Twolegs with bright pelts and gleaming monsters had wrestled the fire into submission; it was safe there now, though devastation stretched in all directions, and the smell of burning still lingered.

Cloud Spots and Dappled Pelt had headed for the river, bringing back bundles of herbs from the waterside. Cats had been out to hunt; life was gradually returning to normal.

As the cats gathered around the rock now to hear what Tall Shadow had to say, Gray Wing noticed that they were still divided into two groups: the forest cats and the moorland cats.

His heart sank to realize it, especially when he spotted Thunder close beside Clear Sky.

"Every cat knows what happened last night in the fire," Tall Shadow continued. "I didn't behave as a leader should. And now, with my brother so badly injured, I don't have the time or the strength to carry on."

Gray Wing winced as he realized what she was about to say. He had expected some kind of announcement, but he still shrank from being singled out.

Tall Shadow glanced around the assembled cats. "I thank all of you for the support you have given me," she went on. *Or not*, Gray Wing thought, with a glance at Shattered Ice and Jackdaw's Cry, whose eyes were fixed on Tall Shadow with intense interest.

"Now Gray Wing will be your leader," the black she-cat finished, and immediately leaped down to sit beside Moon Shadow.

A chorus of surprise and approval rose up from the crowd of cats. Glancing around, Gray Wing realized that Clear Sky's cats looked particularly astonished. *Strange that she would announce this in front of them . . . but I suppose she has her reasons.* And he sensed he wouldn't have long to ponder those reasons.

A tail swiped Gray Wing across the shoulder, and he turned to see Shattered Ice standing beside him. "About time, too," the white tom meowed. "Congratulations."

"Yeah, you'll be a great leader," Jackdaw's Cry added from where he stood at Shattered Ice's shoulder.

Glancing past him, Gray Wing spotted Turtle Tail gazing

at him from the mouth of her den, where she was sitting with her kits. Her eyes were shining with admiration.

Gray Wing could feel himself calming, until he turned and found himself face-to-face with Clear Sky. He braced himself for another argument, but Clear Sky gave him a nod and mewed, "You'll perform well, Gray Wing."

"Thanks." Gray Wing relaxed again; his brother's tone couldn't be called friendly, but it wasn't hostile either. "That means a lot to me. Maybe our two groups can work together more closely now?"

He held his breath, waiting to hear how Clear Sky would respond. The other cat dipped his head.

"Maybe," he said, his tone impossible to read. He shook himself. "It's time we were leaving. Good luck with everything and thank you."

The forest cats were beginning to gather around his brother, ready for the trek across the moor. This was a surprise. Gray Wing had thought it would take several moons for the forest cats to even think about going back to their ruined home.

"Do you have to go so soon?" he asked. "Wouldn't it be better to stay with us, until the forest has healed itself?"

Clear Sky shook his head. "The forest is where we belong," he said. "Nothing can keep us away." Then he raised his voice so all the cats around could hear him. "We thank you for helping us last night," he meowed, "and for the hospitality of your camp." He glanced around until he spotted Jagged Peak. "I especially want to thank you, Jagged Peak. You did so much to make us feel welcome."

Jagged Peak gazed at him in silence for a moment, then turned his head away.

"Now we have to go and see what's left of our home," Clear Sky went on. Quietly he added to Gray Wing, "I want a word with you in private."

Gray Wing had a horrible feeling that he knew what this conversation would be about. "Okay," he murmured.

Clear Sky led the way up the slope and out onto the moor, halting a few tail-lengths away from the hollow. "I hope you won't take this the wrong way," he began, "but the fire has changed things."

"I know," Gray Wing responded. "Even though you're leaving, I hope we can see more of each other now." He was trying to sound enthusiastic. He couldn't see why it would be so terrible for the two groups to work more closely together. It would be the end of so many tensions. *And I'd get to see Thunder more often. . . .*

"I have to be honest," Clear Sky mewed gently. "I doubt we'll be seeing more of each other. I need to prepare for whatever challenges the future holds, and you should do the same, Gray Wing. You're the leader now. Or is that Tall Shadow? Or that rogue . . . what is she calling herself these days . . . Wind? I hear she's a cat with leadership gifts. It's so difficult to make sense of *who* is leading your cats these days."

The shock of Clear Sky's words hit Gray Wing in the face. He was being so cruel and mocking, when their camp had given him a place to rest last night! How could he behave this way? "What are you implying?" Gray Wing growled.

"Nothing," Clear Sky meowed, his eyes widening with innocence. "Only maybe your group needs to be a bit more . . . organized."

If this had been any other cat, Gray Wing would have given him a swift cuff around the ear. *But Clear Sky is my* brother, he thought, forcing himself to be calm, and digging his claws into the ground to stop himself raking them across the gray tom's pelt. *What will it look like if I start a fight in the hollow?*

"I don't think you have the right to tell us how to organize ourselves," he said stiffly. "We were organized enough to save your lives!"

Clear Sky nodded. "True enough. Dangers are all around, and I have to concentrate on making sure my cats are safe now, and back in their rightful home."

Gray Wing felt his neck fur begin to bristle at Clear Sky's use of the word *rightful*. It was harder than ever not to lose his temper. *We're just mountain cats who left our birth home to find somewhere we could live more easily.* Clear Sky and his cats had no more right to the forest than Gray Wing and his group had rights over the moor. *These are simply the places we've chosen to settle.* But he didn't want to see Clear Sky leave on the back of a quarrel.

"We're lucky that the rogue cats like Wind and Gorse have been so welcoming," he gently reminded his brother. "Things could have been very different."

Clear Sky let out a snort of scornful laughter. "Those two bags of bones! I don't know why you bother with them. They just take up precious prey."

Gray Wing remembered what Wind and Gorse had told

him. "But . . . you allow them to hunt in the forest, don't you?" he asked. "I mean, they were here before any of us."

A heartbeat passed before Clear Sky replied, not meeting Gray Wing's gaze. "No," he responded slowly. "They don't hunt in the forest anymore."

"Because you won't let them?" Gray Wing demanded.

Once again Clear Sky didn't reply immediately. Then he spun around to face Gray Wing. "Look—you have to understand," he began. "Thunder is coming with me." Gray Wing opened his jaws to protest, but Clear Sky kept speaking. "I know I sent him away when he was a kit, but I just wanted to test him. He's grown into a brave and clever cat, and that's all thanks to you—I know it is—but I am his father. I'm going to make amends now." He peered into Gray Wing's face as if he was trying to read his thoughts. "You won't try to stop me, will you?"

What can I say? Gray Wing asked himself.

"Good," Clear Sky said. "I knew I could trust you not to get between father and son." He started to walk away.

It can't end here! Gray Wing tried to call his brother back, but as he opened his jaws he felt the breath leave his body. His belly felt tight, as though his rib bones were growing smaller and crushing it. The taste of smoke filled his mouth, and he couldn't speak.

Fear crawled through Gray Wing's pelt from ears to tail-tip. He gasped for breath, and to his relief the crushing sensation faded. But by then, Clear Sky had gone.

Trying to force down his deep uneasiness, Gray Wing returned to the hollow. Clear Sky was standing in the middle, beginning to gather his group of cats around him. At first Gray Wing couldn't spot Thunder; then he noticed him at the far side of the hollow with Lightning Tail. The two young cats were pretending to stalk a pebble, creeping forward with their belly fur brushing the ground. Slowly . . . slowly . . . then pounce!

Pleasure tingled through Gray Wing's paws as he watched them, but the feeling was followed by sadness. *Lightning Tail adores Thunder. . . . How will he cope when he's gone?*

Gray Wing bounded down into the hollow and called to Thunder. As the young ginger tom padded toward him, Lightning Tail started to follow, as he often did. Gray Wing raised a paw to halt him. "I need to talk to Thunder alone."

Lightning Tail looked faintly surprised, then nodded and dashed off to join Acorn Fur, who was batting a feather around at the entrance to their den.

Gray Wing led Thunder to a quiet spot behind the leader's rock. "Clear Sky and his cats will be leaving soon," he began. "I take it you'll be going with them?"

Thunder studied his paws. "How do you know that?" he asked.

Gray Wing reached out a paw and patted Thunder gently on the nose. "I know you better than you know yourself. I raised you from a kit—or have you forgotten that?"

Thunder looked up, his eyes blazing. "I'll never forget that, never!" More quietly he added, "But I'm not a kit anymore, and I think Clear Sky understands that. He'll help me become the best cat I can be."

And you think I wouldn't? Pain clawed through Gray Wing, but he did his best to push his feelings to one side. It wouldn't help Thunder to get upset now.

"I'm sure he will," Gray Wing responded, after a pause. "And I want you to know that you leave with my good wishes."

Thunder's tail went straight up in surprise. "Really?" he asked, sounding relieved.

"Yes," Gray Wing assured him, "but you must do one thing for me. I want you to say good-bye properly to Hawk Swoop. She's done a lot for you. She's treated you as her own son." Gray Wing angled his ears to where Hawk Swoop sat outside her den, watching Acorn Fur and Lightning Tail wrestling together. "Go on, now."

Thunder dipped his head in understanding. "Thank you for everything," he meowed, then padded over to Hawk Swoop.

Gray Wing couldn't hear what they were saying, but he felt that his heart would break when he saw Hawk Swoop's expression change and heard a desolate wail rise up from Lightning Tail.

Hawk Swoop darted a panicked glance over to Gray Wing, who shook his head gently. *Don't try to fight it,* he told her silently. *The best thing we can do for Thunder now is to send him on his way with our good wishes.*

"Forest cats, come on!" Clear Sky called, striding across the hollow to round up the stragglers. "We're leaving now."

His cats gathered quickly, looking confused and startled, exchanging hasty good-byes with the moorland cats. Gray Wing looked around for Tall Shadow, but she was bending over Moon Shadow, and paid no attention to Clear Sky.

Of course, Moon Shadow will be staying here, Gray Wing thought with a hint of bitterness. *Clear Sky has no use for injured cats.*

As the forest cats headed up the slope, Clear Sky gazed across the hollow toward Thunder, who still stood uncertainly beside Hawk Swoop. "Are you coming or not?" he asked.

"I . . . er . . . I thought I'd have more time to say good-bye to the others," Thunder replied.

The fur on Clear Sky's shoulders began to bristle. "Sentiment will get you nowhere," he meowed. "Walk by my side, or stay here in the cozy hollow with the other kits." He turned and followed the rest of his cats without waiting.

Thunder cast a single, regretful glance at Gray Wing, then leaped forward to chase after his father.

Gray Wing watched as he caught up to the others and disappeared over the top of the hollow. *I have no idea when I'll see Thunder again.*

CHAPTER 16

The sun had gone down and stars began to appear in the night sky. A breeze blew across the moor, carrying the smell of smoke and ash from the burnt forest.

Weariness had overwhelmed Gray Wing again as the day-light faded, but he tried to keep his head and tail high as he headed up the slope to the top of the hollow.

"Where are you off to?" Rainswept Flower asked as she passed him with a mouse dangling from her jaws.

"I feel like sleeping in the open tonight," Gray Wing replied.

Rainswept Flower gave a cheerful nod and padded on.

Gray Wing continued out onto the moor. He hadn't lied to Rainswept Flower, but he hadn't told her the whole truth. His instincts told him that the fresh moorland air might help to clear the taste of smoke from his mouth, and he might breathe more easily. But in addition to that, he didn't want the other cats to see him quivering with pain, or licking his injured hind paws.

Now that Tall Shadow has given me the leadership, I can't afford to seem weak.

Once Gray Wing had left the hollow safely behind, he

found a comfortable spot to sleep, in a mossy dip sheltered by a boulder. After giving himself a soothing lick he curled up, but for a long time sleep wouldn't come. His body was tired, but his head was full of racing thoughts.

Will Thunder be okay? He's still so young! And what about Clear Sky? There was something in his eyes—and his tone was so cold when he insulted Jagged Peak, and told Thunder why he should come along with him.

A storm of regret and worry churned through Gray Wing and fought off any tiredness that tried to creep up on him.

Then Gray Wing froze. Tiny sounds warned him that something else was creeping up on him. He opened his jaws to taste the air. *It smells like another cat. . . .*

"Surprise!" Turtle Tail purred, leaping down into the dip to join him.

Gray Wing gazed at her with delight, though he could see the concern in her eyes as she settled beside him.

"Tell me more about what happened in the forest," she meowed.

As briefly as he could, Gray Wing described their struggles during the fire. The pain in his paws, and his anxiety over Thunder's leaving made it hard for him to talk.

"You're scorched and aching, aren't you?" she murmured. "Let me help you lick your pads."

Gray Wing relaxed as he felt Turtle Tail's tongue rasping gently over his burnt paws. *That feels so good. . . .*

"Where are the kits?" he asked after a few moments. *Turtle Tail would never leave them alone.*

"Don't worry; they're fine." Turtle Tail paused in her

licking. "They're asleep in my den, and Rainswept Flower and Jagged Peak are keeping an eye on them."

"Are you okay with that?" Gray Wing asked. "I mean, that Jagged Peak is showing so much interest in your kits?" He'd noticed that his younger brother spent a lot of time involved in the kits' care. Was Jagged Peak in danger of treading on Turtle Tail's claws? He knew it was important for Jagged Peak to find a role, but not if it meant unsettling other cats.

"Yes, it's fine," Turtle Tail replied, looking faintly surprised. "I'm glad of any help. Being a mother is hard work. Besides, I . . . I wanted some time alone with you." She sat up, her green eyes soft and warm as she met Gray Wing's gaze. "I'm so grateful to you, for everything,"

Now that Thunder had left, Gray Wing felt even closer to Turtle Tail and her kits. "I'm glad to help you," he told her, touching her shoulder with his tail.

Turtle Tail let out a contented sigh. Curling up against Gray Wing, she closed her eyes and soon drifted into sleep.

The she-cat's drowsy purring was soothing and comforting to Gray Wing. *I don't want to be on my own anymore,* he realized as he listened to her. He tried to tell himself that it was because he was missing Thunder, but this was something different. Being with another cat like this felt right. *And Turtle Tail is so kind and good-hearted, so smart and resourceful. . . .*

Gradually the night air grew colder. Gray Wing still couldn't sleep, but he felt relaxed. His weariness had melted away like frost in sunlight. He couldn't stop looking at Turtle Tail.

At last she stirred and opened her eyes. "You're thinking about Thunder, aren't you?" she murmured. "Go to sleep. It's not your fault, you know: You couldn't stand in the way of Thunder wanting to be with his father."

Sorrow and relief surged through Gray Wing all at once. He still felt sad that Thunder wasn't with him anymore, but hearing Turtle Tail tell him it wasn't his fault lifted an enormous burden from his back. *She's right. There wasn't anything I could have done.*

A pleasant tiredness crept over him. As his eyes closed and he sank into sleep, he could still hear Turtle Tail's purring.

Low, murmuring voices roused Gray Wing from a dream of brushing through long grass under a bright sun. Struggling awake, he realized that the voices were familiar, not threatening. He opened his eyes, blinking, to see Rainswept Flower with Owl Eyes, Sparrow Fur, and Pebble Heart standing around the edge of the dip in a half circle, gazing down at him, their fur buffeted by a brisk wind.

Rainswept Flower's eyes were alight with mischief. "So there you are!" she exclaimed. "I'm glad you've finally figured out what was obvious to the rest of us."

Gray Wing's gaze slid to one side and he saw Turtle Tail, remembering instantly how they had bedded down together the night before. Embarrassed, he dipped his head.

"You look so cozy, all curled up there," Rainswept Flower mewed teasingly.

"Are you coming to live in our den now?" Sparrow Fur asked.

Turtle Tail was awake, gazing at Gray Wing, happiness sparkling in her green eyes. The three kits let out excited squeaks and launched themselves into the dip, scrambling over Gray Wing and Turtle Tail and burrowing into their fur.

"You've got your paws full there," Rainswept Flower commented, padding off with a whisk of her tail.

A sudden, unexpected warmth flooded over Gray Wing. *Maybe Turtle Tail and I do belong together,* he thought.

CHAPTER 17

Thunder struggled to wake up, like a fish rising from the dark depths
of a pool. Even before he opened his eyes he could feel tension
and a subtle hostility from the cats around him. For a couple
of heartbeats, that confused him, until he remembered . . . *I'm
in my father's camp.*

Ever since Thunder had returned to the forest with Clear
Sky and his cats the day before, he had been aware of suspicious glances from some of the others. He guessed that they
had picked up on Clear Sky's concerns about the future. *They
seem relieved to be back home, but I couldn't call them happy.* Thunder
had tried to ignore the atmosphere, but it was hard when many
of the other cats would only speak to him in a few curt words.

Thunder scrambled out of his nest and arched his back in
a good long stretch. Bright sunlight shone through the leaves
above him, casting patterns on the forest floor as the branches
swayed in the breeze, and dazzling on the pool at the center of
the camp. Clear Sky's cats were already on the move, though
none of them paid Thunder any attention.

Thunder shrugged, trying not to mind their unfriendli-
ness, and settled down to groom himself. He was tugging at

an obstinate tangle in his pelt when Clear Sky padded up to him, followed by the black-and-white tom named Leaf.

"You're coming with me and Leaf on the morning patrol," Clear Sky announced.

Thunder tried hard not to show his dismay. The night before, Leaf had been particularly harsh to him, sliding out his claws and snarling when Thunder had accidentally brushed against his tail.

As they set out from the camp, Thunder deliberately stayed at the back of the group, not wanting Leaf to feel that he was trying to threaten him or take his place.

Then Clear Sky glanced over his shoulder. "Well done, Thunder," he meowed. "It's a brave cat who takes the rear position. A cat who is confident that he can fight off any sneak attacks. Isn't that right, Leaf?"

Leaf muttered reluctant agreement, his amber eyes burning with quiet fury. Thunder gulped. *That's not what I intended at all.*

Clear Sky led the way around bramble thickets and through tight clusters of ferns. Thunder couldn't spot any damage from burning here; the camp had been untouched, too. "How come you were all trapped by the fire?" he asked his father. "You would have been safe if you'd stayed in camp."

Leaf glared at him. "Are you calling us stupid?" he growled. "Or cowards?"

"No!" Perhaps Thunder's question hadn't been the most tactful.

Clear Sky flicked his tail at Leaf. "That's enough. Thunder, you're quite right. We would have been safe if we'd stayed in camp. But it didn't look like that at the time. The wind was blowing the fire toward our camp; the only thing we could do was get out, fast. But then the wind changed, and we were cut off."

"Satisfied?" Leaf demanded.

Thunder nodded. "Yes, thanks, that makes sense. But I didn't mean—"

"We're wasting time." Clear Sky padded on, and Thunder followed.

Maybe it would be better for me to keep my mouth shut from now on.

Thunder took up his position behind Leaf again, noticing patches of burnt undergrowth and swathes of charred bracken. He realized how terrifying it must have been for Clear Sky and his cats to feel that the fire was hunting them in their own home.

"Look—a squirrel!" Leaf's hissed exclamation roused Thunder from his thoughts.

Clear Sky raised his tail in a signal for them to halt. Gazing past him, Thunder noticed a squirrel climbing headfirst down the trunk of a beech tree some way ahead. Leaf had already flattened himself to the ground and was creeping forward with cautious paw steps.

"No," Clear Sky rumbled, his voice deep in his throat. "I want Thunder to catch it. I've seen what he can do; this is his chance to prove himself to you." More quietly, he added to Thunder, "The best way for you to fit in with the rest of them is to show what a valuable asset you are to us."

Leaf sat up with an irritable flick of his tail, and fixed

Thunder with an amber glare. Thunder gazed back at him, trying to look apologetic. *It should be Leaf's prey; he saw it first.*

Clear Sky twitched his ears impatiently. "Come on then," he mewed to Thunder. "Are you waiting for it to walk into your paws?"

A prickle of nervousness ran through Thunder's pads, and he tried to ignore the black-and-white tom's hostility. The squirrel had reached the bottom of the tree by now, and was scrabbling about among the roots. Thunder launched himself toward it, crashing through the outside of a bramble thicket, forcing his legs to drive him on faster and faster.

But he wasn't fast enough. Long before he reached the beech tree the squirrel started, took one glance in his direction, then fled back up the trunk, its tail floating out behind it.

Thunder skidded to a halt at the foot of the tree. The squirrel had disappeared; only the rustling of the leaves told him where it was. He thought of climbing the tree, but the bark was smooth and the lowest branch was many tail-lengths above his head.

Discouraged and furious with himself, Thunder trudged back to where his father and Leaf were waiting. His tail was drooping and his pelt felt hot with embarrassment. *What's the matter with me? I know that's not the way you hunt in woodland!*

"I . . . I guess I've still got a lot to learn," he stammered as he approached the other cats.

"You're right; you have." Clear Sky's blue eyes showed his disappointment. "Maybe I should have brought you into the forest much earlier," he grumbled. To Leaf, he added, "I've got other things to do. You two can finish the patrol, and don't come back to camp until you've caught something."

He stalked into the undergrowth.

Leaf turned to Thunder, his amber eyes narrow. "Follow me," he snapped. "And don't be so clumsy next time."

Thunder padded after the black-and-white tom as they headed farther into the forest. All his senses were alert; his jaws open to taste the air, his ears pricked, and his gaze flicking from side to side. He was determined to make up for his failure with the squirrel.

But the forest was quiet. Eventually Leaf let out a long sigh and lay down in the shade of a clump of ferns. "There won't be much prey stirring after your little performance," he meowed.

Thunder halted beside him. "We should probably wait it out patiently," he responded. "The prey will come back eventually."

"That *is* what I'm doing, in case you hadn't noticed," Leaf hissed. "There's no need to talk to me as if I'm mouse-brained. I know the forest better than you!"

"I'm sorry—" Thunder began, wondering why the cats in his father's group seemed so quick to get angry.

"You should pay attention," Leaf interrupted, apparently not wanting to hear his apology. "That is, if you want to learn the skills that a leader will need."

Thunder gazed at him, his jaws gaping in shock. *Is that what the other cats think? That Clear Sky has brought me here to set me up as leader after him?* "You've got it all wrong," he protested. "I don't want to be leader. I'm sure that's not what Clear Sky—"

"Be quiet!" Leaf snarled. "Your name might be Thunder, but that doesn't mean you have to make so much noise *all the time*."

Thunder suppressed a sigh. Settling down among the ferns beside the older cat, he kept his gaze fixed on the forest, his nose alert for prey. *I'll hunt now, and do the job I was told to do.* But he promised himself that later he'd make sure that the other cats understood he wasn't here to take over the group or push them out. *I just want to fit in*, he thought. *Is that too much to ask?*

Sunhigh was approaching when Leaf and Thunder returned to the camp. Leaf was carrying a squirrel that he had caught in the middle of a clearing after a magnificent bit of stalking. Thunder had managed to catch a mouse that was searching for seeds in a clump of long grass.

Leaf led the way into the camp and deposited his prey near the edge of the pool in the center. Thunder laid his mouse alongside as Clear Sky emerged from his den in a bramble thicket and padded over to inspect the catch. More of the cats appeared, too, exchanging impressed glances as they spotted the prey.

"Very well done!" Clear Sky meowed, his blue gaze resting approvingly on Thunder. "What hunting skills you have!"

Thunder stared at him. It was as if his father had completely forgotten the mess he had made of hunting the first squirrel. "I only caught the mouse," he explained. "The squirrel is Leaf's."

Clear Sky seemed not to have heard him. "I can see it's time I started training you myself in the ways of the forest," he continued. "You show such promise."

"But it wasn't me . . ." Thunder tried to protest again, but Clear Sky had already turned away.

As the other cats closed in to take their share of the prey, Thunder dared to look at Leaf. He hoped that the black-and-white tom would understand. *I'm sorry about what happened. . . . I tried to tell Clear Sky.* But Leaf simply turned his back, hurt and anger glaring from his amber eyes.

Thunder sighed, retreating instead of biting into the prey. He watched the others eat, misery ruining his own appetite. A picture of his adopted littermates, Lightning Tail and Acorn Fur, slipped into his mind. He could see their bright eyes, and the mischievous whisk of their tails.

"I wonder what they're doing now," he sighed. *Life was so much more carefree on the moor. . . .*

CHAPTER 18

Thunder padded along in Clear Sky's paw steps as they headed up the stream away from the river. It was the day after his disastrous hunt with Leaf, and his father was taking him training for the first time. The sky was cloudy, with only the occasional gleam of sunlight; a stiff breeze rustled the leaves and carried with it the reek of the burnt stretch of forest.

Clear Sky didn't halt until they came to the edge of the devastation. Blackened ground and fallen, charred trees lay ahead of them; some of the trees still stood, though their leaves had burned away and their branches looked shaky, ready to crash to the ground.

Across the stream, Thunder could make out the sweep of the moor beyond the outlying trees. He knew they were close to the place where Clear Sky and his cats had crossed the stream, guided by Gray Wing and his group. He opened his jaws to ask Clear Sky if they could cross now and see if Gray Wing was hunting close by, but then changed his mind without speaking. He knew instinctively what Clear Sky's response would be.

"This morning you're going to work on your leaping skills,"

Clear Sky announced, speaking for the first time since they had left the camp.

"Okay," Thunder responded, determined to do his best. "What do you want me to do?"

Clear Sky waved his tail in the direction of the burnt forest. "I want to see you jumping from one tree to the next. It's an important skill if you're hunting squirrels or even birds, and it's a good way to stay clear of your enemies. Out here, where the leaves are burned off the trees, you'll be able to see where you're going."

Like that's supposed to make it easier for me? Thunder thought, gazing up in dismay at the nearest fire-damaged tree. *I'm not even sure it will bear my weight.*

While he hesitated, Clear Sky padded over and faced him. "I can see the doubt in your eyes," he hissed. "That's exactly why you need to climb up the tree right now. The only way you can survive in the forest is without fear." Clear Sky's blue eyes glowed with passion. "Fear is like prey—it only exists to be captured and killed. Fear didn't get me and the rest of us out of the mountains!"

Thunder stretched up to grip the burnt tree trunk with his claws; small chips of black wood flaked away at the touch. He hesitated, but didn't want to turn around and see a disappointed or angry look in his father's eyes.

Bracing himself, Thunder sprang and clambered up the tree, shedding scraps of wood every time he sank his claws into the trunk. At last he reached a branch and clung there, feeling it shake under him and hardly daring to look down at the ground so far below.

"Get moving!" Clear Sky called up to him. "You're showing the tree too much respect."

For a couple of heartbeats Thunder clung tighter as a gust of wind swayed the branch. *It feels like I should respect the tree,* was what he wanted to say. He knew that jumping wasn't his strong point, and besides, he had no idea which branches would support his weight and which would give out and send him crashing down into the undergrowth. *Respecting the tree makes perfect sense!*

"Jump now!" Clear Sky yowled, impatience clear in his tone.

Taking a deep breath, Thunder managed to ignore the creaking of the branch and the stench of dead wood, and launched himself into a leap. He landed awkwardly in the next tree, his forepaws scrabbling at a branch while his hind legs dangled in midair. Clawing desperately, he hauled himself up until he could crouch in a fork between the branch and the tree trunk.

"Far too slow!" Clear Sky's yowl came up from below. "You should have been two trees over by now!"

Stung by the sneering tone, Thunder peered down at his father, who stood at the foot of the tree, his tail lashing.

"What's the *point* of this?" he demanded. "Didn't Jagged Peak injure himself permanently when he fell from a tree?"

Clear Sky didn't bother to answer. "Are you going to perch up there and ask silly questions?" he meowed. "Or are you going to continue to learn new skills? Don't you want to learn the best way to hunt?" He pointed with his tail toward the next tree. "Let me see how strong you are!"

Growing even more irritated, Thunder decided to show his father just how good he was. Pushing off with his hind paws, he leaped from tree to tree, forcing down the fear that stirred in his belly.

This'll show him . . . another tree . . . and another . . .

Crack!

As Thunder's paws hit the next branch, it splintered away from the tree. Thunder felt himself falling, twisting in the air in a frantic effort to turn himself upright. A picture of Jagged Peak, dragging his injured leg across the moorland camp, flashed into his mind. Then he let out a screech of pain as he thumped down, paws first, onto the forest floor. Scraps of bark and chunks of black wood showered down around him.

Clear Sky was watching him with a disappointed look in his eyes. "You showed good courage there," he mewed, dipping his head, "but recklessness can lead to injury." Without another word he turned and headed back toward the camp.

Thunder limped after him, testing each leg gingerly to make sure he wasn't badly hurt. Dull anger was throbbing in his belly. *If I take it slowly, I'm respecting the tree too much. If I go fast, I'm being reckless. What do I have to do to please my father?*

He halted, his anger and confusion becoming too much to bear. "Clear Sky!" he called.

His father stopped and glanced back over his shoulder. "What now?" he asked irritably.

Thunder didn't let his father's tone intimidate him. "Why

are you accusing me of recklessness, when I was only doing what you told me to do?" he demanded.

Clear Sky padded back toward him, sighing patiently. "Do you really not understand yet? I brought you back here because I wanted what's best for you—and that's to fit in and become a useful member of the group. I'm pushing you so you can become the very best you're capable of."

He turned and stalked on.

As they drew close to the camp, a hunting party emerged from the trees. Petal was in the lead, followed by Frost and Falling Feather. All of them were carrying prey.

"How did your training go?" Falling Feather asked around a mouthful of vole. "Are you getting the hang of hunting in trees?"

At least she sounds friendly, Thunder reflected.

"Yes, it was fine," he replied, hoping that no cat would see his disappointment. *I'll show Clear Sky; I'll show all the cats here! I'll do more training, but on my own next time. . . .*

Dawn light was trickling through the trees when Thunder slipped out of the camp on the following morning. The grass was still wet with dew, soaking Thunder's pelt as he brushed against it. Tendrils of mist tickled the trees, and pale cobwebs were stretched on every bush.

Thunder was determined that this morning he would hunt alone, and deserve his father's praise when he came back loaded with prey. He crept through the forest, striving to make every paw step stealthy, so that he would pass as silently as a shadow among the trees.

But that wasn't as easy as he had hoped. He had grown bigger since his foray into the forest with Shattered Ice. Every time he trod on a dead leaf, or a twig snapped under his paw, he halted, cringing, afraid that Clear Sky was following him and would hear.

He had paused beside an oak tree, sniffing carefully for prey, when he picked up the scent of cats and heard the sounds of bodies brushing through the undergrowth. At first Thunder thought it was his father at the head of a patrol, but then he realized that the scents were unfamiliar.

Peering around the bole of the oak tree, Thunder saw two cats emerge into the open. The first was a silvery-furred tom: River Ripple, who had helped them escape from the fire. With him was a black-and-white she-cat Thunder had never seen before.

Thunder's paws tingled with uncertainty. He knew that Clear Sky didn't like other cats hunting in the forest. *But the place is big enough for all of us*, he reflected. *I don't want to drive them off, especially when we owe so much to River Ripple.*

Thunder turned away to head off in another direction. But after a couple of paw steps he had to halt again as a strange black tom appeared around the edge of a bramble thicket.

The black tom thrust his head forward and let out a threatening hiss. Spinning around, Thunder scampered away, only to realize that the black tom was hard on his paws.

Thunder dodged to and fro among bushes and clumps of ferns, but he couldn't shake off his pursuer. Spotting an ash tree with an inviting low branch, he pushed off in a huge leap and clawed the rest of the way up the trunk until he reached the branch.

A furious snarl came from behind him. Turning and looking down, Thunder saw with a stab of fear that the black tom was climbing the tree after him.

Thunder slid out his claws and swiped at the black tom as he came within range, but the tom ducked under the blow and hurled himself at Thunder, almost knocking him off the branch. Thunder tackled him, grabbing the cat's shoulder fur in his jaws. He let out a screech as he felt the black tom's claws rake down his side.

Then he felt his paws slipping from the branch, and a heartbeat later he was falling through the air. He lost his grip on the other cat, who fell with him, paws and tail flailing.

Thunder managed to land on all four paws, wincing at the impact. The black tom was sprawled on his side; Thunder leaped forward and used his forepaws to pin down the black tom's shoulders.

"You stupid furball, I wasn't doing you any harm," Thunder hissed. Glancing up, he saw that River Ripple and his companion had followed and were gazing at them from a couple of tail-lengths away. "I don't want—" Thunder began.

Crashing from the undergrowth interrupted him. Clear Sky sprang into the open and halted for a heartbeat, his gaze raking the three strange cats.

"Get out of here now, and don't come back!" he growled. "Thunder, you can let that mange-pelt up."

Thunder stepped back obediently. As the black tom struggled to his paws, Clear Sky bounded up to him and gave him a warning shove, sending him sprawling.

The black tom scrambled up again and scurried off with the she-cat hard on his paws. River Ripple began to follow them, then paused, looking back at Clear Sky with a long, cold stare.

Clear Sky was unmoved by it. "Cats who attack my son will be punished," he snarled.

"You can't keep doing this," River Ripple mewed simply. "You can't try to tell other cats what to do."

"Come over here and say that again," Clear Sky challenged. "I can do what I like."

Thunder could hardly believe what he was hearing. His own father, acting like some sort of bully.

"I'm sure it doesn't . . . ," Thunder started to say, but Clear Sky's glare was so vicious that the words dried up in his throat.

River Ripple was watching him closely. "No, please, carry on," he said. "I'm interested to know what a young cat thinks about all this."

"Thunder's opinion is none of your business!" Clear Sky hissed. "Thunder doesn't have an opinion!"

Thunder felt his stomach shrivel. Was that really what his father thought? River Ripple was still staring hard at him and Thunder had to look away. Silence throbbed through the air, then there was the sound of River Ripple stalking away.

Clear Sky waited until River Ripple had vanished into the undergrowth before turning to Thunder. "Congratulations!"

he meowed. "You have just expanded our territory. Those cats won't dare come back here again, and hopefully they'll spread the word that we don't tolerate uninvited visitors." Waving his tail for Thunder to follow, he headed back in the direction of the camp.

Is that what I did? he wondered. Thunder had never thought in terms of "tolerating" other cats.

Thunder felt miserable. His morning had been ruined. Instead of training by himself and returning triumphantly to camp with his jaws full of prey, he had ended up in an ugly brawl with rogue cats—including one cat who had probably saved all their lives. *And I'd already defeated the black tom,* he thought with a twinge of resentment. *Clear Sky didn't have to be so protective—or put me down like that.*

"You know, I was fine back there," he began nervously, not wanting to provoke an angry reaction. "The fight was over. You didn't have to shove that cat."

"Fine? The cats were in the forest, weren't they?" Clear Sky hissed impatiently. "How can that be fine?"

"But the rogue cats were here before any of us," Thunder replied, alarmed. "They can go where they like, can't they?" He hesitated then plunged on. "I do have an opinion, you know."

Clear Sky halted, his eyes widening as he gazed at Thunder and his claws working in the grass. "Haven't you listened to a word I've said to you? We need to protect ourselves for the future, and that means no unwelcome visitors." His voice softened. "Of course you have an opinion. I was just putting that cat in its place—you mustn't take any notice. But it's important you understand that we need to guard our home really carefully. You get that, right?"

"Uh . . . right." What else could Thunder say? Of course he wanted the forest cats to have a safe and happy home, although it didn't feel that happy right now.

His tail drooping, Thunder followed his father back to the camp.

What have I done? he asked himself. A moment of doubt pierced him. *Maybe I should have stayed with Gray Wing.* Even thinking that made Thunder feel both disloyal and like a coward. *I had no idea what I was doing—I still don't.*

He watched his father's silhouette, pulling ahead. Thunder's heart felt heavy as a stone. *I'm here now. There's no going back.* Being reunited with his father had once been Thunder's biggest dream, but now it felt like a weight on his shoulders. He wondered where River Ripple and those other cats would be now. Spreading the word of their encounter?

I hope not, Thunder thought. *I wish it had never happened.*

CHAPTER 19

Gray Wing sat at the mouth of the den he shared with Turtle Tail, his paws tucked comfortably underneath him, and watched the three kits playing at the bottom of the hollow. Their squeals of excitement drifted over as they leaped on top of one another and rolled around in the scattered twigs and debris from the gorse bushes.

When Rainswept Flower said we'd have our paws full, she wasn't wrong, he thought. I wonder how I used to fill my days before the kits came.

As Gray Wing slid into a doze, letting the warm sunlight soak into his pelt, he spotted Sparrow Fur racing up the slope toward him. "Gray Wing, come and play with us!" she begged, skidding to a halt in front of him.

Gray Wing's jaws gaped in a massive yawn as he rose to his paws. "Okay," he mumbled. "What do I have to do?"

"Owl Eyes is being a fox," Sparrow Fur explained, looking over her shoulder at Gray Wing as she bounced down the slope ahead of him. "And we have to roll out of his way when he attacks us."

That's a good game for training, Gray Wing realized. One day they might have to do that for real.

When Gray Wing and Sparrow Fur reached the bottom of the hollow, Owl Eyes was racing toward Pebble Heart, with his teeth bared as he uttered tiny, high-pitched growls. "I'm a fox," he declared. "I'm going to eat you up!"

"No!" Pebble Heart shrieked. He dived to one side as Owl Eyes leaped at him, landing on his back and waving his paws in the air.

Owl Eyes spun around and hurled himself at Sparrow Fur. His sister waited until the last moment before darting aside with a yowl of delight and rolling over and over among the scattered twigs.

Drawing his lips back in a snarl, Owl Eyes whipped around to face Gray Wing, his tail lashing to and fro. "I'm the fiercest fox in the forest!"

Gray Wing bared his teeth and snarled back. "And I'm an even bigger fox!"

Owl Eyes flattened his ears and widened his eyes. "I'm so scared!" he meowed, his voice shaking with laughter. He jumped to one side as Gray Wing pounced, landing a blow on Gray Wing's ear before he rolled away out of range.

"Well done!" Gray Wing scrambled to his paws and shook debris from his pelt. "It's a good thing you had your claws sheathed."

Twigs cracking beneath his paws, he whirled to attack Sparrow Fur, but as he charged forward a sharp pain clawed through his lungs and he felt his legs crumple under him. He sank to the ground and lay on his side, chest heaving as he gasped for breath.

The three kits crowded around him, their eyes huge and anxious. Frustration welled up inside Gray Wing as their plump, furry bodies made it harder to breathe, but he knew better than to bat them out of the way.

"Get back!" Turtle Tail's voice rang out from somewhere across the camp. "Give Gray Wing some air."

A moment later she padded up to him, gently thrusting the kits aside. "Is it your breathing again?" she asked.

Unable to speak, Gray Wing nodded.

Pebble Heart poked his nose into his mother's side. "I think Gray Wing needs some coltsfoot for his breathing," he mewed quickly. "Shall I go and see if Cloud Spots has some?"

Turtle Tail turned a puzzled gaze on her son. "How do you know about coltsfoot?" she asked.

"Dappled Pelt told me," the kit replied.

His mother twitched her whiskers in surprise, then nodded. Instantly Pebble Heart darted off toward Cloud Spots's den.

Owl Eyes and Sparrow Fur huddled closer to Gray Wing, touching their noses to his. "Please get better," Owl Eyes begged.

Gray Wing's breathing was beginning to ease, enough for him to reassure the anxious kits. "Of course I will," he croaked. "I promise."

"We've never had a father like you," Sparrow Fur added, brushing her tail along his side. "You are . . . like our father, aren't you?"

Both kits fixed their gaze on Gray Wing, their eyes full of hope and love. Pain pierced Gray Wing's heart, far more agonizing than his trouble with breathing. He opened his jaws to reply, but no words would come. He wasn't sure if it was his illness that closed his throat, or his fear of letting his emotions overwhelm him.

Turtle Tail's gaze met Gray Wing's over the top of the kits' heads. "Of course he is," she meowed briskly. "He's the best father any kit could hope to have."

Pebble Heart, returning with a bunch of coltsfoot leaves in his jaws, dashed up in time to hear what his mother had said. Letting the leaves fall, he hurled himself at her in a wriggling bundle of delight.

"That's the best thing I've heard *ever!*" he announced. "Now we really know we belong!"

Cloud Spots, padding more slowly after Pebble Heart, swept his tail around to gesture the kits away from Gray Wing. "It's time to leave Gray Wing in peace," he told them, dipping his head to Turtle Tail. "I'll look after him, don't worry."

"Yes, it's time for your nap," Turtle Tail mewed, gathering the kits together. "You'll see Gray Wing again later."

"Yes," he called weakly after them as Turtle Tail herded the kits toward their nest. "We'll start training again as soon as I'm better." He watched the kits vanish into their den before turning to Cloud Spots. "I am going to get better soon, aren't I?" he asked. "Tell me the truth."

Cloud Spots rolled his eyes. "You may be ill, but that's no

excuse to behave as if your brain is full of bees. Of course you'll be better soon! You survived the mountains," he added with a snort. "You can survive a bit of smoke in your lungs. Besides, it's not just the kits who need you. You're our leader now, don't forget. You have duties to fulfill."

A scrabbling sound interrupted his last words. Gray Wing looked up to see that Pebble Heart had come back. "Please can I help treat Gray Wing?" he begged.

Cloud Spots paused for a moment before replying, while Pebble Heart worked his claws impatiently in and out.

"Very well," the black-and-white tom replied at last. "Collect those coltsfoot leaves and chew them up so you can dribble the juice into Gray Wing's mouth."

Pebble Heart obeyed eagerly, chomping on the leaves and then letting the juices trickle into Gray Wing's gaping jaws.

"That's enough," Cloud Spots meowed at last. "Good job."

Almost at once Gray Wing could feel the pain ebb away; his breathing relaxed and he was able to scramble to his paws.

Cloud Spots gave a satisfied nod. "No unnecessary exertion for the next moon," he ordered. "After that, you'll be as strong and energetic as one of these kits!"

Gray Wing murmured thanks, though he wasn't sure whether he felt grateful or doubtful. But he was certain of one thing. *I definitely feel hope.*

Gray Wing opened his eyes and stretched his jaws in an enormous yawn. Golden sunrays slanted into his den, showing him that Turtle Tail and the kits had left. *I feel as if I've slept for moons*, he thought, rising to his paws and giving himself a long, luxurious stretch.

As he relaxed again, the sound of loud meowing and yowls of delight broke out in the camp outside the den. Curious, Gray Wing padded to the entrance and looked out.

Most of his denmates were clustered together in the middle of the camp; Wind and Gorse were there too. Apprehension prickled through Gray Wing's pelt, but he shrugged off the feeling. Every cat seemed to be happy about something; surely they couldn't be gathering because danger was threatening.

As Gray Wing gazed down, wondering what it was all about, Lightning Tail broke away from the group and bounded up the slope toward him. "You have to listen to this!" the young tom called out excitedly. He beckoned with his tail for Gray Wing to join him. "Cloud Spots has suggested we give the two rogues longer names like ours. If you'll let us!"

Intrigued, Gray Wing padded down to join the others and slid into the crowd toward Turtle Tail.

This could work well, he thought to himself. *If Wind and Gorse have names like us, then maybe every cat will agree that they should join us.*

As the thought passed through his mind, he glanced at Tall Shadow. The former leader was sitting quietly on the top of the tall rock, keeping watch over the moor as she always did, and her expression gave away nothing of what she was thinking.

"It's good to have you here," Cloud Spots was telling Wind and Gorse as Gray Wing sat down with Lightning Tail beside him. "But I think we all agree your names are kind of short. You should have long names like ours if you're going to spend time with us."

Wind and Gorse let out identical snorts of amusement.

"Okay," Gorse meowed. "Wind, what should we call you? Wind That Chases Rabbits Down Burrows?"

Wind batted at him with one paw. "I'd give up chasing rabbits for good, rather than call myself a mouthful like that. Why don't you call yourself Gorse Prickle Stuck in Paw?"

Cloud Spots let out a *mrrow* of laughter. "Why don't I think you're taking this seriously?"

"Wind, I think you should call yourself Wind Runner," Rainswept Flower meowed. "You're really fast."

Wind thought about that with her head cocked, then nodded. "Yes," she decided, looking pleased. "That's my name now. Wind Runner."

"And what about Gorse?" Jackdaw's Cry asked.

"Gorse Bush?" Hawk Swoop suggested. "Gorse Tail?"

"What about Gorse Fur?" Turtle Tail added. "Because the fur on top of your head sticks up a bit like gorse spines."

Gorse met her gaze for a moment. "It'll do," he decided, then licked his paw and drew it across his spiky head fur. "Thanks."

Lightning Tail blinked thoughtfully at the two rogue cats, and let out a long sigh. His earlier excitement had vanished like mist in sunlight.

"What's the matter?" Gray Wing asked.

Lightning Tail hesitated, as if he was reluctant to share his thoughts. "I wish Thunder could be here to see this," he mewed at last. Trying to sound optimistic, he added, "At least now there are new cats here in the hollow who will help to lead the group."

Gray Wing felt his fur begin to bristle with hostility. "Lead?" he asked. "I thought that was my job now."

Even as he spoke, he realized that however much he had fought against taking over the leadership from Tall Shadow, his position already was important to him.

"I didn't mean—" Lightning Tail began to protest.

"Then what did you mean? Gorse Fur and Wind Runner aren't even part of our group yet, and you talk about them leading?"

Lightning Tail looked injured, and Gray Wing wondered if he had been too harsh with the young tom. "I only meant . . ." Lightning Tail cast a glance toward Wind Runner and Gorse Fur; they were standing in the middle of a group of cats, who were all eagerly congratulating them on their new names. "Well, the more strong cats we have, the better, right?"

Gray Wing still felt unsettled. "What do you mean by strong?" he asked.

Lightning Tail scrabbled at the ground with his forepaws, looking more uncomfortable with every heartbeat that passed. Glancing around, he suddenly exclaimed, "Look, there's Acorn Fur! I have to talk to her."

Gray Wing stretched out a paw to halt the young cat as he

sprang to his paws. "You haven't answered my question," he meowed. "What do you mean by strong?"

Lightning Tail turned back to Gray Wing, his whiskers quivering with indignation. His claws raked the ground as if he had to let out some inner turmoil. "I mean cats who can stand up to Clear Sky!" he blurted out at last. "There, I've said it! I can't believe Thunder went away with him, after all the stories we've heard." His neck fur fluffed up in anger as he met Gray Wing's gaze. "Don't pretend you don't know what I'm talking about," he growled. "Every cat knows that Clear Sky is trying to push other cats around."

As Gray Wing stood staring at him, too astonished to speak, Acorn Fur came bounding up to them. She glanced uncertainly from Gray Wing to her brother and back again. "What's going on?" she asked. "Are you two arguing?"

"Oh, no," Gray Wing replied. Between shock and anger, his voice was cold. "Why would I stop to argue with such a young cat, barely out of his nest?"

Lightning Tail reared back at the insult. He opened his jaws to respond, then clearly thought better of it. Whipping around, he stalked off toward Wind Runner and Gorse Fur, followed by his sister, who still looked bewildered.

Gray Wing stood where he was, watching. As his anger ebbed, he realized that he might be missing an opportunity. *If I'm going to lead, I need to know that these cats are on my side.*

Racing across the camp, barely thinking about Cloud Spots's advice not to exert himself, he leaped onto the top of the rock beside Tall Shadow. The black she-cat gave him a surprised glance, then edged back to make room for him.

Facing the gathered cats, Gray Wing sought out Wind Runner and Gorse Fur, and dipped his head to them. "Congratulations on your new names," he began. "We hope that they will bring us closer together in friendship in the seasons to come."

I'd like to welcome them as full members of the group, he thought to himself. *But I'm not sure every cat is ready for that yet. And I want to be certain of myself as leader before I let Wind Runner in, because as sure as snow falls in the cold season, she'll try to take over.*

"Thank you," Wind Runner responded to his words.

By now all the cats had realized that something unexpected was happening. They turned toward the rock and gazed up at Gray Wing while he waited for silence to fall. It wasn't a long wait; he could see that every cat was eager to listen to what he had to say. He spotted Turtle Tail at the back of the group, looking surprised.

I never told her I was going to make a speech. I didn't know it myself until a moment ago.

Standing as tall as he could on top of the rock, Gray Wing cleared his throat. "When my brother left here with Thunder," he began, "he said that sentiment didn't count for anything. I'm not sure that I agree with him."

Pausing, he let his gaze travel over the assembled cats. His three kits were huddled together with Jagged Peak, while Acorn Fur stood protectively beside Lightning Tail, whose fur was still ruffled from their argument. Gorse Fur and Wind Runner stood side by side.

At last Gray Wing's gaze settled on Turtle Tail. Strong feelings began to surge through him at the sight of her, powerful as the waterfall that crashed into the pool outside the mountain cave.

"Sentiment counts for *everything*," he went on, letting his voice ring out clearly across the camp. "Where would we be without each other? I'm so proud of you all for making friends with Wind Runner and Gorse Fur."

For a moment he could feel Tall Shadow's stare boring into his back from where she sat behind him at the edge of the rock. He knew she had always been cautious around the two moorland cats, but he also knew she would have to accept them eventually, and he paid no attention to her now.

"But if I'm to truly lead," he continued, "I need to know that you're all with me." He paused before he asked the question that meant everything to him. "Are you?"

When he had finished speaking Gray Wing closed his eyes and waited. His belly began to churn as the silence seemed to stretch out for seasons. *What if I've got it all wrong?*

Then his eyes flew open again as the air was split with yowls of delight and enthusiastic support.

"Yes, Gray Wing!"

"We're with you!"

"Gray Wing! Gray Wing!"

Gray Wing blinked down at them, stunned and overwhelmed. He was aware of Tall Shadow padding up behind him, and felt her breath warm in his ear as she murmured, "I think you should get down now."

For a heartbeat Gray Wing felt as though his paws were frozen to the rock. Then he pulled himself together and leaped down into the crowd of his friends. They all pressed around him, brushing their pelts against his, resting their tails on his shoulders or pushing their noses into his fur. Hawk Swoop, Jackdaw's Cry, Shattered Ice, Rainswept Flower . . . Confidence thrilled through Gray Wing, filling him from ears to tail-tip, at this proof of their loyalty.

At last he found himself facing Lightning Tail. "This is what it's about," Gray Wing told him. "This is true strength."

Lightning Tail dipped his head in understanding, his hostility gone. "Where you lead, we will all follow," he meowed.

And that's all I need to hear, Gray Wing thought.

CHAPTER 20

Dawn light woke Gray Wing where he lay in the den with Turtle Tail and the kits. They were still sleeping, the kits sprawled over their mother's body. Turtle Tail's tail was wrapped against her nose, its fur riffling with every breath she took.

Gray Wing watched her, his heart swelling with affection. He remembered how pleased she had been when he caught up to the others on their journey from the mountains. She had observed him silently when he fell in love with Storm. Now Gray Wing understood why she had left the moor to go and live with Bumble and the Twolegs.

I drove her to it, he realized. *All this time, she's cared for me as more than a friend, and what did I do? I ignored her. But not any longer,* he resolved.

Turtle Tail's escape from the Twoleg den, and the comfort she'd given him over the moon they'd been denmates, had made Gray Wing see her with new eyes. Turtle Tail had always been beside him.

We care for each other. No, it was more than caring. Gray Wing knew that he loved this cat.

"Hey!" A paw prodded him in the side. "Go and catch me some prey, flea-pelt."

Turtle Tail was awake, her green eyes alight with mischief. Gray Wing let out a snort of laughter.

"Who are you calling flea-pelt? Okay, okay, I'm going."

Gray Wing rose to his paws, gave his fur a shake and padded to the mouth of the den. The dawn chill enveloped him as he stepped into fresh air. The pale sky was streaked with clouds, only the faintest rosy flush showing where the sun would rise.

Heading out of the hollow, Gray Wing felt more alive than ever before. His injured paws had healed and even his breathing seemed to feel better, despite his recent collapse. *Leaving the mountains was the best decision I ever made.*

Gray Wing knew that if he hadn't made that choice, he would never have become the father to Sparrow Fur, Pebble Heart, and Owl Eyes, kits he now loved as his own. And if the next cold season was as easy as the last, the kits would grow up strong and healthy. He wouldn't have felt the same confidence in the mountains, where the cold could kill.

As Gray Wing reached the top of the hollow and struck out across the moor, he heard paw steps following him, and a high-pitched squeak of excitement. He stopped and turned, knowing exactly what he would see.

The three kits scampered up to him.

"We want to hunt with you," Owl Eyes announced, his whiskers quivering. "For real this time. No more pretend foxes!"

Gray Wing shook his head. "Sorry. You're too young."

"Please!" Sparrow Fur fixed him with beseeching green eyes. "No kit is too young to learn good hunting skills."

Gray Wing fixed her with a stern look. *Where did she pick that up, I wonder?* "If you think you can get around me . . . ," he began.

"We'll be good!" Pebble Heart mewed, jumping up and down.

Gray Wing found he couldn't resist their pleading. "Okay," he agreed. "But stay close together, and close to me, and do *exactly* what I tell you. Understood?"

All three kits nodded vigorously.

"Come on, then."

Gray Wing led the way onto the moor, his ears and nose alert for the signs of prey. The kits followed him, behaving themselves for once, their excitement showing only in the twitching of their whiskers and their wide, shining eyes.

Soon Gray Wing picked up the scent of a hare, and located it in the long grass at the edge of a stream. At first he could only see the black tips of its ears, but gradually he distinguished the outline of its body among the grass stems. It seemed to be a young one, not yet fully grown.

"Be very quiet," he murmured to the kits, pointing with his tail. "Look over there."

The kits stared in the direction his tail was indicating. Then Pebble Heart turned to him, blinking a little in distress. "It's only a kit!" he mewed.

"Yes, won't its mother and father be upset when it doesn't come home?" Sparrow Fur added.

Owl Eyes was looking upset, too.

For a moment Gray Wing didn't know how to answer. Then he sat down and gathered the kits closer with a sweep of his tail. "I understand how you feel," he meowed. Clearly they weren't as ready for hunting as they thought they were. "But we can't take our hearts hunting, not if we want to survive. We have to be tough. I've seen a cat die of hunger. . . ." His voice quivered a little as he remembered his sister Fluttering Bird. "I don't want to see it happen ever again. Do you understand?"

The kits exchanged uncertain glances. "I . . . I guess so," Owl Eyes replied at last.

"Then I'm going to show you how to hunt this hare," Gray Wing went on more briskly. "And I want you to remember that hares can be dangerous. Their back legs are very powerful. One kick could break a cat's spine. Now watch."

Gray Wing checked the hare again; it was sitting with its back to them, and so far it hadn't noticed them. "The breeze is blowing toward us," he murmured. "Do you know why that's good?"

All three kits thought for a moment.

"Because we can scent the hare," Sparrow Fur responded brightly. "But it can't scent us."

"Right." As the little kit puffed out her chest proudly, Gray Wing added, "Now stay here and don't move."

Gray Wing began stalking cautiously toward the hare. There was no cover between him and the clump of grass where the hare was hiding, and he didn't want to alert it by a sudden movement.

He had covered about half the distance before the hare suddenly sat erect. Knowing it had sensed him, Gray Wing hurtled toward it, calling on every scrap of speed he could manage. He leaped upon the hare as it bounded out of cover, swerving to avoid its back legs, and to break its neck with one skillful twist of his jaws. The hare fell to the ground and lay still.

Gray Wing turned to beckon the kits with his tail. As they padded toward him, sudden spots began to dance before his eyes and his vision was obscured by glittering darkness. Pain was gnawing at his lungs, and he could hardly breathe. *Not again!*

The kits gathered around him, letting out anxious squeaks. Their small, furry bodies pressed up against him.

"You're not ill again, are you?" one of them asked.

He pushed them away as he filled his lungs with air. *Yes, yes . . . not so bad this time. If I can just gather myself.* But he heard one of the kittens yowl with pain and he realized he hadn't been as gentle as he'd hoped. Panic must have made his paws strike out harder than he'd meant.

"I'm sorry," he gasped. "I didn't mean to hurt you."

The kits looked at each other. Finally Owl Eyes muttered, "It's okay."

Pebble Heart came scampering up. He dropped something small on the ground and cautiously approached Gray Wing. "May I listen to your chest?" he asked.

Gray Wing eyed him doubtfully. *I'm not in the mood for games.* But Pebble Heart's expression was deeply serious, and some instinct told Gray Wing to agree. "Okay," he mewed, lying down again and rolling onto his back. He allowed Pebble Heart to place his ear against his chest and listen to his breathing.

After a moment Pebble Heart pulled away. "It's not too bad," he mewed. "But I brought you a juniper berry to help." He picked up the small object and dropped it beside Gray Wing.

Gray Wing stared at it for a moment, blinking. *Well, I don't suppose it can do any harm....* He licked the berry up, chewed, and swallowed it.

Almost at once Gray Wing felt the last of his tight breathing subside. Astonishment spread through him as his pain ebbed. "How did you know to do that?" he asked, sitting up again.

Pebble Heart studied his paws, looking a bit embarrassed. "I just sort of worked it out for myself," he admitted.

Gray Wing felt a pang of anxiety. "I hope you don't start eating random stuff to see what it does," he meowed.

"Oh, no!" Pebble Heart relaxed a little. "I listen to Dappled Pelt and Cloud Spots, so I know which herbs are good and which are dangerous."

Gray Wing nodded thoughtfully. There was something special about Pebble Heart. Which other kit of his age would want to learn about herbs and know just the right one to bring back in a moment like this? He remembered Stone-teller, back in the mountains, who had so recently visited his dreams. *I know she had visions sometimes,* he thought. *I wonder if this young kit is born to be like the Stoneteller?*

"Do you ever have dreams?" he asked the kit gently.

Pebble Heart looked away quickly. "No."

Gray Wing knew very well that Pebble Heart wasn't telling the truth, but he decided to say no more for now. *There'll be a better opportunity to discuss this, when the other kits aren't listening.*

"Well, thank you," he meowed. "I feel much better. Let's head back to camp now."

He grabbed up the hare and the kits helped him to carry it as he led the way back to the hollow. When they arrived, Turtle Tail was sitting outside her den, grooming herself. The kits dropped the hare and pelted over to her as soon as they saw her, huddling close to her as she gave each of them an affectionate lick behind their ears.

"You're trembling!" she exclaimed. Looking past them to Gray Wing as he approached more slowly, she asked, "What happened out there?"

Gray Wing set the hare down in front of her. "Are you proud of your kits?" he asked. "They did well on their first hunt."

Turtle Tail fixed him with a long stare. "Answer my question," she meowed. "What happened out there?"

Before Gray Wing could think how to reply, Sparrow Fur exploded into speech. "Gray Wing killed a hare, but then his breathing went funny again. He pushed us away."

"Pebble Heart brought him a berry," Owl Eyes added.

Gray Wing saw fury flash into Turtle Tail's eyes, but her voice was quiet as she mewed, "Kits, take the hare down into the center of the camp so that we can all share. Now," she snapped as the kits hesitated.

"I'll help them," Jagged Peak offered, padding up. "Come on, kits."

"Thanks, Jagged Peak," Turtle Tail meowed.

Gray Wing couldn't suppress an irritated twitch of his tail. *Jagged Peak is always nearby when the kits need anything.*

With Jagged Peak supervising, Sparrow Fur, Pebble Heart, and Owl Eyes began dragging the hare away, while Turtle Tail and Gray Wing gazed at each other. Once the kits were out of earshot, Turtle Tail rose to her paws.

"Let's go for a walk." She led the way up the slope without waiting to see if Gray Wing was following.

Turtle Tail didn't speak again until she and Gray Wing had reached the shelter of the gorse bushes near the top of the hollow. Then she turned and faced him. "What's going on?" she demanded.

Gray Wing understood very well what she was getting at, but he had no idea how to reply. "Uh . . . what do you mean?" he asked, playing for time.

Turtle Tail gave her tail a single lash. "Too much time has already been wasted by the two of us not talking to each other," she began. "Not anymore. I'm not stupid, you know! I've seen you struggling with your breathing, ever since the forest fire. You can't even teach your own kits—or as good as your own kits—to hunt without there being a problem. And then to push them aside like that? What were you thinking?"

Gray Wing felt as though everything was piling up on him,

like an avalanche in the mountains.

"Do you have any idea what it's like?" he demanded when Turtle Tail stopped at last for breath. "Trying to keep a camp of cats happy? Asking myself if Tall Shadow made the right choice when she wanted me to take over as leader? I didn't ask to be any cat's leader, and now I can't sleep for worrying about the others! Do you really think the other cats need to know that I'm struggling with my health?" He let out a long sigh. "I don't *feel* like a leader," he continued. "I couldn't get the cats out of the forest when the fire spread. If it hadn't been for Thunder taking the lead and River Ripple guiding us . . ." His head drooped in shame, listening to the rattle of his breathing.

When he looked up again, he saw that the anger had died from Turtle Tail's eyes. "I'm sorry," she murmured. "I didn't mean to upset you. It's only because I care. I don't want to see you become more ill. And I definitely don't want to hear about you pushing the kits away."

"It won't happen again," Gray Wing meowed, struggling against the fog of depression and inadequacy that surrounded him. "I needed some air, that's all it was."

"And next time?" Turtle Tail asked.

"There won't be a next time," Gray Wing assured her. He could tell that his breathing was getting better—he was sure of it.

He met Turtle Tail's steady gaze. Thankfully, she didn't pursue the argument.

Together, their pelts brushing, they turned back toward the camp.

Turtle Tail opened her jaws to say something, but there was a scuffling in the undergrowth. A hot, unwelcome scent hit Gray Wing in the throat.

"Dogs!" he exclaimed.

Two of the panting beasts leaped out of the bushes and stood growling on the path in front of them. Gray Wing thrust Turtle Tail toward a nearby stunted thorn tree and scrambled after her into the branches.

The dogs had seen them, and snuffled around their tree, leaping up to plant their huge paws on the trunk. Gray Wing looked down, not daring to move. The dogs were both huge, with sleek black pelts and flopping ears. Their jaws gaped and their tongues lolled as they panted in their eagerness to get at the cats.

"Now what do we do?" Turtle Tail asked, frozen with fear as she dug her claws into the branch.

Gray Wing didn't reply. He remembered what Shaded Moss had once said about dogs: *It's an animal you don't want to meet.* And here were these two, not many tail-lengths from the camp!

His chest tightening, Gray Wing felt it was almost as if the dogs had turned up to prove Turtle Tail's point. Everything began swirling in front of his eyes. *Don't let me fall out of the tree!* he thought desperately.

Sensing his distress, Turtle Tail pressed her body against Gray Wing's flank, gently pinning him between her and the tree trunk. "Thanks," he whispered, realizing that he wouldn't fall now that she was supporting him.

Loud paw steps sounded from beyond the gorse bushes, and a Twoleg voice was raised in a loud yowl. One of the dogs glanced around, but neither of them moved away from the tree.

Then two Twolegs appeared farther down the path and stomped up to the dogs on their heavy paws. They spoke harshly; Gray Wing didn't understand the words, but he recognized the angry tone. The Twolegs pulled long tendrils from their pelts and fastened them to the dogs' necks, dragging them away from the tree.

The dogs resisted, their paws skidding on the ground as they went on snarling and snapping at the two cats. Finally the Twolegs gave the tendrils a vicious jerk, and the dogs stopped pulling and walked quietly alongside them down the path.

Gray Wing puffed out his breath in relief. "Imagine being under orders like that!" he exclaimed with a disgusted snort. "Those dogs are pathetic. And the Twolegs must be flea-brained to want them around."

Too late, he remembered that Turtle Tail had once lived in a Twolegplace, but she was already climbing down the tree trunk to the ground. Gray Wing hurried to follow her, his paws slipping on the rough bark. "I'm sorry," he called out. "I didn't mean anything by it!"

When Turtle Tail turned to face him, Gray Wing was thankful to see that her eyes were glimmering with laughter. "It's okay. You don't need to worry," she told him. "You looked pretty scared, though, for a cat who thinks dogs are pathetic."

Gray Wing breathed a sigh of relief. He never wanted to

quarrel with Turtle Tail; her anger over the hunt and his treatment of the kits had struck him like a claw in his heart.

"Thank you for agreeing to keep my secret a bit longer," he meowed as he and Turtle Tail padded back to the camp. Turtle Tail drew ahead a couple of paw steps, and glanced back over her shoulder.

"I never agreed to any such thing," she pointed out. "Come on. Let's get home."

CHAPTER 21

♣

When he arrived back at the camp, Gray Wing left Turtle Tail to check on her kits, while he padded over to the tall rock and leaped up onto it. "Let all cats gather around to listen!" he yowled.

Hawk Swoop emerged from her den with Acorn Fur and Lightning Tail just behind her, tails waving as they scurried up to sit below the rock. Jagged Peak dragged himself over and sat nearby. Cloud Spots and Dappled Pelt looked up from where they were sorting herbs. Rainswept Flower went to meet Turtle Tail, and both she-cats gathered the kits together and made them sit down quietly. Jackdaw's Cry and Shattered Ice appeared at the top of the hollow; Shattered Ice was carrying a mouse. Only Tall Shadow paid no attention to Gray Wing's summons, remaining crouched over Moon Shadow, who, as always, lay unmoving.

"Turtle Tail and I just met a couple of dogs," Gray Wing announced when all his denmates had gathered. "Some Two-legs took them away, but we still need to be careful. For the rest of today we should all keep together, and stay close to the hollow until we're sure that the dogs have gone home with their Twolegs. Understand?"

"Sure, Gray Wing," Shattered Ice responded, while the rest of the cats murmured agreement.

"I'm a dog and I'm going to get you!" Sparrow Fur squealed, leaping on top of Owl Eyes.

While Turtle Tail separated the scuffling kits, the meeting broke up and Gray Wing jumped down from the rock. He padded over to Tall Shadow and described to her what had happened, but he realized that even now she was only half listening. Her face was taut with worry as she looked down at her brother.

Moon Shadow's breathing was fast and shallow. His eyes were closed and his fur dull. The wound on his side wasn't healing, in spite of the herbs spread on it; blood was oozing out, darkening the covering of chewed-up leaves.

"Is there anything I can do?" Gray Wing asked. He could feel the distress coming off Tall Shadow in waves.

She shrugged. "Not unless you suddenly learned the art of healing," she replied. She looked older than Gray Wing had ever seen her and he touched the tip of his tail to her shoulder.

"He'll get better," he mewed.

"Don't say that," Tall Shadow hissed. "You don't know that and neither do I. Just leave us alone, please."

She lay on the ground beside her brother, and kept her gaze focused on his breathing. Gray Wing might as well have not been there.

As he paced back to his old nest his chest began hurting again. That scramble up the tree hadn't done him any good, but at least he wasn't in as bad a state as Moon Shadow. *Why did that fire ever have to happen?* Cats were ill and injured and he'd lost Thunder to Clear Sky. *What are they doing now?*

Pebble Heart scampered up to him as he reached his nest. "Are you okay?" he asked.

"Yes, I'm fine," Gray Wing responded.

"He's been keeping an eye on you, you know," Turtle Tail mewed as she came to join them.

"That's good." Gray Wing brushed his tail over the tabby kit's head. "But I've had enough talk of sickness for one day!"

He lowered himself into his old sleeping place, burrowing deeply into the dried ferns. *The others can share the prey. I just want to sleep.*

When Gray Wing woke again, clouds had covered the sun, stretching gray and threatening above his head. The air felt damp, as if rain was on the way.

A small movement in the bedding beside him made Gray Wing turn his head. Pebble Heart was sleeping at his side, his body twitching and his paws working as if he was running in his sleep.

He's having a vivid dream, Gray Wing thought.

He didn't want to wake the kit, because he knew it could be dangerous to jerk cats out of their dreams. *Besides, if I'm right, and Pebble Heart has special skills, this dream might mean something.*

Gray Wing waited patiently for Pebble Heart to wake. Suddenly the kit exploded into movement, leaping to his paws, his eyes wide and staring. He turned on Gray Wing with a hiss, but Gray Wing stretched out a paw to calm him.

"Take it easy," he murmured. "It's okay. You were having a dream, that's all."

Gradually Pebble Heart returned to the waking world, his gaze focusing on Gray Wing's face.

Gray Wing could see bleak misery in his eyes. "You've had this dream before, haven't you?" he asked.

For answer, Pebble Heart curled himself into a small ball, pressing himself against Gray Wing's side. Gray Wing could feel his trembling. Gently he licked the kit's pelt with strong, soothing strokes of his tongue. "It's okay," he whispered. "You can tell me."

Gradually Pebble Heart's trembling subsided. "I've had dreams for a while now," he confessed. "Owl Eyes and Sparrow Fur sleep so soundly, I knew it was only me having them. And there's something about them that makes them feel . . . well, more than dreams. Am I being mouse-brained?" he asked hesitantly.

Gray Wing shook his head. "Not at all. Tell me more about the dreams," he mewed.

Pebble Heart's eyes grew distant with memory. "There's one particular dream I've had a few times," he began. "I was walking down a long, dark tunnel, and there was a glittering light at the end, as if a star was shining underground."

"And that scared you?" Gray Wing asked, stroking the kit's back with his tail.

"Oh, no!" Pebble Heart's eyes shone. "It was exciting! I really wanted to get to the end of the tunnel and find out what the light was. And it was weird . . . I couldn't see any other cats, but I felt like there were cats there, trying to tell me something. Only I couldn't hear what they were saying. I thought if I could get to the star thing, I would understand, but every time I have the dream, I wake up before I reach the end of the tunnel," he finished, sounding disappointed.

Gray Wing couldn't make sense of that at all. "You don't have to worry," he reassured Pebble Heart. "You're not the only cat who has dreams. You remember Turtle Tail and I told you about Stoneteller and the other cats in the mountains, where we came from?" Pebble Heart nodded. "Well, Stoneteller had dreams like yours sometimes. Just the same as you."

The little kit's eyes were bright with interest. "Really?"

"Really. And she's a very wise cat." More hesitantly, he asked, "What was your dream about this time, Pebble Heart?"

"A fight—a big fight," Pebble Heart replied, beginning to tremble again. "Cats were screeching and clawing each other. I think I saw Clear Sky there. I've dreamed that one before, too."

Apprehension clawed at Gray Wing, though he took care not to let the kit see that he was worried. *Has he had some kind of warning?*

"It's all right," he soothed Pebble Heart. "You don't have to talk about it anymore."

Glancing toward the mouth of the den, Gray Wing noticed that Jagged Peak was crouched nearby, watching them intently. *I think he's too far away to have heard what we said, but even so . . .*

Protectively Gray Wing curled his body around Pebble Heart, bending over so that both their faces were hidden. This was something that he didn't want Jagged Peak or any other cat to see.

If Pebble Heart is special, then he needs to be kept safe, he thought.

"For now, don't tell any other cat," he mewed. "But let me know if you have any more—"

He broke off as a grief-stricken yowl rose up from the other side of the camp. Springing to his paws, Gray Wing saw Tall Shadow standing over the body of her brother. Other cats were already rushing toward her.

Gray Wing joined her with Pebble Heart scampering hard on his paws. Moon Shadow lay still, his legs splayed out as if in a last spasm of pain. A drying, sticky pool of blood stained the ground near his mouth.

Oh no! He must have died while the kits and I were sleeping, Gray Wing thought.

He pushed his way through the gathering crowd of cats until he reached Tall Shadow's side. The black she-cat was rocking back and forth, her claws tearing up the ground in her anger and grief.

"It wasn't his time to go!" she wailed.

The other cats had encircled them and stood watching, wide-eyed and silent, stunned by Moon Shadow's death. Gray Wing realized there was only one thing left to do. He reached out a paw to touch Moon Shadow's body; it was already cooling. A shudder of grief passed through Gray Wing. No cat's death was ever easy to witness.

We have to bury him. Gray Wing remembered how they had laid Fluttering Bird to rest under a pile of stones, and his heart twisted. The sooner they got through this, the better. "Are you ready?" he mewed gently to Tall Shadow.

The black she-cat didn't need to ask what he meant. She had seen too many cats die in her time.

Glancing around, Gray Wing spotted Jagged Peak, and beckoned to him with his tail. "We're going to bury Moon Shadow," he told his brother when Jagged Peak had limped up to him. "I want you to stay here and look after the kits. They're too young to witness this."

Jagged Peak stood taller, looking confident. "You can trust me, Gray Wing."

Owl Eyes and Sparrow Fur scampered up to join Pebble Heart, who was gazing sadly at the body of Moon Shadow. Gray Wing could see that Pebble Heart knew there was nothing more he could do to help this cat.

"Jagged Peak is going to look after you while we're out of camp," Gray Wing meowed, gathering the kits together with his tail.

"Great! He knows really cool games," Sparrow Fur agreed enthusiastically.

"But why can't we come with you?" Owl Eyes argued.

"Because there are some things young kits don't need to see," Gray Wing told him.

"Quite right." Turtle Tail padded up to join the group. "You kits stay here with Jagged Peak." She hesitated and looked at Gray Wing's younger brother. "Thank you," she said. "We couldn't do this now, without you."

He dipped his head in acknowledgment, then shook himself. "Come on, kits," he called, as he started limping away.

Once the kits had withdrawn, bouncing around Jagged Peak as he led them across the camp, Gray Wing and Tall Shadow picked up the body of Moon Shadow. It was lighter than Gray Wing had expected—clearly the injured cat hadn't been eating well. Moving slowly and respectfully, they carried the body up the slope and out of the hollow. The other cats followed them, the soft fall of their paw steps the only sound.

As they emerged onto the moor, Gray Wing spotted Gorse Fur and Wind Runner approaching from a few tail-lengths away.

"We'll help," Gorse Fur offered immediately as he joined them.

"Thank you," Gray Wing meowed gratefully.

"Okay, every cat get into a line." Wind Runner took over immediately. "Don't crowd Moon Shadow. Show him a bit of respect."

There were a few startled glances at Wind Runner as she spoke, but the cats were too grief-stricken to protest. Gray Wing was thankful for her calm efficiency. *She can see what's needed because her feelings aren't as deeply involved.*

With the rest of the cats following, Gray Wing and Tall Shadow carried Moon Shadow to a quiet spot in the shelter of a rock and stood back while Wind Runner and Gorse Fur scratched away the earth and stones.

At last there was a hole deep enough for Moon Shadow's

body. Gray Wing and Tall Shadow rolled him into it; Gray Wing winced as he spotted streaks of blood in the dirt. *No cat deserves to die in this way.*

Moon Shadow's belly was exposed so that every cat could see the burns on his pelt. Tall Shadow let out a wail of distress. Scrambling into the hole after her brother, she tried to turn him over so that the terrible wounds weren't exposed. But the hole wasn't big enough, and his body was already stiffening.

Turtle Tail padded to the edge of the hole. "Come on out, Tall Shadow," she mewed gently. "Leave him be."

Tall Shadow looked up with a brief flash of anger that gradually faded to quiet misery. Reluctantly she heaved herself out of the hole and watched with dull eyes as Jackdaw's Cry and Shattered Ice piled stones and rocks until Moon Shadow had disappeared forever.

Gray Wing felt that they hadn't done enough. *This is the first burial since we came to the moor. It's important for me to say something.*

As Jackdaw's Cry and Shattered Ice stood back, cleaning earth from their paws, Gray Wing turned to face the other cats. "Moon Shadow was a brave cat," he began. "He survived so much, in the mountains and on our journey here. His death is a sign of all the changes we have experienced since we left the mountains. I know there will be more changes to come. But whatever happens, no cat will ever forget Moon Shadow. I'll make certain of that."

Before he had finished speaking, Tall Shadow had already turned and walked away, heading back to the camp. Gray Wing felt his heart begin to break, to see her so alone.

The rest of the cats followed. Gray Wing was the last to reach the camp. He paused for a moment at the top of the hollow, watching as the cats dispersed after the burial. As he stood there, he saw Jagged Peak come hobbling up to him. His fur was bristling and his blue eyes wide with apprehension.

"Gray Wing!" he gasped. "I've lost Owl Eyes!"

Gray Wing couldn't believe what he was hearing. "What do you mean, lost? All you had to do was look after three young kits!"

Guilt and shame flooded into Jagged Peak's eyes. "I was giving them a training session, teaching them how to climb a rock. Obviously I can't show them, but I can give them directions. I was helping Pebble Heart and Sparrow Fur, when I suddenly realized Owl Eyes wasn't with us anymore."

Gray Wing dug his claws into the ground in anxiety. "That's no excuse. You're supposed to be watching all three!"

He knew how harsh his words sounded when he saw Jagged Peak flinch, but he was too worried about Owl Eyes to care. His gaze raked the hollow. The other two kits were standing close together a couple of tail-lengths farther down the slope, their eyes wide and frightened, but there was no sign of Owl Eyes.

"Have you checked the dens?" he asked Jagged Peak.

The young cat gave a tense nod. "He's not there."

Turtle Tail padded up to stand beside Gray Wing. Her face and her voice were calm—*too calm*, Gray Wing thought—as she spoke to Jagged Peak. "You mustn't worry," she told him, sounding as if she could barely get the words out. "This isn't your fault."

Gray Wing beckoned the other kits with his tail. "Do you know anything about this?" he asked them both.

Pebble Heart shook his head. Sparrow Fur scuffled her forepaws in the soil, her head lowered.

"Sparrow Fur!" her mother mewed sharply. "If you know anything, you have to tell us!"

"Owl Eyes said he was going out to hunt a hare," the tortoiseshell kit admitted reluctantly.

"A hare!" Turtle Tail turned to Gray Wing, her eyes wide and frightened. "He's not big enough to tackle a hare. And on his own!"

"And there are dogs on the moor," Gray Wing added, feeling his chest beginning to tighten again as he realized what might happen to Owl Eyes. "Why didn't you tell Jagged Peak?" he asked Sparrow Fur, his tone harsh with fear and anger.

She flinched away. "Because I didn't think he meant it!" she wailed. "I thought he was just boasting. I never believed he would be flea-brained enough to actually *do* it."

Gray Wing paused for a heartbeat. He knew that Owl Eyes had good hunting instincts, but deciding to go out alone was one of the most reckless things he had ever heard of. "We have to go after him," he decided.

No way am I going to leave a kit to be killed in a dog attack or a fight with a hare.

With a wave of his tail, Gray Wing called the other cats to him. "Turtle Tail, Wind Runner, you stay here and look after the kits," he ordered, ignoring Jagged Peak's hurt look. *I can't trust him with the kits again!* "Jackdaw's Cry, I want you with me. Gorse Fur, will you take charge of another group?"

As the cats began to organize themselves, Gray Wing padded across to Tall Shadow, the only cat who had not answered his summons. She was sitting at the foot of the tall rock, staring into the distance.

"Tall Shadow, Owl Eyes has gone out onto the moor by himself to hunt," Gray Wing explained. "We're going to look for him. Will you come with me?" When Tall Shadow didn't respond immediately, he added, "I know you're grieving for Moon Shadow, but I need you by my side now."

Tall Shadow rose and gave her pelt a shake, as if she was trying to get rid of clinging burrs. She finally turned to look at Gray Wing, and her eyes were blazing.

"My brother is buried," she meowed. "I won't see another cat die. Of course I'll help. Where do we start?"

CHAPTER 22
❧

As *Gray Wing led the way* up the slope, he paused to speak to Rainswept Flower, who was watching, her eyes wide with concern. Angling his ears toward Jagged Peak, he meowed, "Look after him, will you?"

Rainswept Flower nodded. "Don't worry, Gray Wing. I will."

At the edge of the hollow Gray Wing sniffed around until he picked up Owl Eyes's scent. "This way!" he exclaimed, waving his tail to beckon Tall Shadow and Jackdaw's Cry.

But as the three cats headed across the moor, the kit's faint scent was drowned in the reek of dogs.

"We'll never find him at this rate," Jackdaw's Cry muttered.

Fear crept through Gray Wing as if the blood in his veins had turned to snowmelt. Gazing around, he realized how unlikely they were to find the kit he'd come to love as his own before he fell into danger. *It could already be too late.*

"He seemed to be going this way," he meowed, setting out in the direction the scent had led.

His denmates followed as he forged onward, all his senses at full stretch to pick up the least trace of the kit. Weaving a path through a clump of gorse bushes, he spotted a smear of blood on one of the low branches. For a heartbeat his paws froze to the ground, he was so afraid that the blood belonged to Owl Eyes.

Tall Shadow padded across and sniffed at the smear. "I'm sorry," she mewed. "The dog-scent is so strong, I can't tell where the blood came from."

That wasn't much comfort for Gray Wing, but he forced himself to get moving again.

On the other side of the gorse bushes all three cats cast around to try to pick up Owl Eyes's scent again. Eventually Tall Shadow raised her tail. "Over here!" she called out. "The trail is leading toward the forest."

Gray Wing gazed at the line of trees in the distance. Somewhere among them was Clear Sky's camp. *Would he protect Owl Eyes if the kit was in danger?*

The moor gradually sloped downward into a valley with a narrow stream trickling along the bottom. The dog-scent wasn't as strong here, and everything seemed peaceful, but Gray Wing's pads prickled with apprehension.

It's too peaceful. . . .

Glancing around he realized that if they were attacked there was nowhere to hide, not a tree or bush they could scramble into. The only cover was sparse clumps of reeds and long grass by the waterside.

They were heading downstream, still following Owl Eyes's scent trail, when Gray Wing heard a shrill voice calling his name. He stiffened, gazing across the stream, and spotted

Owl Eyes's head popping out between the reeds.

"Look what I caught!" the kit called triumphantly, tossing a dead vole into the air.

Relief surged through Gray Wing, followed by a hot rush of anger. "You stupid, *stupid* furball!" he yowled, leaping the stream and bounding toward the kit. His chest had begun to ache again from stress and the effort of running.

Tall Shadow and Jackdaw's Cry crossed the stream behind him, but as they reached Owl Eyes the clouds which had been lowering over the moor for most of the day suddenly released their rain. Fat drops splashed onto Gray Wing's pelt and stippled the surface of the water.

"Now we'll get soaked through!" Jackdaw's Cry grumbled.

Gray Wing's breath was wheezing in his chest. He couldn't face racing back across the moor to the shelter of the camp. Hunching his shoulders as the rain grew heavier, he spotted a hole in the bank of the stream above their heads. "Up there!" he snapped at Owl Eyes, thrusting the kit in front of him and following him into the hole. "Come on!" he called to the others.

Little light filtered in from the entrance to the burrow, and there was a stale scent of rabbit. But there was enough space to move forward, Gray Wing's pelt brushing the earthen sides. He could scent Tall Shadow and Jackdaw's Cry following him, and when he glanced over his shoulder he could just make out Tall Shadow's ears outlined against the dim light.

In the next heartbeat there was a slippery sound and the light was cut off, leaving the cats in pitch darkness.

"What happened?" Gray Wing called out, feeling his belly clench with the first stirrings of panic.

"The entrance collapsed," Jackdaw's Cry replied, sounding more annoyed than frightened. "The rain must have weakened it."

"Then we're trapped," Tall Shadow rasped.

Guilt washed through Gray Wing, as overwhelming as the rain outside. He struggled to catch his breath, knowing that the others would be able to hear his wheezing in the silence. He had never felt so useless in his life. *If it wasn't for my bad chest, we would be halfway back to the camp by now.*

"I . . . I'm sorry . . . ," he choked out. "I shouldn't have . . ." His voice was trembling too much from his sense of failure and he couldn't finish what he wanted to say.

"It's not your fault," Jackdaw's Cry meowed sturdily. "And it's no big deal. All we have to do is keep going. There's bound to be another way out."

Gray Wing began to creep forward, gently pushing Owl Eyes ahead of him. "This is exciting!" the little kit squeaked, then added, "Mouse dung! I dropped my vole by the stream."

Gradually Gray Wing realized that the darkness was giving way to a faint gray light, coming from up ahead. At the same time he began to pick up a strange scent: a strong reek that reminded him of the smell of foxes, though it wasn't quite the same. The fur on his neck and shoulders began to prickle.

A few paces farther on, the tunnel widened into an open space where the cats could stand side by side and look around. More than one tunnel led away from the central cave where they were. Light was trickling down through small chinks in the roof, the earth held up by a tangle of roots. The floor of the cave was covered with dead leaves and bracken; Gray Wing wrinkled his nose at the smell.

"This place is yucky!" Owl Eyes announced. "I don't like it here."

Jackdaw's Cry gave him a gentle cuff over one ear. "It's your own fault for running away from Jagged Peak," he meowed. "What were you told about not leaving camp? You can't ignore Gray Wing's orders like that, especially when he is our leader, and the most respected cat in camp."

Even though Gray Wing knew that Jackdaw's Cry was trying to make him feel better, guilt gnawed at him even more deeply. *Respect? I don't deserve that!* But he had the sense to stay silent and not reveal to Owl Eyes how bad he was feeling.

"It was just a bit of fun!" Owl Eyes protested. "And I *did* catch a vole."

"Fun!" Jackdaw's Cry exclaimed. "You bee-brained kit, you—"

"That's enough, both of you," Gray Wing interrupted. "We need to decide which of these tunnels is best," he went on, gesturing with his tail toward the exits from the cave. *I can't wait to get out. This damp air is making my chest hurt even more.*

But as he led the way across the cave to the nearest tunnel, there was movement inside it. Gray Wing stared as an animal paused in the entrance. It had black fur with a white stripe down the middle of its narrow head, a wet nose, bright beady eyes and small ears. Its short legs ended in powerful, blunt claws.

Gray Wing froze with a mixture of fear and curiosity. "What's *that*?" he whispered.

"It's called a badger," Tall Shadow replied in a no-nonsense tone. "I remember Shaded Moss telling me about them. He said they live in groups like us, and they're really fierce."

And we just walked into its den, Gray Wing realized. Struggling to think clearly, he could see that they only had one advantage: speed. This great hulking creature couldn't possibly move as fast as a cat. *We're trapped down here—but we have to try to get away.*

The badger heaved itself out of the tunnel and reared up in front of the cats, opening its jaws to show huge yellow teeth.

"Run!" Gray Wing screeched.

Making sure that Owl Eyes was following, he raced for the next exit tunnel and plunged into it. Almost at once he realized that he had made a mistake. They could only go as fast as his breathing would allow, and that wasn't as fast as he would like.

I should have let the others go first. I could have faced the badger while they escaped.

But it was too late now. The tunnel was so narrow that the other cats couldn't get past him.

Thankfully he realized that after the first few tail-lengths the tunnel opened up into a network with connecting tunnels on either side. Gray Wing twisted and turned, hoping to lose the pursuing badger. More chinks in the roof let in enough light for him to see his way.

Gray Wing hesitated at a screech of pain behind him, followed by the sound of a scuffle. *Some cat is injured!* But there was no way he could get back to help; he had to go on.

At last Gray Wing spotted an irregular patch of light ahead of him and realized that they had found the way out. He forced a last burst of speed from his paws and tumbled into the open.

The heavy rain had turned into a thin drizzle. Through it Gray Wing saw that they were close to the edge of the forest. One of the outlying trees was a few tail-lengths away. Checking with a swift glance to make sure all his cats were following, he hurled himself at the tree and clawed his way up the trunk until he could crouch trembling on a branch, his breath coming in great gasps. His denmates joined him and shrank back into the cover of the leaves.

Gray Wing gazed down and saw the badger thrust its striped snout out of the tunnel mouth. It raked the surroundings with a glance from its small, malignant eyes, then let out a grunt and withdrew underground.

Tall Shadow let out a gasp of relief. "It's gone!"

"Owl Eyes, are you okay?" Gray Wing asked.

The kit was pressing close to him, shaking with fear. Gray Wing spotted a scratch down one of his back legs; it was slowly oozing blood. "You're hurt!" he exclaimed. "It was you I heard back there."

"It's nothing. I'm fine," Owl Eyes mewed bravely, though his teeth were chattering.

Jackdaw's Cry flexed his claws. "I gave the badger something to think about."

Gray Wing could hardly believe that the kit had been

injured while he was still so young. *It's my fault*, he thought despairingly. *What sort of leader am I, when I can't even protect my own kit?*

The last of the rain stopped and the clouds began to clear. Gray Wing could see the sun dipping toward the horizon.

"I don't think the badger's coming back," he meowed. "We'd better get back to camp. If we're out here after dark, we'll be in more trouble."

Tall Shadow was first to jump out of the tree; she took the lead as the cats headed back across the moor. Gray Wing and Owl Eyes brought up the rear, Gray Wing still struggling for breath and Owl Eyes limping from his scratch.

"I'm sorry," Owl Eyes murmured, blinking apologetically at Gray Wing. "I shouldn't have left the camp on my own like that."

Gray Wing twitched his ears to acknowledge the kit's words, but he didn't have any energy left to speak.

He looked up and saw the shape of Highstones outlined against the setting sun. It reminded him of his own more distant mountains. *If only I had Stoneteller here to guide me*, he thought. *But she's so far away. She can't help me now.*

As Gray Wing reached the top of the hollow, he saw his denmates huddled together in the middle of the camp, exchanging anxious meows. Then Rainswept Flower looked up and spotted them.

"They're back!" she yowled.

Instantly Turtle Tail raced up the slope, flinging herself at Owl Eyes and covering him with licks. "I'm so angry with you!" she mewed. "What were you thinking, going off on your own like that? And you're hurt!"

"I caught a vole," Owl Eyes announced proudly.

"I don't want to hear about it!"

Turtle Tail nosed her son down into the hollow, and the other cats followed, while their denmates crowded around, questioning them about what had happened. Gray Wing was still having trouble breathing, so he sat down and let Tall Shadow tell the story.

He noticed Jagged Peak wincing at the mention of their frantic scramble up the tree, and knew that the young cat must be remembering his own injury.

Pebble Heart and Sparrow Fur rushed up to their brother, burying their noses in his fur. Spotting the wound the badger had given Owl Eyes, Pebble Heart began licking it vigorously.

"This will help stop an infection," he declared confidently between licks. "You have to keep wounds clean."

"How do you know that?" Owl Eyes asked.

"Cloud Spots told me," the little tom replied. "He's teaching me all about herbs, too. He says when I'm bigger he'll take me to gather herbs with him and Dappled Pelt."

Meanwhile Gray Wing realized that Turtle Tail was giving him a long, hard glance. "How could you have allowed this to happen?" she asked. "That badger could have killed our son."

"Me?" Gray Wing found himself forgetting his vow never to quarrel with Turtle Tail. "How is it my fault? I went to rescue him! If Owl Eyes hadn't been so disobedient . . ." His voice trailed off. His chest felt tighter than ever and he found it hard to breathe. He felt himself swaying; the air sparkled in front of his eyes.

"That's it!" Turtle Tail snapped. Through the glitter Gray Wing saw her turn to the rest of the cats, and her voice rose above their anxious murmurings. "Look at Gray Wing! Can you see how he can barely sit upright? Can you all hear the breath rattling in his chest? He's ill—seriously ill. Am I the only cat with eyes in my head?" Her tail lashed furiously as she glared at the rest of the group. "If Gray Wing won't face up to the truth, I will," she went on. "He needs time to recover. He can't lead this group of cats anymore. He can't . . ."

A roaring like a gale sweeping through the forest rose in Gray Wing's ears, until he could no longer hear Turtle Tail's words. His vision began to fade, and he was faintly aware of his body collapsing to the ground.

The world shrank to a tiny dot of light and then winked out.

CHAPTER 23

Thunder padded through the undergrowth, following Frost and Petal as they patrolled the boundaries of Clear Sky's territory. Clouds covered the patches of sky he could see through the trees. The air was damp and chilly, and the ground soggy underpaw; he winced at the cold touch of water on his pads.

He felt more comfortable with Frost and Petal than with most of Clear Sky's other cats. But the other cats' caution had had an effect on Thunder—now he didn't know who to trust, either.

He couldn't help feeling sorry for Frost, who was still limping from when he trod on a burning branch during the forest fire. The injury wasn't healing as it should, and there was always a layer of pain in the white tom's eyes.

As they did so often now, Thunder's thoughts strayed back to the camp on the moor and his life with Gray Wing. *What would he think if he could see me now?* The borders made Clear Sky's group feel safe and guarded, but Thunder knew how uncomfortable Gray Wing was with these perpetual patrols, and that he thought there was no need to be so rigid about where cats were allowed to hunt.

He had heard stories about Petal's brother, Fox, who had attacked Gray Wing for trespassing. Gray Wing had defended himself, and Fox had died in the fight. *I'm sure Gray Wing wouldn't have wanted that to happen,* Thunder thought.

He felt a sudden impulse to question Petal and Frost about that fight, but he realized how stupid that would be. *It's none of my business. I'd probably get my fur clawed off.*

Frost, who was in the lead, halted suddenly at the sound of a scuffling in the undergrowth. Thunder's pelt began to prickle as he picked up the scent of a strange cat. He thought he ought to recognize it, but he couldn't remember when he had smelled it before.

"Come out!" Petal called sternly. "We know you're there."

There was a moment's pause before the fern fronds in front of the three cats parted and a skinny tortoiseshell cat stumbled out.

"Bumble!" Thunder exclaimed. "What are you doing here? Aren't you a kittypet? Shouldn't you be with your Twolegs?"

"You know this cat?" Petal snapped, looking suspiciously at Thunder.

Oh, mouse dung . . . now she thinks I'm friends with kittypets! "Er . . . she just came to our camp on the moor once," Thunder replied.

"I'm *not* a kittypet—not anymore." Bumble drew herself up proudly. "I told the moorland cats that I wasn't going back to the Twolegplace, and I didn't. I really didn't. I'm a wild cat now."

Thunder couldn't help noticing that Bumble was much thinner than when she came to the moorland camp to ask to live there. Her ribs were showing, and for all her proud words, the look in her eyes was desperate. And she seemed a bit too insistent that she hadn't gone back to the Twolegplace. *Is she trying to convince us that she's wild now . . . or herself?* Thunder wondered.

"Wild or not," Petal mewed tartly, "you can't be here."

"That's right," Frost added. "You're trespassing. This is Clear Sky's territory."

Bumble hesitated, glancing indignantly from Frost to Petal and back again. "I can go where I want," she responded, but there was a betraying quiver in her voice.

Frost didn't reply in words, just slid out his claws and took a threatening step forward. Bumble stood up to him for a couple of heartbeats more, trying to puff her chest out bravely, but when Petal snarled she whipped around and fled.

"Get out and stay out!" Frost yowled as he and Petal raced after her.

Thunder stayed where he was as the other three cats vanished into the undergrowth. For a moment he tracked them by waving fern fronds and a bird that rocketed upward with a shrill alarm call; then all was silent.

I hope they don't hurt her, he thought apprehensively. *Why can't they just let her go?*

A faint, mournful wail drifted to Thunder's ears, and he recognized Bumble's voice. It didn't sound as if she was injured, just frightened and hurt by the cats' rejection of her.

Moments later, Frost and Petal reappeared. "We won't

have any more trouble from *her,*" Frost meowed with a satisfied whisk of his tail.

"Right," Petal agreed. "She's just a confused kittypet, that's all; it's not like she's going to catch anything. The sooner she goes back to her Twolegs, the better off she'll be."

But Thunder couldn't shake off his anxiety. *Bumble is so thin now!* "Maybe we could have helped her," he murmured half to himself.

Petal let out a contemptuous snort. "No cat helped me or my brother when our mother died. We were only kits then."

"That must have felt very lonely," Thunder mewed.

Petal's eyes hardened. "It was lonely, until Clear Sky rescued us. I'll never stop being grateful for his help. And if supporting him means defending the boundaries with every tooth and claw I've got, then that's what I'll do. I *owe* Clear Sky."

"Let's keep going," Frost grunted.

As they headed farther along the border, the clouds began to clear away and the sun peeped through. It was already beginning to dip toward the horizon, casting a reddish light into the forest.

"We'd better get a move on," Petal murmured, excitement creeping into her voice. "Clear Sky will be starting his meeting soon, and we have to be back in camp."

Frost's eyes gleamed. "Yeah, no way I'm missing that. Hey, Thunder, do you know what it's all about?"

Thunder shook his head. The first he had heard about the

meeting was when Clear Sky had announced it that morning.

"Oh, come on," Petal urged him. "You're Clear Sky's son. He must have told you *something*."

"No, sorry, he didn't," Thunder responded, feeling slightly disappointed that his father hadn't seen fit to confide in him. "He doesn't share his secrets with me. We'll all find out in good time."

Petal rolled her eyes as if she didn't entirely believe him, but didn't question him any further. "What do you think Clear Sky is planning?" she asked Frost.

"Maybe he wants us to expand our boundaries," Frost suggested. "Wouldn't it be great to get as far as that hollow with the four oak trees?"

Thunder was horrified. *That's too far away! How would we ever defend that much territory? And what about all the cats who hunt there now? What would they do?* But he was careful to hide his reaction from Frost and Petal.

"I don't think so," Petal meowed, to Thunder's relief. "I think it's more likely that Clear Sky wants to give certain cats more responsibilities."

"Hmm . . . maybe." Frost sounded dubious. "Which of us, do you think?"

Petal's gaze grew calculating, and Thunder guessed she was considering the possibilities. "Falling Feather and Quick Water have been with Clear Sky from the beginning," she began. "But Quick Water is such a scaredy-mouse! Always moaning about getting her paws wet. Falling Feather's okay, I suppose, but there's nothing special about her."

"Maybe Leaf," Frost suggested. "He's a good hunter."

"You think?" Petal twitched her whiskers dismissively. "*I* think he couldn't catch a squirrel if it leaped into his paws."

"Yeah, and if it comes to a fight I can beat him, no problem," Frost meowed. "You know, if Clear Sky is going to pick some cat, you and I have a good chance, better than those useless furballs."

Thunder couldn't stand this any longer. "Is that really the way you talk about your denmates?" he asked, shocked.

Frost and Petal both halted and gazed at Thunder with surprise in their eyes.

"Where have you been living for the last two moons?" Frost asked. "Hasn't your father taught you anything? Every cat knows that we all have our place in the camp, and that place depends on how much Clear Sky likes us. He made it quite clear from when he first moved into the forest—his opinion is final."

Thunder shook his head, completely bewildered. "I thought—"

"He doesn't *need* to understand all that," Petal interrupted with a spiteful note in her voice. "As Clear Sky's own son, he goes straight to the top."

When she finished speaking, there was a flicker of movement just ahead, and a mouse appeared from the shelter of a dead leaf. Without waiting for Thunder to respond, Petal hurtled off to chase it.

Which cat named her "Petal"? Thunder wondered. *There's nothing soft about her.* Coming to the end of the patrol, the cats set out back toward the camp. Thunder brought up the rear, not wanting to listen to Frost and Petal talking anymore. He had only taken a few paw steps when he heard a faint rustle behind him. Glancing over his shoulder, he spotted yellow eyes peering out from under a bush. A heartbeat later the cat emerged: a she-cat with a wiry brown pelt who crossed the border without hesitation and stood with her ears pricked and her jaws open as if she was searching for prey.

Wind!

Thunder realized that the she-cat hadn't noticed him; he was partly screened from her by the edge of a bramble thicket. He knew that he ought to chase her off, but he remembered how friendly and helpful she had been to the moorland cats. He didn't want to turn her into an enemy.

Hesitating with one paw frozen in midair, Thunder hoped that Wind would just stroll away again, and there would be no reason for a scene.

Frost and Petal won't take her trespassing as lightly as they did Bumble's. And she won't be as easy to scare off.

Before Thunder could make his mind up, Frost dashed ahead, shouldering him out of the way, and confronted Wind. "Get out of here!" he snarled.

For all his bravado, Thunder could see that Frost was wincing from the pain of his wound. *He'd do better to be kinder to other cats,* he thought. *He's not exactly ready for a fight.*

Wind didn't budge a single paw, but gave Frost a disdainful stare.

"You've crossed our boundary, flea-pelt," Frost snarled. "Get off our territory!"

The other cat widened her eyes and gazed around her with an elaborate pretense of confusion. "My name is Wind Runner," she meowed. "And I lived here long before any of you newcomers showed up. I think you should be the one to get out of my way."

Her cool tones clearly infuriated Frost. With a growl of rage he flung himself on top of Wind Runner, and the two cats rolled over and over on the forest floor in a hissing, clawing tangle of fur.

Thunder started forward a couple of paw steps and stopped, not sure what he wanted to do. He saw that Petal had come up, too, and was watching the fight with steady green eyes. Thunder guessed she would join in if Frost seemed to be getting the worst of it.

But there was no need for Petal to intervene. Frost, who was bigger and more powerful, soon had Wind Runner pinned down underneath his body. Thunder tried to hide his surprise. Frost's injuries hadn't stopped him from being a formidable fighter.

Wind Runner's eyes rolled in her head. As she gazed at Thunder, who stood watching helplessly, he had no doubt what message she was trying to send.

Help me!

But Thunder was conscious of Petal watching him across the fighting cats' bodies, and knew that she would report any betrayal to Clear Sky.

Wind Runner saved him from having to decide. Twisting her neck, she sank her teeth into the big white tom's paw. With a hiss of shock at the unexpected pain, Frost pulled away, giving Wind Runner the chance to wriggle free. Petal started forward, but within a heartbeat Wind Runner had vanished down a nearby rabbit hole.

Thunder let relief wash over him. *She'll escape through the tunnels. She'll be fine.*

But the feeling didn't last long. Both Frost and Petal rounded on him, standing shoulder to shoulder.

"You saw that cat!" Frost accused him. "Why didn't you attack sooner?"

"Yeah, why are you even out on patrol if you won't guard the borders?" Petal demanded.

Thunder didn't try to defend himself. He could easily imagine a fight developing, and he didn't want an account of the incident getting back to Clear Sky. *Maybe if I let it go, they won't say anything. . . .*

Petal and Frost glared at him for a moment longer, then Petal gave a snort of disgust. "Come on, let's get back. We don't want to miss Clear Sky's announcement." She turned and padded off with Frost beside her.

Feeling thoroughly depressed, Thunder followed.

* * *

Darkness had fallen over the camp. Thunder sat unobtrusively in the shelter of a bramble thicket while the rest of Clear Sky's group, fluid shadows in the black night, gathered around the pool in the center of the clearing. The air tingled with excitement as the cats murmured together, speculating about the reason for the meeting.

At last, when Thunder thought he couldn't endure the waiting a heartbeat longer, Clear Sky leaped onto the tree stump from which he usually addressed the group and surveyed his cats. His eyes glittered in the moonlight and his gray pelt shone with a silvery gleam. Thunder drew in a sharp breath, in awe of his father, who stood above every cat with such authority.

Clear Sky waited until the murmuring voices had sunk into silence. "Greetings, everyone," he began. "I have called you here tonight because I have decided it is time to adjust our territory lines."

Thunder heard a few cats gasp with surprise. His belly stirred uneasily. *What does he mean by that?*

"The forest fire has made hunting harder than ever," Clear Sky continued. "It's my duty as your leader to make sure that no cat goes hungry." A pained look crossed his face as he added, "I would never forgive myself."

Thunder heard one or two cats let out mews of sympathy. Frost raised his head and called out, "You have nothing to forgive yourself for, Clear Sky. Tell us what to do!"

Clear Sky dipped his head in acknowledgment. "Thank

you, Frost. Your loyalty means a great deal to me."

Thunder was feeling even more uneasy, as if ants were crawling all through his pelt. *He talks about* adjusting *the borders, but I know he means to* expand *them.* Thunder blinked unhappily. *Why am I doubting him? He's my father!*

Thunder glanced around at the other cats to see if any of them shared his discomfort. The gaze of every cat was fixed on their leader; only Quick Water met Thunder's glance and then quickly looked away.

"The territory adjustments will begin first thing tomorrow," Clear Sky continued. "At dawn I will personally summon the cats I have chosen to help me on this first expedition. For now, you should all get a good night's sleep. Who knows what lies ahead of us?"

Excited mewing broke out again as the cats moved away to their resting places. Clear Sky remained on the tree stump until the gathering had broken up. Then he beckoned with his tail. "Thunder! Over here!"

Surprised and a little intimidated, Thunder sprang to his paws and bounded across the clearing to the stump.

Clear Sky leaped down to meet him. "Come with me," he meowed. He led the way to a sheltered spot among the roots of an oak tree just outside the camp. Glancing around to make sure they weren't overheard, he continued, "Thunder, there's a reason why I've been taking you out in the morning for training. I want you to be part of the first group that sets out at dawn to mark the new borders."

Thunder couldn't stop himself from gaping. "Me?"

His father nodded. "I'm calling on you to do your duty. It's a great honor—are you up to it?"

Thunder felt as if he was being torn in two. He wasn't sure that it was right to expand the territory, and yet he wanted desperately to prove himself to his father.

"I . . . I know the forest needs time to recover from the fire," he stammered. "But I haven't seen any cats struggling to find something to eat."

Clear Sky turned his head away with that same look of anguish. Thunder waited, realizing that he had said the wrong thing, until his father returned his attention to him, looking deep into his eyes. Thunder tried not to shrink beneath that brilliant blue gaze.

"Of course, you can't see the signs of starvation," Clear Sky explained patiently. "You've never had to struggle for food. You can't possibly recognize the slow, cruel progress of hunger."

"But—" Thunder tried to interrupt, knowing perfectly well how easy it was to find prey, and how hunting patrols never came back empty-pawed.

Clear Sky ignored his interruption. "I know it only too well, from my time in the mountains," he continued. "One day a cat looks healthy, and then after a few sunrises you can count their ribs. I've already seen some of the early warning signs." He dug his claws hard into the ground. "I won't let the mountain tragedies of hunger visit any of my cats!"

Thunder saw how deeply moved his father was, and regretted that he had ever questioned him. *We've only been together two moons,* he thought. *I have to learn to trust his judgment.*

"Of course I'll come with you tomorrow," he meowed, trying to sound excited. "I'll do everything I can to help."

Clear Sky dipped his head and touched Thunder's ear briefly with his nose. "Then we'll meet at dawn. You will be the first cat to mark the new territory boundary."

CHAPTER 24
❧

White mist curled through the trees, drenching the grass and under-growth and striking a chill across Thunder's pelt as he padded through the camp. Clear Sky was waiting for him at the edge of the clearing, his gaze distant, fixed on something only he could see.

A deeper cold invaded Thunder's body, as if all the blood in his veins were turning to ice. *What is my father planning?*

As Thunder reached his father's side, Clear Sky acknowl-edged his presence with a nod, but made no move to leave. Thunder sat silently beside him; embarrassment flooded over him and he shifted on his haunches as his belly rumbled with morning hunger.

A heartbeat later, a rustle in the long grass announced the arrival of Petal.

"Good," Clear Sky meowed. "Let's go."

He led the way out of the camp and through the trees, heading in the direction of the clearing with the four oak trees. *Will he try to include that in his territory?* Thunder wondered as they crossed the old boundary.

But Clear Sky halted at the edge of a stream, still far short of the four oaks, its banks edged with lush growth of ferns and brambles. "This will be our new boundary," he announced. "Thunder, you may have the honor of setting the first scent markers."

Thunder heard a derisive snort from Petal, as if she thought the honor should have been hers, but he forced himself not to react.

Relieved that for once his task didn't involve fighting, Thunder began working his way along the bank of the stream, setting the markers as he went. Soon he came to a large bramble thicket that grew so close to the water's edge, he had to circle around it and set the markers on the landward side.

Clear Sky let out a hiss of annoyance. "Can't you get any closer to the stream?" he asked.

Yes, if I want the thorns to tear my pelt off, Thunder thought, but didn't dare say so out loud. "Okay, I'll—" he began, only to break off as a gray-and-white she-cat leaped out of the thicket in front of him, her lips drawn back in a snarl.

"Get out of here, dungface!" she spat.

For a heartbeat Thunder stared at her, too taken aback by her aggressive stance to react at all.

"Well?" Clear Sky growled from behind him. "What are you waiting for? Do what you have to do."

Thunder crouched to spring, but in the same heartbeat the gray-and-white cat swiped him hard across the side of the head, throwing him off balance. His ears rang with the force of the blow as he scrabbled to regain his paws. A hot flash of humiliation passed through him.

"Leave this to me!" Petal snarled, diving past him. "I know this cat!" She flung herself on the gray-and-white she-cat, and the two of them rolled over together at the edge of the thicket, spitting and clawing at each other, paws and tails flailing. The forest echoed with their furious screeches.

Thunder managed to stand at last and gave his pelt a shake. He knew he should help Petal, but the two she-cats were locked so closely together that if he had tried to strike he would have risked injuring his denmate. He started to pad forward uncertainly, until a voice made him freeze.

"Don't," Clear Sky meowed. "This isn't your fight."

Thunder's father was watching the skirmish from a couple of tail-lengths away. He looked calm, as if he was used to seeing cats grappling together with such ferocity.

"Petal has a history with this cat," he explained after a moment. "Her name is Misty. When Petal and her brother were kits their mother died. They asked Misty for help, and she refused. Petal has never forgotten that."

"I can't blame her," Thunder murmured. *I might have been that kit, if it hadn't been for Gray Wing.*

Meanwhile Petal had managed to pin her opponent down. Misty writhed under her paws, her green eyes glaring in rage. Both cats were bleeding from scratches along their sides, and blood was trickling down Misty's muzzle.

"This is our territory now," Petal hissed. "Get out of here, and no cat will hurt you."

"No chance, mange-pelt!" Misty snarled. Heaving herself up, she threw Petal off and jumped on top of her. Her teeth snapped as they met in Petal's ear. Petal let out a shriek, lash-ing out with her hind paws, but she couldn't make contact.

"Fox dung!" Clear Sky bounded forward and flung himself into the battle, thrusting Misty aside so that she had to let go of Petal. Between them they pinned Misty down again, with Petal lying across her hindquarters. Clear Sky kept one paw clamped on her shoulder while the other was raised to strike at her throat.

"Give her a chance to leave!" Thunder gasped, before the killing blow could fall.

Clear Sky flicked him a glance. "She's *had* a chance. Will you leave quietly?" he asked Misty.

"Never!" the gray-and-white she-cat replied.

She surged upward, her teeth bared and the claws of her one free paw aimed at Clear Sky's face. But Clear Sky was faster. His claws tore at her throat and sank deeply through her pelt. Blood gushed out, bubbling as Misty tried to yowl a last few words. Then she fell back, limp, her blood spattering over the grass and brambles.

Clear Sky stepped back. "Stupid flea-pelt," he meowed. "If she hadn't been so stubborn, she wouldn't have had to die." In spite of his harsh words, he sounded as if he genuinely regret-ted the she-cat's death. He glanced at Petal, who had risen to her paws and was shaking bits of debris out of her fur. "You fought well," he told her with an approving flick of his tail. "Now she has finally paid for what she did to you and Fox."

Petal made no response except for a curt nod.

Thunder forced himself not to flinch as his father turned and padded up to him. *Does he think I'm a coward because I didn't join in the fight? I would have helped Petal if he hadn't stopped me!*

But to his surprise Clear Sky's eyes were shining as he spoke. "Congratulations. You showed compassion when Misty was defeated. That takes spirit—the spirit of a leader."

He padded around Thunder, inspecting him closely, making Thunder feel nervous rather than relieved that his father wasn't angry. "I see so much of me in you," Clear Sky mewed.

Thunder felt every hair on his pelt begin to rise with the tension. *Why does it feel like he's threatening me?*

"Gray Wing trained you well," Clear Sky continued, coming to stand in front of Thunder. "But I will make you a leader. You've shown promise today. Now, let's get on with marking the new boundary. Petal," he added, pointing with his tail, "you can go that way."

"Right." Petal bounded off upstream without a backward glance at her enemy's body.

As he padded over to the bramble thicket and started to look for a way down to the bank of the stream, Thunder struggled to feel pleased by his father's praise. *How many more cats will have to die before Clear Sky is satisfied?*

As he was wriggling through the outer tendrils of the thicket, he heard a faint squeaking that came from farther inside. *Mice*, he thought hopefully, his belly rumbling again to remind him that he hadn't eaten that morning. *Surely Clear Sky won't mind if we stop for a moment or two to hunt.*

Though Thunder tasted the air in an attempt to pinpoint his prey, everything was blotted out by the reek of Misty's blood. But he could still hear the squeaking, so he pushed his way through the brambles toward it.

A couple of heartbeats later he halted, his heart beginning to pound uncomfortably. Lying in a nest of bracken among the brambles, their tiny jaws gaping as they let out shrill cries, were two tiny kits. Their eyes were open, but Thunder could see that they were still very young.

So that's why Misty fought so fiercely! he thought. *And that's why she wouldn't leave. She was protecting her kits . . . and now we've killed their mother.*

Thunder cleared his throat. "Clear Sky!" he called. "You have to come and see this!"

There was a rustling beside him and a moment later Clear Sky pushed up beside him. "This had better be worth a peltful of thorns," he grumbled, "or I'll—" He broke off, staring. "Oh, mouse dung!" he mewed softly.

"What are we going to do?" Thunder asked. The pitiful cries of the kits were piercing his heart.

For a moment Clear Sky did not respond. Then he stepped forward, stooping over the kits. "We'd better get them out of here, at least," he meowed, picking up the closest kit by the scruff. She was a gray-and-white she-cat just like her mother, Misty, and she waved her paws frantically in the air as Clear Sky carried her off.

Thunder picked up the second kit—a ginger tom—and backed carefully out of the thicket, making sure that the thorns didn't snag in the little one's pelt.

When he emerged into the open, Clear Sky had already set the she-cat down and was gazing at her with a somber expression. Thunder put the little ginger tom down beside his littermate. The two kits huddled together on the grass, letting out shrill, frightened mews.

"We can't leave them here. They'll die," Thunder mewed, positioning himself between the kits and Misty, so that they wouldn't see their mother's body.

Before Clear Sky could reply, Petal came bounding up from setting scent markers farther upstream. "What have you got there?" she asked.

Clear Sky's only reply was a wave of his tail.

"Misty had kits!" Petal's voice was shocked. "So that's why she fought so hard," she added more thoughtfully. "She was brave . . ."

Thunder could see deep distress in Clear Sky's blue eyes. "They'll die without their mother," he mewed. "Perhaps we should kill them quickly so that they don't suffer."

"No!" Thunder let out a yowl of protest.

"Then what do you suggest?" Clear Sky asked. "There's no she-cat with milk that I know of."

Petal stepped forward, placing herself between the kits and Clear Sky. "I will look after them," she asserted.

Clear Sky stared at her. "But Misty was the cat who rejected you and Fox when you were kits."

"And now Misty is dead," Petal retorted. "These kits haven't done me any harm. I'll take care of them, because I know what it feels like to be a helpless kit with no cat to give me food or warmth or teach me how to live."

Thunder gazed wonderingly at the yellow tabby she-cat. He had always thought of Petal as harsh, hard-bitten perhaps because of her brother Fox's death. He would never have expected her to show so much compassion for the kits of her enemy.

"I'll help you," he blurted out. "I can hunt for you, while you look after the kits."

Petal dipped her head. "Thank you. You can help me now by carrying one of them back to camp." Stooping over the squirming, terrified kits, she murmured, "Don't be afraid, little ones. You shall soon have a warm nest and something to eat."

She picked up the little she-cat, her teeth meeting gently in her scruff, and headed for the camp without a backward glance at Clear Sky. Thunder hesitated, not knowing how his father would react.

But Clear Sky merely shrugged. "Go on," he meowed to Thunder. "Do as she says."

Thunder picked up the tiny ginger tom and followed Petal. As he brushed through the undergrowth, keeping the soft waving paws just clear of the grass, he couldn't rid his mind of the picture of Misty, lying dead with her blood pooling around her.

She didn't have to die, he thought sorrowfully. *Clear Sky doesn't need all this territory. If we hadn't come here, none of this would have happened. And would he really have killed these kits, if Petal hadn't offered to take them?*

Horror filled Thunder, a cold, creeping fungus, as he realized he didn't know the answer to that question.

CHAPTER 25

Gray Wing stretched luxuriously in his nest of moss and bracken, and finished the last mouthfuls of the portion of young hare Hawk Swoop had brought him. The sun was rising over the moor and he let the warm rays soak into his pelt. The sky was a pale, clear blue, with scarcely a wisp of cloud.

The cats are doing a fantastic job of pulling together while I'm ill, he thought. *And they're being so good to me . . . if only it didn't make me feel so useless.*

He spotted Lightning Tail dragging a rabbit across the camp toward him, and reflected on what a fine hunter the young cat was becoming. *But he can hardly manage the weight of his prey!*

Rising to his paws, Gray Wing padded over to Lightning Tail and helped him carry the rabbit into the center of the camp, where most of the cats were gathering around prey brought in by Rainswept Flower and Shattered Ice. All of them drew back to let him eat first.

"No, go ahead," Gray Wing meowed, gesturing toward the rabbit with his tail. "I've already eaten."

The portion of hare was all he could manage; his appetite

still hadn't returned, although it had been several days since the badger attack.

As Acorn Fur wriggled into the group beside her brother and the rest of the cats tucked in, Gray Wing noticed that Turtle Tail was watching him from the other side of the camp. He had never seen her so angry or upset as when he came back to the camp with Owl Eyes. *She said I wasn't fit to lead, and she was right.* She was only now beginning to soften toward him again.

Fresh misery pulsed through Gray Wing. *I never meant to make Turtle Tail unhappy!* Then he gave his pelt a shake, forcing himself to be more hopeful. His breathing had been much better since he had been forced to rest. *Soon I'll be chasing mice again! And I know Turtle Tail was only angry because she cares about me.*

As he let his gaze rest on Turtle Tail, Gray Wing felt a small paw prodding him in the side. He looked down to see Pebble Heart standing beside him, his eyes wide and troubled.

"What's the matter?" Gray Wing asked him.

The kit pressed against his side; Gray Wing could feel him shivering. "I had another dream," he whispered.

"What kind of dream?" Gray Wing let his tail rest gently over Pebble Heart's shoulders. "Was it the fight again, or the long, dark tunnel?"

Pebble Heart shook his head. "No, worse than that. There's something bad at the edge of the forest . . . something very bad. I think some cat ought to go and look."

Puzzled, Gray Wing studied his son. The kit obviously believed every word he was saying, but Gray Wing wasn't sure he could ask cats to go and investigate, so close to Clear Sky's territory, on the basis of a kit's dream.

"Did you see anything—?" he began, only to break off as Wind Runner raced over the top of the hollow, with Gorse Fur at her shoulder. She bounded down into the hollow and scrambled up to the tall rock. The other cats slowly gathered around her. Jagged Peak was gazing at her with hero-worship in his eyes. Ever since Owl Eyes had run off, Jagged Peak had kept his distance from the kits. As Gray Wing watched, Tall Shadow padded over and sat beside him, neatly curling her tail over her forepaws. Pebble Heart drew back a pace, to let the two senior cats talk in private.

Wind Runner's voice suddenly rang out over the camp. "Can all cats gather around the tall rock for a meeting!"

Gray Wing felt a twinge of anxiety in his pads. *Since when has Wind Runner called meetings, instead of me or Tall Shadow? And since when did all the cats obey her like this?*

Lightning Tail and Acorn Fur bounded eagerly across the camp; Hawk Swoop and Jackdaw's Cry were close behind them and sat next to the kits. Shattered Ice hesitated as if he was wondering whether to answer the summons, then stalked forward to join Cloud Spots and Dappled Pelt.

Gray Wing slowly followed. He was painfully aware of the other cats waiting for him to arrive and settle down, but his legs still felt shaky and he couldn't go any faster.

Jagged Peak was sitting at the base of the rock. Turtle Tail was close to him, and Gray Wing noticed that she was giving Wind Runner a long, hard stare.

Oh, no! Turtle Tail, please don't cause a scene. I know Wind Runner is pushy, but she looks as if she has something important to say.

As Gray Wing reached the group of cats, Wind Runner gave her pelt a shake as if she was saying, *At last! Now we can get on.*

Gray Wing noticed that some of the cats were glancing uncertainly from him to Tall Shadow and then to Wind Runner, as if they weren't sure which cat was in charge. Rainswept Flower and Cloud Spots looked particularly unhappy. Tall Shadow glanced away, refusing to meet their gaze.

Okay, Gray Wing thought. *If she's not going to assert herself, then I will. Thanks so much, Tall Shadow.*

"Thank you for gathering us, Wind Runner," he meowed. "What news?"

He hoped that he sounded more confident than he felt. *I never asked to become leader,* he thought. *But now that Wind Runner is pushing herself to the top . . .* Gray Wing realized with a jolt that he didn't want to let go of all he'd achieved. *No rogue cat is going to come in and usurp me!* Gray Wing hadn't joined the cats' journey out of the mountains just to lie down and let another cat stomp heavy-pawed over everything he'd done.

Wind Runner dipped her head respectfully to him. "Hunting has become more and more difficult," she replied. "As you know, Clear Sky is defending his territory fiercely and is using guards. I crossed over into Clear Sky's territory, and I was challenged by his cats. When I told them I'd been here far longer than any of them, I was viciously attacked. Look at this!"

She held up one forepaw and Gray Wing saw that part of her fur had been ripped off. Gasps of shock rose from the other cats at the sight of it.

"Who did that to you?" Jagged Peak demanded, his pelt bristling. "Who?"

"Frost, one of Clear Sky's guards," Wind Runner answered. "I had to escape down a hole, as if I were a rabbit! But there's more. . . ." She hesitated, looking at Gray Wing.

"Go on," Gray Wing responded, feeling his pads prickle with apprehension. "Tell us everything."

"Well . . ." Wind Runner still seemed reluctant, glancing nervously around the group while her claws scraped the surface of the rock. "Thunder was in the group of guards, along with Petal. He stood back and watched while Frost attacked me."

"No, not Thunder!" Hawk Swoop gasped.

"This is bad," Tall Shadow murmured.

Turtle Tail was staring right at Gray Wing. He felt himself stagger to one side and then sink to the ground, his vision blurring for a heartbeat. *Thunder . . . the kit I brought up as my own son . . . he's become one of them. . . .*

Gray Wing remembered his fight with Fox, the fight that had finally torn Gray Wing and Clear Sky apart. He regretted killing Fox, but he still believed he had been given no choice when the huge tom attacked him. He felt as if all the blood in his veins had turned to ice when he thought of Thunder becoming such a cat. *But what choice would he have, now that he's joined Clear Sky?*

Gray Wing glanced around and realized that all his den-mates were looking at him, waiting to hear what he would say. Only Turtle Tail turned toward Wind Runner.

"Are you sure?" she asked. "It's so hard to believe that Thunder—"

"If you don't believe me," Wind Runner interrupted, "perhaps you'd like to see where Gorse Fur and I buried Misty."

"Who's Misty?" Jackdaw's Cry asked.

Gray Wing felt his apprehension growing at the mention of another dead cat, but he made himself keep quiet and let Wind Runner tell her story.

"Misty was a rogue, a gray-and-white she-cat," Wind Runner began. "She lived mostly at the edge of the forest. Gorse Fur and I found her body. She had terrible wounds along her sides and across her belly, and there was blood everywhere. Clear Sky's scent marks were there, too, and Thunder's."

"He's expanded his territory yet again," Gorse Fur added, raising his voice to make himself heard above the horrified exclamations from the other cats. "And this time he had to kill a cat to do it."

Screeches of outrage and distress rose from the other cats. Jackdaw's Cry and Shattered Ice leaped to their paws and began to pad around, quickly joined by Rainswept Flower and Dappled Pelt. Shocked and appalled, the cats huddled together in small groups. The meeting was beginning to break up in disorder.

"Wait—there's more!" Wind Runner yowled, raising her tail for silence. "Misty had two kits. Gorse Fur and I searched all around Misty's nest, but we couldn't find them. They were gone. Either Clear Sky killed them, too, or they wandered off when their mother was killed. And they were far too young to survive alone. Don't you see," she went on, her voice tight with fury. "Clear Sky is extending his territory, and he doesn't care what he does to make it happen. If we don't act fast, we'll lose everything we ever had! We can't trust any cat—not even Thunder."

Everything we *ever had?* Wind Runner's words jolted Gray Wing. *Since when did Wind Runner help us escape from the mountains or set up this camp?* He sat in stunned silence as exclamations of pity and outrage erupted all around him.

"Killing kits—that's the worst he's ever done!" Turtle Tail exclaimed.

"And what are *we* going to do?" Shattered Ice asked.

Desperately trying to shut out the sounds of panic and rage, Gray Wing turned to Pebble Heart, who had followed him to the rock and was crouching close to his side again. "Is this the bad thing in your dream?" he asked.

Pebble Heart's eyes were filled with horror at what he had heard, but he looked puzzled, too. "No . . . ," he responded. "I'm not sure, but I don't think the bad thing has happened yet."

Gray Wing shook his head in confusion. He wanted to believe the kit, but he couldn't imagine what Pebble Heart's dream might have meant if it wasn't about the death of the she-cat and her kits. *Another bad thing in the forest . . . where will it all end?*

While Gray Wing had been talking to Pebble Heart the

caterwauling had died away. Jackdaw's Cry's voice rang out strongly. "We need a leader!"

Gray Wing looked up to realize that the cats were all focused on Wind Runner, who was still standing on top of the rock. Even Tall Shadow was glancing uncertainly from Gray Wing to the brown she-cat.

Gray Wing wasn't sure what to do. He was acutely aware that he still hadn't recovered completely from his illness. And Tall Shadow was staying on the outskirts of the group, clearly unwilling to take the leadership again.

But do we really want Wind Runner as our leader? A cat who was a rogue until a few sunrises ago?

He cleared his throat. "Tall Shadow, what do you—" he began.

Wind Runner interrupted him, speaking to all the cats who were gathered around her. She wasn't even looking at Gray Wing. "I suggest taking a patrol to talk to Clear Sky," she meowed. "We need to find out what happened to those kits."

Yowls of agreement came from the surrounding cats.

"If he killed them I'll rip his pelt off!" Shattered Ice threatened, digging his claws into the ground.

"I'll help you," Jackdaw's Cry agreed.

Gray Wing knew that he had to take control. "Good idea, Wind Runner," he mewed, rising to his paws. "Will you and Gorse Fur come with me? And I'll take Turtle Tail and Cloud Spots too." Turning to Shattered Ice and Jackdaw's Cry, he added, "Not you two. There'll be no pelt ripping until we find out exactly what's going on."

"We *know* what's going on," Shattered Ice growled, but to Gray Wing's relief neither he nor Jackdaw's Cry challenged his decision.

Good. You insisted on making me leader, so let me lead.

Gray Wing bent his head to speak quietly to Pebble Heart. "I'll keep an eye out for the bad thing. Now find your brother and sister, and don't worry."

"I'll look after them," Rainswept Flower meowed, sweeping her tail around Pebble Heart and leading him away. "Good luck, Gray Wing."

Turtle Tail followed for a few paces. "Good-bye, kits," she mewed, touching each one on the head with her nose. "Behave yourselves for Rainswept Flower. I'll be back soon." Then she turned and hurried back to Gray Wing.

Gray Wing glanced around at the cats in his patrol; they were all pressing closely around him, their eyes eager. "Right," he snapped. "Let's go."

CHAPTER 26

❧

The sun was rising higher as Gray Wing led his cats across the moor. Ahead of them, the forest was a rustling green wall; the breeze carried scents of heavy green growth and prey.

Once he got going, setting the pace at a steady lope, Gray Wing found that his breathing was easy and he didn't have any pain in his chest. "Maybe I'm really over this at last," he mewed to Turtle Tail.

His mate twitched her ears. "Let's hope so. But don't you *dare* hide it from me again."

Gray Wing was leading his patrol toward the edge of the forest nearest to Clear Sky's camp. As they drew closer, his senses were alert for anything that might explain Pebble Heart's dream. *I trust him*, he realized. *Pebble Heart is going to be an extraordinary cat.*

They passed the first of the outlying trees, and plunged into the undergrowth. As lush ferns brushed against his pelt, Gray Wing was watching for any sign of Clear Sky's guards. But nothing halted their progress until an eerie shriek rose up in front of them, splitting the peaceful morning air.

"That was a cat!" Turtle Tail gasped.

"This way!" Wind Runner took the lead, racing toward the sound.

The shriek wasn't repeated, but as he bounded after Wind Runner, Gray Wing could hear the faint noises of a cat in pain. He began to pick up the scent of fox. *Is this Pebble Heart's bad thing?* he asked himself. Fear of what he was going to find throbbed within his heart.

Wind Runner led the way between two oak trees and vanished into a clump of ferns. As the patrol burst through after her, Gray Wing found himself in a small clearing. In the middle of a circle of trampled grass, a skinny tortoise-shell cat lay splayed out, blood trickling from wounds all over her body.

"Bumble!" Turtle Tail exclaimed. "Oh, no!"

Outstripping Wind Runner and Gray Wing, Turtle Tail raced across the clearing and flung herself down beside her friend. "Bumble, we're here now," she mewed, pressing her nose against Bumble's shoulder. "We'll help you."

Gray Wing and the others padded across to stand beside the injured cat. The reek of fox was overwhelming now, drowning all other scents.

Bumble's eyes were half closed and her breath came in shallow pants. Her glazed eyes were fixed on Turtle Tail.

Cloud Spots pushed forward and began to examine Bumble's wounds. Gray Wing could see that there were slits down her belly and sides that were slowly leaking blood. Though he didn't have Cloud Spots's skills, Gray Wing guessed that none of the wounds alone would have killed her, but there were so many, and she was losing so much blood, that it was clear she was dying.

Cloud Spots looked up at him and gave a tiny shake of his head, confirming what Gray Wing already knew. "There's nothing I can do," he murmured. "This is beyond the power of any healing herbs."

Turtle Tail shot him a grief-stricken look, and began licking at her friend's wounds with a soothing murmur as if she were tending to her kits.

Gray Wing bent his head close to Bumble's. "Who did this to you?" he asked. "Was it a fox?"

Bumble opened her jaws to reply, but she was so weak that only a faint sigh came out.

"I'm picking up another scent here," Cloud Spots muttered. "Another cat . . ."

Gray Wing tasted the air carefully, trying to distinguish other scents beyond the stink of fox. At once he realized that Cloud Spots was right. Horror and disbelief broke over him like an avalanche of snow as he recognized the cat scent that clung to Bumble's fur.

"Clear Sky!" he gasped. *Yes! This is Pebble Heart's bad thing, no question.*

Cloud Spots's eyes widened and he took another sniff. "You're right," he mewed. "I know you're right, and I still can't believe it."

"I can," Wind Runner responded grimly. She began to sniff around the circle of trampled grass. "It looks as if there was a fight here."

"So Clear Sky did this to Bumble." There was a sick look in Gorse Fur's eyes. "She's just a poor, pathetic kittypet. What could she have done to deserve this?"

"Maybe he didn't," Gray Wing protested, desperate to believe that his brother could be innocent. "There's all this fox scent—"

"Don't try to defend him!" Turtle Tail interrupted, springing to her paws. "Which cat has been determined to expand his territory, never mind who gets hurt? Clear Sky! And now he's attacked poor Bumble." Her voice choked and she crouched beside her friend again.

Bumble opened her jaws again and this time managed to speak, her voice a faint tendril of sound. "This was my fault. I was so hungry . . . I couldn't think straight. It was stupid. I should never have hunted here. . . ." Her voice grew shaky, blood pumping from her wounds. "The cat was only—"

"I was only warning her," a new incisive voice interrupted.

Gray Wing spun around to see a cat half hidden among the leaves of a tree at the edge of the clearing. He narrowed his eyes, trying to make out who it was. Then he stiffened as Clear Sky jumped down and paced forward toward the other cats, his eyes glaring a challenge to attack.

Even with Bumble dying beside him, Gray Wing couldn't help admiring his brother's bravery. *What other cat would leap into the midst of a hostile group?*

Gray Wing was acutely aware of the other cats around him, all of them waiting for him to take control. "Do you know anything about this, Clear Sky?" he demanded, his voice cracking as he forced out the words. "Did you injure Bumble? Or do you know who did?"

"And what about Misty's kits?" Wind Runner snarled with a lash of her tail. "Did you kill them?"

Clear Sky was prowling around the group, his gaze shifting from cat to cat. His eyes showed mingling guilt and horror as he looked at Bumble. When Gray Wing thought that he would have to let out a screech to break the tense silence, his brother finally spoke.

"Hello to you too." He paused and gave Gray Wing a long, hard look. Gray Wing felt as though his belly was shrinking under his brother's gaze—a gaze that seemed to accuse him of betrayal.

"Petal is caring for Misty's kits," Clear Sky went on. "They're fine. As for this cat . . ." He angled his ears toward the dying Bumble. "What do you think?" He looked around the group, and now it was impossible to read his expression. "Do you believe I'm capable of this?"

Gray Wing's denmates all eyed one another nervously, as if none of them wanted to be the first to answer.

Taking a deep breath, Gray Wing drew himself up. "No," he meowed. "I don't believe it."

Hisses of outrage came from Wind Runner and Gorse Fur.

Gray Wing felt movement beside him and saw that Turtle Tail had stepped up to his shoulder.

"I do," she growled, all her neck fur fluffed up. "I believe you could do this. Since I returned to the moor, I've heard nothing but horrible stories about the way you treat other cats. You're power-mad, Clear Sky. You don't care who you hurt to get what you want. And now . . . you're not the cat I came down from the mountains with. You're . . ." She switched her tail to and fro. "You're an *apology* for a cat."

The group exploded into yowls of agreement, pacing back and forth with their claws extended and their shoulder fur bristling, as if all their anger and hurt had to burst out somehow.

Wind Runner glared at Gray Wing. "Well, *leader?* What do we do now?"

Every muscle in Gray Wing's body tensed with anxiety. *If I let them know with one twitch of a whisker that I doubt Clear Sky, they'll attack. He'll be torn apart. But he's my brother! And if we do that, we're no better than he is. The life we've tried to build will be over.*

He stepped forward between Clear Sky and his own cats, not sure which of them he was trying to protect. "Get out of here, Clear Sky," he ordered.

Clear Sky's eyes widened. "Then you believe I'm innocent?"

His words gave Gray Wing a tiny chink of hope. "If you didn't harm Bumble, who did?" he asked. *If only Clear Sky can explain . . .*

"This kittypet was hunting here, in the new part of my

territory," Clear Sky began, speaking more quickly now, as if he was glad of the chance to tell the others what happened.

Gray Wing heard a low growl from Wind Runner, but to his relief she didn't interrupt. *This is no time to start arguing about boundaries!*

"I wanted to give her a warning," Clear Sky went on. "Nothing too painful, just a little cuff around her kittypet ear. How was I to know she was so weak from hunger that she would faint? But I could see her paws twitching, and I knew she would come around soon. So I left her and headed back to camp." He paused, wincing. "Then I heard a fox bark, and I ran back. But I was too late. I was going to get help when I heard you all arrive."

"Liar!" Turtle Tail spat out the word, shouldering Gray Wing out of the way to confront Clear Sky. Her back was arched and her pelt bristling with fury.

Clear Sky faced her, his lips drawn back in a snarl. "I won't be spoken to like that!" For a moment he locked his gaze with Gray Wing's, silently challenging him to speak in his defense.

What can I say? Gray Wing asked himself, staring at the furious cats. *I'll only make things worse.*

When Gray Wing didn't speak, Clear Sky gave a final flick of his tail and stalked off. "I see where I stand now," he meowed as he went.

Gray Wing watched his brother leave. He wanted to call after Clear Sky, but he could feel the hostility from the other cats in his group. *If I don't let him leave now, there will be a fight.*

Turtle Tail turned away, her tail drooping, as Clear Sky vanished into the ferns. She crouched beside Bumble, avoiding the spreading pool of blood, and began licking her head gently. "I'm here," she murmured between licks. "I won't leave you."

Bumble fixed her eyes on Turtle Tail's face. "I'm sorry if I ever hurt you," she whispered.

"I wish you could have found happiness," Turtle Tail replied, her voice quivering. "I know you could never have lived wild with us in the hollow, but I was so unhappy to learn how much you were suffering in the Twolegplace."

Bumble's eyes closed while Turtle Tail was speaking. Her breath wheezed and her face twisted with pain. Her body jerked once or twice as her breathing grew shallower still, fading with each heartbeat until her chest stopped moving.

"She's dead," Cloud Spots mewed.

Even though Gray Wing had never especially liked Bumble, he felt as though his heart would crack with sorrow. *This isn't just the death of a kittypet. It changes the way my cats think of Clear Sky, and that changes everything.*

As he gazed, stunned, at his denmates, the most mournful sound Gray Wing had ever heard rose up into the air. It was the wail of Turtle Tail, grieving for her dead friend.

"Clear Sky told us that a fox must have killed Bumble. There was certainly fox scent all over the clearing."

Gray Wing stood on the tall rock at the end of the hollow, with his cats gathered around him. He was coming to the end of the story of what the patrol had found when they went to the forest.

"And do you believe him?" Rainswept Flower asked.

"I don't know what to believe," Gray Wing confessed. "But I do know that starting a fight with Clear Sky wouldn't help any cat."

"So what did you do then?" Jackdaw's Cry asked.

"We buried Bumble and came home."

Jackdaw's Cry let out a hiss of anger, his claws raking the grass. "You mean you let him get away with it? That's flea-brained!"

"That's what I told him." Wind Runner looked just as furious, her tail lashing. "Clear Sky will just think we're *weak*! Is that what we want?"

"No!" Jagged Peak yowled; Shattered Ice and Jackdaw's Cry echoed him.

"Now, wait a moment." Tall Shadow rose to her paws and padded into the middle of the group. "What would be *really* flea-brained would be to attack Clear Sky when we're all worked up about Bumble's death. After all, she was only a kittypet."

"She was my friend!" Turtle Tail flashed.

"I know." Tall Shadow's voice was calm. "All I'm saying is, we need time to think."

"And suppose Clear Sky won't give us time?" Wind Runner challenged her.

Gray Wing realized he would have to intervene. He was relieved that Tall Shadow was recovering some of her old leadership skills, and she deserved his support.

"Tall Shadow is right," he meowed. "We'll wait, and starting tomorrow we will send out extra patrols toward the forest, so that we can keep an eye on Clear Sky." He locked glances with Wind Runner, half expecting her to argue, but after a moment's pause she gave him a reluctant nod.

Gray Wing was glad to see that the other cats were calming down too. He leaped from the rock and padded over to Tall Shadow. "Thank you for that," he mewed. "You said exactly the right thing."

Tall Shadow dipped her head. "Should we talk about this?" she suggested.

With a murmur of agreement Gray Wing led the way to the shelter of a gorse bush. The sun had set over the moor, but the sky was still streaked with scarlet. Some cats had obviously been out hunting while Gray Wing's patrol had been away, and a pile of prey lay at the bottom of the hollow. Most of the others gathered around to start eating, while Wind Runner leaped up onto the rock to keep watch, and Turtle Tail headed to her den to see her kits.

"Tall Shadow, what do you think we should do now?" Gray Wing asked.

The black she-cat thought for a moment. Gray Wing noticed that she was looking more energized, more like the leader she had once been. *She doesn't have to worry about Moon*

Shadow any longer, and she knows as well as any cat that we have to deal with Clear Sky.

"Do you want to take over as leader again?" he asked.

Tall Shadow shook her head. "I'm happy to share responsibility with you, Gray Wing," she replied. Her mouth twisting wryly, she added, "I don't even mind much that Wind Runner has started organizing us all. She's a valuable cat, and once all this is over I think we should welcome her and Gorse Fur formally into our group."

"Good idea," Gray Wing meowed, pleased that Tall Shadow was losing some of her caution around other cats. *Working together is the best way forward.* "We need every cat on our side."

"As to what we do now," Tall Shadow went on, "some cat has to stop Clear Sky, before more damage is done."

Gray Wing nodded. "You're right, but it won't be easy."

Tall Shadow gave one forepaw a thoughtful lick and drew it over her ear. "Let me think about it," she meowed.

Fighting off a sense of foreboding, Gray Wing padded down to the prey, chose part of a hare, and carried it up to Turtle Tail's den to share with her and the kits.

Turtle Tail was sitting at the entrance to the tunnel, her paws tucked neatly underneath her. The kits were sleeping behind her in a heap of fur.

"Are they okay?" Gray Wing asked as he set the prey down in front of her.

Turtle Tail sighed. "I think they are now. But they were upset when I had to tell them that Bumble is dead. Pebble

Heart in particular took a long time to drift off."

Gray Wing glanced at his mate, faintly surprised at the note of accusation in her voice.

"I didn't make any of this happen," he mewed. "We could never have accepted Bumble into our group. She wouldn't have been able to cope."

Turtle Tail's shoulders sagged. "I know," she murmured, her voice so full of grief that she could hardly get the words out. "I believe in you, Gray Wing. I know this isn't your fault. It just broke my heart to see her lying there, bleeding. I wish things could have been different."

Gray Wing pressed himself close to her side and covered her ears with comforting licks. "I'm sorry you're hurting, Turtle Tail," he murmured. "You and the kits are the most important things in my life. I never dared hope for such happiness . . . ," he mewed. "After the fire, I wondered if I could carry on as leader, but you made me rest, and now I'm ready to lead again—with Tall Shadow, if that's what she wants."

"But how will you lead?" Turtle Tail asked, looking up and gazing into his eyes. "Innocent cats are being slaughtered— and for what? So Clear Sky and his cats can have enough to eat?"

"No," Gray Wing replied. "I'm not sure that Clear Sky killed Bumble. I think it was the fox, and besides, I don't believe this is about hunting anymore. Clear Sky already has more territory than any cat could possibly want. I think he has some kind of plan. I have no idea what it is, but in part of his mind, Clear Sky honestly thinks he's doing this for a good reason." He let out a long sigh. "Some cat has to get to the bottom of it all somehow."

"And that cat has to be you?" Turtle Tail asked.

Gray Wing blinked at her. "What other cat is there?"

CHAPTER 27

Thunder ducked underneath a low-growing elder branch and headed into the clearing, a mouse dangling from his jaws.

Skirting the pool in the middle of the camp, he padded to Petal, who had made a new nest for herself and Misty's kits underneath an arching clump of ferns. The kits had survived for the three days since their mother's death, and Thunder was hopeful that they would grow up into healthy cats.

"There you go," he mewed, dropping the mouse in front of Petal.

"Thanks, Thunder," Petal responded, dipping her head gratefully. "My belly's so empty, they can probably hear it rumbling on the moors."

Thunder saw that she had chewed up some squirrel into a mush, and was encouraging the kits to lap it up. The little she-cat turned her head away and pressed herself against Petal's belly, rooting for milk.

"No, little one," Petal murmured gently, guiding the kit back to the squirrel mush with one paw. "This is what you need to eat now that you're getting bigger."

"Big kit now," the tiny she-cat agreed, sniffing at the squirrel mush and then starting to suck it down.

Thunder was amazed to see the kind and loving look in Petal's eyes as she gazed down at the kits. *Petal—the toughest she-cat you could wish to meet!* "Have you given them names yet?" he asked.

"Yes," Petal replied. "The little tom is Birch and the she-cat is Alder."

"Those are good names," Thunder mewed.

Most of Clear Sky's other cats were lazing in the clearing, enjoying the after-sunhigh warmth. Quick Water was curled up drowsing in a patch of sunlight, while Falling Feather was giving her white pelt a thorough wash. Frost was licking the wound that he had gotten in the fire; it still refused to heal.

Everything's peaceful now, Thunder told himself. *Maybe Clear Sky will be satisfied with this new territory.*

But he couldn't convince himself that was true. Clear Sky was the only restless cat in the camp, pacing backward and forward and occasionally stopping to stare into the trees, though Thunder had no idea what he was staring at. *He's been weird ever since he got back yesterday . . . reeking of blood and fox. Something happened that he's not telling any cat.*

Thunder headed for his nest, but before he reached it he was intercepted by Fircone and Nettle, two young rogues who had joined Clear Sky's group a half-moon before.

"Did you want something?" Thunder asked.

"There's something we have to say . . . ," Fircone began, in a low voice and with a furtive glance at Clear Sky to make sure the leader wasn't within earshot. "Can we find somewhere that's a bit more private?"

"Private?" Uneasiness stabbed at Thunder like a thorn. "Why does it have to be private?"

"Just come over here and we'll tell you," Nettle mewed nervously, beckoning Thunder to a sheltered spot beneath the roots of a fallen tree.

Thunder hesitated, then followed the two toms. *If something's going on, it's best if I know what it is.*

"It's like this," Fircone went on when all three cats were settled among the roots. "When we came to join your group, we weren't really sure what we were getting into. And we're not sure we like it."

Thunder wondered what they expected him to do. "You don't *have* to stay," he pointed out.

"Mostly it's good here," Nettle mewed. "We like having the support of a group. But some of this stuff . . . chasing cats off—"

"Killing cats," Fircone added. "We thought—"

He broke off as Leaf padded past, heading for his nest with a bundle of fresh ferns in his jaws. He halted, giving the three cats a curious glance.

"Clear off, we're not talking to you," Nettle snarled.

Leaf let the ferns drop. "Are you looking for a clawed ear?" he demanded, beginning to bristle.

"Sorry, Leaf," Thunder meowed hastily. "They're okay, they

just don't know how to behave in a group yet."

"They won't get the chance to learn if they don't shape up," Leaf snapped, picking up his bedding and padding off with a final glare at Nettle.

"That really wasn't a good idea, antagonizing the older cats," Thunder muttered. "Anyway, what do you expect me to do about the way Clear Sky runs his group? I don't enjoy the way things are, any more than you do."

"We wondered if you would have a talk with your father," Nettle suggested. "If he realized that his cats aren't happy . . ."

"We're worried about where all this is leading," Fircone added. "Soon, Clear Sky won't listen to what anyone has to say, and we won't have any choice about what he asks us to do."

"And he might ask us to do *anything*," Nettle finished.

Thunder couldn't help thinking that the young cats were optimistic if they thought that a talk from him would turn Clear Sky aside from anything he wanted.

"I suppose you have a point," he sighed. "I'll see what I can do."

Thunder could feel his belly shaking with apprehension as he realized what he was getting into. *I might be the one with a clawed ear—or worse!* Reluctantly he snagged a piece of rabbit from the prey the hunting patrols had brought in, and carried it over to Clear Sky.

"What can I do for you?" Clear Sky asked, not looking at him.

"I wanted you to have this." Thunder set down the rabbit at

his father's paws. "You haven't eaten today."

"I'll eat when I'm ready. I'm not hungry now." Clear Sky turned an intense blue gaze on Thunder. "I saw you talking to those young rogues. Why have they sent you over here?"

Thunder hesitated, clearing his throat. *So much for being private* . . . He realized that other cats were looking interested, too, beginning to edge closer to hear the conversation. Frost in particular was watching with ears pricked, and Falling Feather had halted her grooming with one paw in the air.

"Nothing really . . . ," Thunder began, trying not to cringe under his father's scrutiny. "We were just saying how green the forest was looking. When I was out hunting just now I saw that green shoots are springing up in the places the fire damaged. Soon no cat will know that there was a fire here. And have you seen the number of bugs and small prey that are returning? There isn't any reason for a cat to go hungry at all. No reason to extend our territory any farther, don't you think . . . ?"

His voice trailed off as Clear Sky narrowed his eyes, then glanced around at the other cats. Frost stiffened as that blue gaze flicked over him. Thunder realized that most of them were listening, thoroughly awake now; Nettle and Fircone had hopeful expressions on their faces.

"Does Thunder speak for all of you?" Clear Sky asked. "Is this what you think too—that what we're doing here is a waste of time?"

Silence fell as the other cats glanced at each other but

didn't reply. *Am I the only one brave enough to say all this?* Thunder thought in frustration. He didn't know whether to think that the other cats had betrayed him, or to feel a thrill of exhilaration.

"Can't we agree to look after what we have?" Thunder plunged on. "Can't we forget about expanding our territory?"

Clear Sky took a pace forward to loom over Thunder. "It's too late to stop what's begun," he meowed. Thunder thought that he could make out a flicker of regret in his father's face. "Tell me, this forest fire . . . ," Clear Sky went on. "If it meant so little, why are there places where the land is still scarred? I've seen patches of earth where no grass has returned, and pools still choked with ash. No cat could drink that water."

"But they won't always be like that," Thunder protested. "There's fresh growth too—we've all seen it." Looking at his father's implacable expression, he began to wonder if he should have started this conversation. But it was too late now, and he realized he meant every single word. *I'm not just saying this because some other cats asked me to.* Thunder had felt the same himself for a long time, and it hadn't helped when his father had returned broody and mysterious after his solitary walk. *Whatever's started, it has to stop. For the camp, for Clear Sky—and for myself. I didn't leave Gray Wing to live in fear. I'm sure this can't be what my father truly wants.* "I'm only trying to help," he continued. "I just thought—"

Clear Sky silenced him with a wave of his tail. "Frost, come here," he mewed.

The big white tom looked up from where he was still licking his wound, then rose to his paws and limped painfully to Clear Sky's side. Thunder thought that he was moving more slowly than the last time they had been on patrol together.

"Show every cat your injury," Clear Sky ordered.

Frost's eyes widened in surprise. Clearly reluctant, he turned so that he was exposing his injured leg to the gaze of his denmates. The fur hadn't grown back over the wound, and the exposed flesh was red around a weeping sore.

"This is an injury from the forest fire," Clear Sky proclaimed in a loud voice. "An injury that has not healed."

Frost lowered his head in shame.

"It's not Frost's fault that he was burned in the fire," Thunder meowed.

"No." Clear Sky spun around to glare at him. "But see how the forest fire really damaged us? Now one of our group puts us all in danger. Frost can't carry out his patrols properly."

Thunder had never liked the way Frost behaved, but he couldn't bear to see the white tom humiliated like this.

"Frost *has* been hunting and patrolling," he protested, his pelt prickling with apprehension as he contradicted his leader. "He still contributes to our group. And his wound just needs care to get better. Isn't that right?" He looked around at the other cats, waiting for one of them to come out in support of Frost, but they all stared hard at the ground or busied themselves with grooming. *Cowards!* Thunder thought.

As he was looking around, Thunder felt a sudden shove in

his back. It was Clear Sky, forcing him down to the ground so that his nose was less than a mouse-length from the wound on Frost's leg. The scent of rotting flesh flooded over him, and bile rose in his throat. Some of the cats mewed with anxiety, but still they did nothing.

"If you care so much, why don't you lick his wound clean?" Clear Sky asked.

I won't be treated like this!

Wriggling free, Thunder turned to face his father. "What has happened to you?" he demanded. "Why don't you care about Frost anymore? You always say that you're acting in the best interests of *all* of us."

"That's right." To Thunder's surprise, Quick Water rose to her paws and faced Clear Sky. Finally one of the other cats was standing up to have their voice heard! Quick Water had known Clear Sky all his life. *If any cat can reason with my father, it's her.* "What are you doing?" she asked in a quiet, certain voice. "You're our leader, not our tormentor. Think of Quiet Rain— would she want to see this?"

"Leave my mother out of it," Clear Sky snarled.

Quick Water ignored his interruption. "Is this why she wished you good luck when we left the mountains?" she asked.

Instead of exploding into anger, Clear Sky took a deep breath, letting his gaze travel over all his cats. "I owe you all an apology," he mewed, stepping back. "Clearly you don't understand what I'm trying to do. I should have explained it better." Turning to Thunder and Frost, he continued, "Frost must leave us. It's time for him to go, before he spreads disease among us. This is for the greater good."

Frost's jaws opened in a gasp of shock, as he gazed incredulously at Clear Sky.

"Thunder, I want you to escort him to the boundary and leave him . . ." Clear Sky seemed to hesitate, then plunged on. "Leave him where the maggots will find him. Do you understand?"

Thunder felt his neck fur beginning to bristle. *I want no part of this.* "No, I'm not sure I do understand," he replied, letting a trace of anger creep into his tone. "Where the maggots will find him? Are you asking me to abandon Frost somewhere to die alone, with no cat to take care of him?"

Clear Sky didn't respond, but from the icy look in his blue eyes Thunder realized that was exactly what he was asking.

"No!" Frost wailed as he took in for the first time what his leader meant to do to him. "Please, Clear Sky, don't send me away! I can still hunt—I caught a vole yesterday. And I've done all my patrols. I'll die out there! Please give me another chance."

Thunder watched, appalled as this once-proud cat begged his leader for his life. *This* can't *be what it means to belong to a group of cats.* Once Frost had roamed free as a rogue cat; perhaps it would have been better for him to have stayed like that. *Perhaps it would be better for me.*

Thunder's thoughts winged back to Gray Wing and Hawk Swoop. Why had he ever left them? *But I could never go back and ask to join them again, not after everything that's happened . . . or could I?*

When Thunder imagined telling Gray Wing about how he had stood by when Wind Runner was chased off, and when Misty was killed, he knew that he would never be able to stand the disappointment in the older cat's eyes.

I've let every cat down—including myself. But no more. It ends here.

Thunder leaped up onto a tree stump, his gaze raking across the cats in the clearing.

"What are you doing?" Clear Sky hissed.

"Yes, get down, you stupid furball," Quick Water meowed.

What? Thunder gaped at the she-cat. *I thought you were on my side!*

"I won't do this," he announced, recovering himself quickly. "I won't lead Frost to his death. I can't help any of you, but I can help myself and Frost." He suddenly understood what he had to do. "We're leaving. And neither of us is coming back."

Yowls of protest or agreement rose from the cats who surrounded them, and furious arguments broke out. Not bothering to listen, Thunder bunched his muscles to leap down from the stump.

But before he could jump, a familiar stink hit Thunder in the throat, heavy and menacing, and he spotted a fox prowling into the clearing, its pointed snout raised and its tail straight out behind it.

"Now see what you've done!" Clear Sky growled, dragging him down from the tree stump. "Bringing danger into the camp with your noise."

He gave Thunder a shove. Off balance, Thunder stumbled straight into the path of the fox. In the midst of his danger, a thought flashed through his mind. *Did Clear Sky do that on purpose?* He remembered the time Clear Sky had come back to camp, stinking of foxes and in a foul mood. The fox's eyes lit on Thunder and in a flash it was running at him. Some cat let out a yowl of distress. Thunder had just enough time to recall Gray Wing's story of how he and Clear Sky had once tackled a fox. One had jumped on its back, while one clawed its face. *But it looks as if I'm on my own here!*

As the fox bounded toward Thunder, he reared up on his hind legs and swiped at the creature's muzzle, a double blow with both sets of claws. At the same moment Leaf and Falling Feather appeared, one on each side of him, their paws raised to strike.

But there was no need. The fox let out a bark of pain, whipped around and vanished into the undergrowth.

"Thanks," Thunder gasped to the two cats who had come to support him. His heart was pounding as if he had run all the way to the moorland camp and back.

"No need," Leaf mewed; Thunder was surprised to see respect dawning in the black-and-white tom's eyes. "You managed fine on your own."

"Yes," Clear Sky agreed, padding up to join them. "Some cat taught you well."

"Not you," Thunder retorted coldly. He knew that whatever

bond he had felt with his father was truly gone. *I'll never trust Clear Sky again.*

Clear Sky made no reply.

Thunder looked around at the other cats, but none of them were meeting his gaze. Nettle and Fircone, who had been so eager for him to talk to Clear Sky, were slinking away with their heads lowered.

So that's how it is, Thunder thought.

"Come on." Falling Feather touched Thunder on the shoulder with her tail-tip. "Let's get this over with. I'll come with you and Frost as far as the border, just in case that fox is still hanging around."

"What border would that be?" Thunder asked drily. "They change so often around here, I've lost track."

"Don't get clever," Clear Sky snarled. "You do know, if you leave now, you don't come back."

"I don't *want* to come back," Thunder responded.

Beckoning to Frost with his tail, he headed out of the camp, setting a slow pace so that the injured cat could keep up. Falling Feather padded along with them.

Thunder forced himself not to look back. *I don't care if Clear Sky is watching me leave or not. He's nothing to me now.* But even as he thought this, he knew it would take longer than the walk from camp for his wounds to heal. He'd trusted Clear Sky—he'd left Gray Wing to be with him!—and for what?

The three cats walked on in silence, pushing through the ferns.

"Why are you doing this?" Frost asked eventually, when they had left the clearing behind them. "We were never friends."

Thunder snorted. "I might think you're an annoying mange-pelt," he replied, "but I still don't want to see you dead."

"You'll be disappointed then," Frost growled. "This wound isn't going to heal."

"No cat has tried to heal it," Thunder meowed. "But there are cats on the moor who know everything there is to know about healing herbs. You'll be chasing prey for many seasons yet, Frost."

"That's right," Falling Feather agreed. "Thunder, I almost wish I was coming with you."

Thunder tried to hide his surprise. "Then come," he mewed in a soft voice.

The white she-cat shook her head. "I made my choice. The forest is where I belong now."

She halted as they reached the edge of the trees. The moorland slope swelled up in front of them, warm in the light of the setting sun. Bees buzzed among the wild thyme and a white butterfly zigzagged past in front of their noses.

"We're going up there?" Frost asked, sounding intimidated.

Thunder nodded. In spite of his earlier doubts, he was certain now that the only place he could go was back to the moorland camp and Gray Wing. He would have to tell them how sorry he was, and try to make it up to them however he could. *And I have to warn them about what Clear Sky is doing.*

"How fast do you think you can walk?" he asked Frost, seeing how the white tom was already wincing with pain.

"Fast enough." Frost's voice was grim. "I'll get there, don't worry."

"Good-bye," Falling Feather meowed. "And good luck."

"Thanks," Thunder responded, dipping his head.

As the sun shed scarlet light across the moor, Thunder and Frost began the long climb to the top of the ridge. About halfway up, Thunder halted and glanced over his shoulder. Falling Feather had disappeared; all he could see was the green barrier that marked the edge of the forest.

Beyond a clump of ferns, he made out the shape of a cat and spotted the flash of a gray pelt. *So my father came to see me leave, after all,* he thought. But even as he watched, the older cat sprang out of sight and disappeared into the gloom of the forest, where he belonged. *Where he should stay,* Thunder thought.

"Come on," he meowed to Frost. "The faster we walk, the sooner we arrive."

He began to lead the way from Clear Sky's camp. Thunder had tried to fit in there, tried to be everything his father had wanted him to be. *But I failed,* he thought. Or had he? Whatever had brought Clear Sky and Gray Wing out of the mountains with the other cats, some part of the hunger and desperation had sown a rotten seed in Clear Sky's heart. Even now, Thunder knew his father hadn't been born bad. *But he's changing. And that can't be good for any cat. Whatever I shared with my father, it's over,*

Thunder thought, guilt and regret mingling in his heart.

Now all that was left was to find Gray Wing and the others and tell them everything. It would be hard, but Thunder knew he had to share every awful detail.

He started to pick up speed.

"Hold on!" Frost called after him. "I can't run as fast as you, remember."

Thunder sat on his haunches and waited, his gaze grazing the moorland ahead of them. Out there was the other cats' camp. Out there was Gray Wing. Out there was hope.

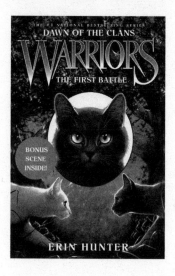

DAWN OF THE CLANS
WARRIORS
THUNDER RISING

BONUS SCENE!

Read on to see how River got his name . . .

PROLOGUE

A loud yowl roused Ripple from a dream of scampering after butter-flies over sunlit grass. As he struggled back to consciousness, he recognized the Call of Awakening ringing clearly across the Park. Blinking sleep away from his eyes, he slid out of his sleeping place, a mossy nest under the low-growing branches of a bush.

Dawn light filled the sky, and one spot on the horizon was flushed with pink and gold, showing where the sun would rise. Ripple turned toward it, his fur beginning to bristle in happy anticipation.

Soft grass stretched all around him, broken by clumps of bushes and the bright flowers the Twolegs planted. Here and there a tree let fall its blossoms, scattering the ground with tiny white petals like stars. Ripple couldn't imagine anyplace more beautiful.

Now his friends and elders were appearing from their own nests. Each turned like Ripple to face the light, and as the blazing sun edged its way into sight, they raised their voices in a loud caterwaul to welcome the new day. Ripple stretched his neck and let his yowl ring out clearly, watching the last shadows flee the powerful rays.

Once the sun had completely cleared the horizon, the cats turned away and began to wash. Ripple found a warm patch of grass beside a clump of scarlet Twoleg flowers, his nose wrinkling at their strong scent. He knew how important it was to wash thoroughly, remembering the correct order.

Paws first, then face and ears . . . chest and belly next, he told himself, rolling over to reach his soft belly fur. *Now back and tail . . .*

There was an order to everything for the Cats of the Park. From kithood, they knew when and how to wake, to wash, and to perform every one of the small acts that made up their lives. It was peaceful, and good.

Hunger ached deep inside Ripple as he struggled to reach the awkward spot at the base of his spine, and he hurried to finish his washing with long strokes of his tongue.

With a last swift lick at his tail, Ripple sprang to his paws and joined the end of the orderly line of cats heading across the Park for their Morning Meal. After a few paw steps he realized that his mentor, Arc, a sleek and elegant black tom, had fallen into step beside him. When Ripple was just a kit, Arc had chosen to teach him, and the older cat had educated Ripple in all the ways of the Cats of the Park.

"Greetings, Arc," Ripple meowed with a respectful dip of his head. "Isn't it a lovely morning?"

"It is," Arc agreed. "The sun is warm above our heads, and the grass is soft under our paws. Ripple, you should give thanks to the sun and the earth for the way they care for you. We're lucky that our life is so comfortable."

"I do give thanks," Ripple responded, puzzled. "Every day.

I know how lucky we are." *Why does Arc feel he has to tell me this?*

"Don't let these gifts make you soft," Arc warned him, his tone suddenly somber. He flicked his dark tail, gazing across the sunlit grass. "Always be aware, life can be hard, even for us."

Now Ripple was even more confused. Why would Arc want to spoil this bright morning with such dark words? *Life has never been hard for us!*

He dismissed the matter from his mind as he approached the row of bowls at the edge of the park. Twolegs laid out food every morning and evening at the far side of the Park. There was plenty for every cat; no need for pushing and shoving as they clustered around the bowls, each making sure that the cat beside him had enough space. Ripple began to eat, remembering not to gobble or gulp the food down. He wondered where the Twolegs hunted this weird prey that ended up as hard little nuggets. It wasn't very tasty—not as good as the occasional mouse that Ripple caught in the Park—but it filled his belly and kept his limbs strong and his pelt glossy.

"Time for Morning Meditation," Arc meowed as Ripple stepped back from his food bowl, swiping his tongue around his jaws. Whatever had been bothering Arc before their meal seemed to have passed. He was more cheerful now, his green eyes bright.

Ripple followed him across the Park, leaping up to sit next to him on top of one of the boundary walls. On the other side, the hill fell away steeply to where a river ran between banks edged with thick vegetation. None of the cats ever went there; the drop was too long to leap safely.

Besides, who would want to? Ripple reflected. *We have everything we need, right here.*

But Ripple was named for the movement of the river water, and he found special pleasure in focusing on that for his meditation. He was proud, too, of the way the movement was repeated in the rippling stripes of his silver-gray pelt.

"We'll practice hunting later," Arc told him as he folded himself into the correct pose for meditation, his paws tucked underneath him and his tail curled around them.

"Great!" Ripple purred, copying his mentor's position.

Through slitted eyes he watched the rippling river below and felt the warmth of the sun soaking bone-deep into his fur. A contented sigh escaped him.

We do this every day. We have an order and a routine, and we do things right. Nothing will ever change. It's so good here.

CHAPTER 1

Ripple stretched drowsily in the shade of a bush with glossy dark leaves. His belly was comfortably full, and he could still taste the mouse he had caught in his hunting session with Arc. Half asleep, he remembered the small gray body scuffling through the grass, and the sense of triumph as he pounced and felt his claws grip his prey.

This is one of the best days ever, he thought.

A panic-stricken yowl flew into Ripple's ear like a claw. He sprang up, shooting out from the shelter of the bush and staring around wildly. Nearby stood Arc, his back arched and his black fur bristling to twice his size. As Ripple stared at him in dismay, he let out another desperate yowl.

"What's the matter?" Ripple cried. He had never seen his calm, wise mentor like this before.

Arc didn't reply. Following his horrified gaze, Ripple saw that the edge of the Park was surrounded. *Twoleg monsters!* They were much bigger than any he had seen before on the Thunderpath that passed the Park.

Their shining yellow bodies edged forward with throaty roars, and the nearest one opened glittering jaws with teeth as long as a cat's body. Ripple stared in disbelief as it clamped those jaws deep into the earth. It was eating the Park!

"What's happening?" Ripple wailed.

His mentor seemed to pull himself out of his panic. Racing over to Ripple, Arc gave him a shove toward the far side of the Park. "We have to get out of here!" he snarled. "Come on!"

Pelting along beside Arc, Ripple dodged through a crowd of Twolegs who were using some fierce, growling creature to bite through a tree. Its shining fangs sliced through the wood as easily as Ripple's claws had sunk into the mouse.

"They're destroying everything!" he gasped. "Why? It's so peaceful here!"

"Not anymore," Arc grunted. "Run!"

As the two cats raced past, the wounded tree let out a massive groan, tilted slowly to the side, then crashed to the ground. Birds flew upward, letting out loud alarm calls, and the wind of the tree's fall ruffled Ripple's pelt as he fled.

Twolegs were rampaging through the Park. Everywhere Ripple darted his frantic gaze, he could see destruction. *Why... why?* But there was no answer to his anguished question.

Then Ripple spotted a group of Twolegs heading across the park, carrying small dens of shiny mesh. There were cats trapped inside, clawing at the mesh and yowling to be let out. Ripple's jaws gaped in disbelief.

"Look!" he meowed, halting for a moment in sheer horror. "There's Dart . . . and Shine . . . and that's your sister Flutter!"

Arc gave him another shove. "I know," he responded, his voice full of grief. "But we can't help them. Keep moving!"

He dodged to one side to avoid a Twoleg who was bearing down on them, and Ripple followed, racing along in Arc's paw steps until they reached the wall overlooking the river. This was the farthest part of the Park, and so far no Twolegs had appeared. Ripple could hardly believe that only that morning they had sat there to meditate.

Arc glanced back as they reached the wall. "This way!" he panted. "If we run along the top we can escape."

He leaped up to the top of the wall, and Ripple followed.

As he landed, a louder roar from one of the monsters broke out behind him. Startled, Ripple jumped backward. His paws slid from under him; gray stone rushed past him. He let out a screech of terror as he found himself falling.

Ripple whirled through the air, his legs and tail flailing. *I'm going to die!*

A heartbeat later he plunged into the river, all the breath driven out of his body. He sank into darkness, with nothing to hold on to. His senses began to spiral away.

Then there was a burst of light as his head broke the surface. Gasping and coughing up water, Ripple thrashed his limbs in a panic.

One paw struck something solid; he drove his claws into it. He was gripping a floating log. He managed to haul himself onto it with a frantic scrabble.

A caterwaul sounded overhead. Sunlight on the water dazzled his eyes, but as Ripple looked up he caught a glimpse of Arc, still standing on the wall high above him.

"Ripple!" he yowled.

With a last, desperate effort, Ripple lunged for the river-bank. But a wave washed over him, and his head went under again. When he first resurfaced, he could see nothing but surging water. Then, as he twisted his head, he spotted the log bobbing in the current beside him. Gulping and choking, he managed to scramble back onto it.

I'll be carried away . . . or drown . . .

As the river swept him along, Ripple looked back at his mentor, now no more than a small black shape on top of the wall. Spread-eagled on the log, Ripple gazed back until Arc, and with him everything Ripple had ever known, had vanished out of sight.

Ripple was shaking with cold and terror. When he had caught his breath again, he drew his paws up until he was crouching in the very middle of the log, as far away from the water as he could get. His pelt was soaked, plastered uncomfortably to his sides.

The river carried him past Twoleg dens and gardens stretching down to the water's edge. Gradually the current was carrying the log closer to the bank, and as the sun dried his fur Ripple began to feel more optimistic.

Maybe I can get to shore and find my way back to Arc.

Surely the Park would not be completely destroyed. Ripple's life would return to the way it had always been.

As the river bent into a wide curve, the log was driven toward a place where the current had scoured a hollow in the bank. Branches and bits of Twoleg rubbish had collected there. The log bumped gently up against the floating debris and stopped.

Ripple sized up the distance to the bank. *Can I jump that far?*

As he bunched his muscles for the leap, he heard a high-pitched yowling, and a couple of Twoleg kits came running along the bank. Ripple blinked at them hopefully. He had never had much to do with Twolegs, even the ones who left food for the Cats of the Park.

Maybe they'll help me, he thought. "Hey! Over here!" he called out, rising shakily to his paws.

The Twoleg kits halted, pointing at him. Then to Ripple's utter amazement, one of them bent down, scooped up a rock, and hurled it toward Ripple. With a splash, it struck the debris nearby, making his log bob dangerously up and down.

"What did you do that for?" Ripple meowed, full of indignation.

The Twoleg kits let out weird yelping sounds, showing their teeth. The second kit threw a rock, too. This time it hit Ripple on his shoulder, stinging him and almost making him lose his balance.

Why are they trying to hurt me? Ripple wondered.

Ducking to avoid another pebble, Ripple slid to one side, losing his balance, and splashed into the water again. This time he was close enough to the log to grab hold of it before he sank, and kicked out at the floating debris with his hind paws.

His struggles dislodged the log, and the current carried him away from the bank, out of range of the flying rocks. As Ripple hauled himself back on top of the log, he puffed out a breath of relief to see the Twoleg kits dwindling into the distance.

Thank you, river, he thought.

The Twoleg dens on either side of the river became more widely spaced, with stretches of open ground between them. A Thunderpath ran along one side of the river, glittering monsters roaring past in both directions. Ripple crouched down on his log, hoping the monsters wouldn't spot him; he wasn't sure if they could swim out and attack him.

Then the Thunderpath took a sharp turn and rose up until it spanned the river in a shallow arch. Ripple gaped at it in astonishment and flinched as he was swept underneath, the water gurgling with a weird echo as the shadow of the Thunderpath covered him.

He went limp with relief as he shot out into sunlight again and the river carried him away, leaving the Thunderpath behind. Now there were open fields on both sides of the river. The grass was divided into sections, sometimes by lines of shining metal, sometimes by rows of bushes. Huge black-and-white animals were champing at the grass; they raised their heads and watched Ripple as the current carried him past.

Here and there in the distance Ripple could make out a Twoleg den, and from time to time he passed trees, not growing neatly in order like the trees of the Park, but straggling far apart, or growing tightly together in dark bunches that looked vaguely threatening.

By now the sun was going down, streaking the sky with scarlet and casting long shadows across the water. Ripple began to shiver in the cool air of evening. Hunger ached deep in his belly. It was way past the time of the Evening Meal, and even longer since he had caught and eaten the mouse, back in the safety of the Park.

If I could get to the bank I could catch another mouse, he thought longingly, but the river was wide and his log was drifting almost in the middle.

As he looked down into the water, Ripple spotted small shapes flickering here and there, slender creatures with pelts that flashed silver in the last of the light. *They must be "fish,"* he realized, remembering something Arc had told him. *He said you can eat them. I hope he was right.*

He had never tasted fish, but his jaws began watering at the sight of them. *Everything is different out here,* he told himself. *I can't trust Twolegs anymore, so I'll have to look after myself. I'll have to learn to hunt fish.*

Balancing carefully on the log, Ripple dabbled one paw into the water, trying to snag a fish. But the creature easily darted away from his outstretched claws. Ripple felt hungrier than ever to think of all that food just a tail-length away. He could see the fish, but he couldn't reach them; he almost felt as if they were mocking him.

The sun had gone down, and the river became a sheet of silver, reflecting the pale sky above. Something dark broke the surface a little way ahead. As the current swept him closer Ripple recognized the spiky shape of a dead branch, clearly caught on something on the river bed. As the log collided with it, the branch shifted, then settled again, bringing the log to a halt.

Ripple glanced around. Water slipped quietly past him,

stretching away in all directions. "Now what do I do?" he meowed aloud.

He reached out a paw to the branch, hoping that he could push himself off and continue his journey, when he heard a couple of loud splashes behind him. His pelt prickled with alarm as he struggled to his paws and turned to meet this new threat.

Two heads were poking out of the water close to the bank. As Ripple watched, the creatures swam into the current, then veered around and headed for the bank again. Scrambling out, they revealed long, muscular bodies covered in sleek brown pelts. When they reached the top of the bank they dived back into the river, one chasing after the other, clearly playing and reveling in their strength and skill.

Ripple felt a pang of envy. *I wish I could swim like that!*

A moment later, one of the creatures vanished beneath the surface, reappearing with a gleaming fish in its jaws. Both animals swam back to the bank, where they shared the catch, chomping it down with gusto.

Ripple's belly bawled with hunger, and he barely stopped himself from letting out a yowl of protest. *I want some of that!*

When the creatures had polished off the fish, they turned back to the river. For a moment they stood still, gazing across the water and exchanging weird chattering calls. Then together they plunged into the river and swam out, heading straight for Ripple.

They've spotted me!

As the creatures drew closer, Ripple could make out their

broad, whiskered muzzles and rounded ears. They bared their strong teeth threateningly at him. They were still letting out their strange, birdlike calls; they sounded angry and fierce.

It's not my fault I'm in their territory. I don't want to be here!

Terror flooded through Ripple from ears to tail-tip. In the Park, all the cats had lived peacefully together. He had never fought in his life.

Maybe I can warn them off, he thought, determined not to let them see how frightened he was.

He fluffed his fur and slid out his claws, giving a furious snarl as the creatures approached his log. But his defiance only seemed to make them angrier. They swam faster, closing rapidly on him, their calls deafening. Ripple braced himself for battle.

They're bigger than me, and there are two of them. But I'm going to do my best.

The log lurched beneath Ripple's feet as the leading animal climbed onto it, lunging forward to snap at him. The creature's teeth met in his pelt. Ripple jumped back in a panic and kicked out at it, fending it off.

The log bobbed wildly in the water. The creature lost its balance and fell back with a splash. The log moved as the creature fell, and the current tugged it loose, bearing Ripple away from the threatening creatures. As Ripple stared back at them, they called out to him with angry chittering, but they didn't try to follow. Ripple lost sight of them as the river curved around a rocky outcrop with a thick growth of bushes.

Ripple had escaped, but he felt no relief. Instead, he

despaired. The world outside the Park was huge and cruel. Until now, he had always been protected by the other cats, by the sun and the earth, by kindly Twolegs. He had believed things would always be that way.

Now Twolegs and other creatures attack me. And I'm starving. Everything has fallen apart, just as the Twolegs destroyed my home.

Ripple huddled miserably on his log as the last of the light died and the river carried him on into the night.

CHAPTER 2
❧

Ripple was exhausted, but he didn't dare to sleep. He was too afraid of falling off his log and drowning in the river. Stars appeared, their reflections glittering on the surface of the river, but he was too wretched to appreciate their beauty.

Full darkness had fallen when Ripple heard a soft splash close to his log. He tensed and struggled to his paws, looking around for the new threat.

Maybe those animals followed me after all!

There was another splash, and this time Ripple caught a glimpse of a fish arcing out of the water. Another followed, and another . . . They're all around me, he thought hungrily.

With a smacking sound, one landed directly in front of Ripple on the log. Instantly he slapped down his paw, digging in his claws before the fish could flap back into the water. It writhed underneath his pads as it struggled to free itself. For a heartbeat he didn't know what to do; hesitantly he bent down and bit into it at the back of its head.

The fish went limp, and Ripple tore off a mouthful of its flesh and gulped it down. "Wow!" he exclaimed aloud. "It's delicious!"

He ate the rest of the fish in huge, famished bites, amazed and pleased that the river had given him food.

He remembered how Arc had taught him that the sun and earth protected him. Now he realized that the river had protected him, too, ever since he fell from the wall at the edge of the Park. The river had sent the log that had saved him from drowning, and carried him away from the Twoleg kits and the strange, savage animals.

"Thank you!" he breathed out, feeling less alone for the first time since he fell from the wall and saw his mentor disappearing into the distance.

His log floated on through the darkness. With a full belly, Ripple managed to doze, feeling more secure in his hope that the river would go on caring for him.

He came fully awake to see the pale light of dawn in the sky. The lush enclosures on either side of the river had given way to bleak slopes of short, tough grass, broken up by clumps of thornbushes and stony outcrops. Far away in one direction, jagged spikes of rock stood out against the sky. A chilly wind swept across the river, ruffling the surface. Ripple shivered, hoping for the sun to rise and warm his fur.

There'll be no morning caterwaul today, he thought with a pang of loss, wondering what had happened to Arc and the rest of his friends in the Park. *At least my fur should get properly dry.*

But when the sun eventually rose, it was mostly hidden behind clouds, and there was no warmth in the day. The log stayed in the middle of the river; Ripple had no hope of getting to shore, and in any case the bare hills on either side

looked uninviting. The river had grown narrower, too, and
the current was faster.

Maybe I'll come to a better place soon, he thought.

Then from somewhere ahead Ripple heard a distant roaring. At first he thought it must be another Thunderpath,
but the noise was too steady to be the passing of monsters. It
rapidly grew louder as the current hurried him on, faster and
faster. Ripple dug his claws deep into his log, his heart beginning to pound with alarm as he drew closer to the unknown
sound.

Staring ahead, Ripple saw the weirdest thing yet: the river
seemed to come to a sudden stop. Beyond it was only the sky.

"What . . ." he muttered.

Then he reached the edge. His eyes widened in pure panic
as he caught a glimpse of water pouring over rock in a smooth
curve. Far below him, there was turmoil as the river cascaded
into a pool in a chaos of spray and foam. Ripple let out a
screech as his log tipped over the edge.

The thunder of the falling water was all around him. He
lost his grip on the log. His paws flailed helplessly as the
weight of water bore him down and plunged him into the
pool. The river closed over his head and rolled him over and
over until he didn't know where the surface was.

His senses were spinning away into darkness when his head
bobbed up into the light. He took in a gulp of air, but when he
opened his jaws to let out a yowl of terror, water gushed into
his mouth and he sank again.

But Ripple refused to give in. He pumped his legs with

all the strength he had left, forcing himself back upward. A moment later he reached the surface. To his amazement, the river was bearing him up, supporting him as it swept him along. He kicked out in the turbulent water, managing to stay afloat as the current whirled him onward.

I can swim! he thought triumphantly. *Just like those creatures who attacked me!*

Forbidding walls of rock stretched above his head on either side. Panic clawed at Ripple as he saw no way of climbing to safety up the sheer face of the cliffs.

But gradually the river grew wider again and the speed of the current slackened. The rock walls gave way to grassy banks. Ripple glanced from side to side, knowing that his strength was ebbing and he would have to find somewhere to come ashore soon.

Before he could strike out across the current, the river washed him gently against a boulder. Ripple grabbed at it with his claws and scrambled up until he could collapse on the flat top of the rock. He lay limp, his paws splayed out, and coughed up a few mouthfuls of water. Then a sparkling darkness filled his head, and he knew nothing more.

A long time later, Ripple became aware of warmth beating down on him. He blinked his eyes open and raised his head to look around. While he was unconscious the clouds had cleared away and the sun shone in a bright blue sky.

Muscles shrieking in protest, Ripple tottered to his paws and looked around. He was standing at the edge of a group of flat rocks that rose above the surface of the river. Deep channels of fast-flowing water separated him from the banks on either side.

Ripple gazed longingly across at the banks. They sloped upward, covered with long grass and clumps of fern, to where bushes and trees grew at the top. A little farther downstream a willow tree leaned over a reed bed, its branches trailing in the current.

As he watched, a mouse darted out of a clump of ferns and scuttled across the grass to the shelter of a tree stump. It was so close that Ripple could pick up its scent, and water gushed into his mouth. His belly was complaining again, and there was nothing to eat among the sunbaked rocks.

Ripple worked his legs, stretching and relaxing his muscles until the aches faded. Then he crouched down at the edge of the rock and lapped a few gulps of water, reveling at the cool touch in his parched mouth.

There were fish here too, he noticed, resting in the shade cast by the rocks. Ripple dipped in a paw and tried to catch one, but it swam off with a flick of its tail before he could get anywhere near it. *There must be a way of doing this,* he thought determinedly.

After a few more failed attempts, Ripple worked out that he had to position himself so that his shadow didn't fall on the water, and not lean over so far that the fish could see him. He let his paw slide into the water so slowly that it didn't disturb the flow of the current, edging closer to a plump fish that lay close to the rock. When he thought he was near enough, he flashed his paw upward as fast as he could.

To his delight, the fish flipped out of the water and landed beside him on the rock. Ripple slammed his paw on top of it and bit down hard. The fish stopped wriggling, and Ripple devoured it in eager mouthfuls.

That's so good. . . .

But when he had eaten the fish and sat cleaning his whiskers, Ripple still yearned for the grassy comfort of the riverbank. The rocks where he was sitting were bare. *They're great for snoozing in the sun, but I don't want to live here.* The shady spot under the willow tree looked like a perfect place to hide and hunt. *This place is beautiful,* he realized, *even though it's nothing like the Park I came from.*

Ripple stared across the channel, waving his tail in indecision. He had managed to swim when he fell down the waterfall, but it was a different matter to actually make the *choice* to jump in.

The sun and earth have protected me all my life, he thought. *Just like the river has taken care of me, over and over again. It gave me a soft landing when I fell from the wall. It carried me away from the danger that was destroying the Park. It saved me from those fierce creatures, it fed me, and now it has brought me to what could be a wonderful new home. Maybe it will help me to get to the bank, if I can just trust it.*

Ripple rose to his paws and lifted his head to let out a clear meow. "Thank you, river, for all you've done for me. If you can help me again, one last time, and get me to the bank, I will stay beside you and praise you all my life."

Without giving himself the chance to change his mind, he plunged into the current.

At once, Ripple found that he was swimming strongly. The river bore him up, carrying him to the bank just upstream of the willow tree. Almost before he knew it he felt his paws touch solid ground. He waded out and scrambled up the bank, shaking water from his long, silvery fur.

"What *are* you?" a voice asked. "A water rat?"

Spinning around, Ripple spotted a young black-and-white she-cat watching him from beneath an arching clump of ferns a couple of tail-lengths away. She was staring at him with a stunned expression, but in spite of her amazement her voice was friendly.

Ripple dipped his head toward her. "Greetings," he mewed. "I've come from the Cats of the Park. Will you and your Cats allow me to stay here?"

Amusement glinted in the she-cat's eyes. "I'm not part of any group of cats," she told him. "This land belongs to wild cats who hunt alone. You're welcome to stay here, as long as you don't steal the prey out from any other cat's paws."

"Hunt?" Ripple asked uneasily. He had only hunted a few times before, and only for fun. And he had always been with other cats. "The cats here hunt . . . *alone?*"

Loneliness stabbed through Ripple at the thought. His tail drooped as he remembered Arc and the other Cats of the Park. He had always lived in a group, and an intense sense of loss swept over him like a chill wind through his fur. *What will I do without them? Will I ever see them again?*

The she-cat let out a sympathetic purr, as if she understood his sorrow. "Even though we hunt for ourselves," she meowed, "that doesn't mean that we can't hunt with a friend. Would you like to join me today? I'll introduce you to my brother, and we can all hunt together."

"Really?" Ripple felt hope rekindle inside him. "Thank you!"

"Maybe we can give you some tips," the she-cat went on. "And maybe you can show us what a water rat can do."

"I'd be glad to," Ripple agreed happily, wondering if these cats knew how to catch fish.

"My name is Night," the she-cat meowed. "What's yours?"

Ripple looked back at the river flowing by. It had given him food and protected him from his enemies, and he had to believe it was still protecting him and taking him where he was meant to be.

I'm not the young Cat of the Park anymore, he realized. *Not really. I'm something else now, something more—a Cat of the River. And I should honor my protector.*

"I'm River," he told Night. "River Ripple."

THE TIME HAS COME
FOR DOGS TO RULE THE WILD

SURVIVORS

BOOK ONE:
THE EMPTY CITY

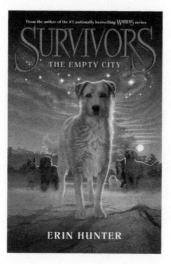

Lucky is a golden-haired mutt with a nose for survival. Other dogs have Packs, but Lucky stands on his own . . . until the Big Growl strikes. Suddenly the ground splits wide open. The longpaws disappear. And enemies threaten Lucky at every turn. For the first time in his life, Lucky needs to rely on other dogs to survive. But can he ever be a true Pack dog?

DON'T MISS

RETURN TO THE WILD

SEEKERS

**BOOK ONE:
ISLAND OF SHADOWS**

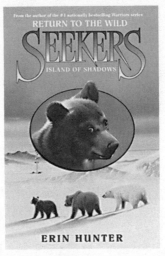

Toklo, Kallik, and Lusa survived the perilous mission that brought them together, and now it's time for them to find their way home. When the group reaches a shadowy island covered in mountains and ice, Kallik is sure they're almost back to the Frozen Sea. But a terrifying accident leads them into a maze of abandoned tunnels, unlike anything they've ever seen before—making them question their path once again.

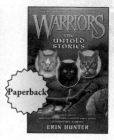

Warrior Cats Come to Life in Manga!